MW00780163

WOOD'S REEF

MAC TRAVIS ADVENTURES - BOOK 1

STEVEN BECKER

THE WHITE MARLIN PRESS

WOOD'S REEF

Join my mailing list
and get a free copy of my starter library:
First Bite

Click the image or download here: http://eepurl.com/-obDj

PROLOGUE

STEVEN BECKER

A MAC TRAVIS ADVENTURE

WOOD'S
REEF

KEY WEST, October 27, 1962

"November, 2442. Truman ATC. Low on fuel, over," the pilot radioed to the air traffic controller. He rubbed his sweaty palms against his flight suit and waited, hoping the air traffic controller would respond quickly

"Truman ATC, N2442. Can you make Key West, over."

"Negative. Fuel is low. Truman, request permission to jettison cargo, over."

"N2442, Truman ATC, if no alternative, permission to jettison granted. Mark location, over."

"Roger Truman, will do. Permission to land, over."

"N2442, Truman ACT. Roger, runway 21 from west. Please note east wind at 18 knots. Do you require emergency equipment, over."

"Negative Truman, just overweight. Copy that runway 21 from west. ETA twelve minutes."

"N2442, Truman ATC. Roger that. Call back when you have feet dry and visual."

The jet took a wide turn toward the west to look for a good spot to jettison its cargo. Below, the late-afternoon sun clearly showed the transitions in color between deep water and shallow. The dark blue spots indicated deep water — what he was looking for. At the apex of his turn, the pilot spotted a hundred-yard-long dark blue line indicating a trench. That was the spot. With the low fuel alarm sounding, he dropped altitude to 500', and air speed to just short of a stall. The cargo doors opened.

Seconds later, two projectiles broke the surface of the water and quickly sank to the bottom.

————

The jet taxied to a stop by the service hanger, and two crewmen looked up from their card game, reluctant to leave the shade. Finally they stood and walked out. Crossing the tarmac, shimmering in the heat from the tropical sun, they made their way to the pilot.

"Heard you had some trouble out there," Machinist Mate Woodson said to the pilot.

"Spent too much time chasing that Russian B-29 sub off San Juan. We forced her to surface, and I had to stay on site. Took a lot of fuel with that payload." The pilot climbed down from the cockpit, the afternoon sun reflecting off his visor causing the machinist to squint. "Had to drop two bombs to get light enough to make it back."

Aviation Ordnanceman Jim Gillum pressed the release outside the cargo doors and looked in. "You dropped the nukes."

The pilot came around and looked inside the bomb bay door, surprised. "Well, they must have been loaded wrong then. The nukes should have been on the sides, not the middle." He wiped the sweat from his brow with his sleeve, suddenly worried. He'd thought he made it home safely, but this ... this was a complication. "This is big trouble boys. There are all kinds of unexploded ordnance at the bottom of the sea, but not nukes."

Joe Ward was due a promotion, and had no intention of letting this get in his way. He started his less than stellar career as a Naval Aviator at the end of the Korean War. "This is your fault, not mine. Just check them in like they should have been loaded. Fudge the paperwork — whatever you have to do. Just make sure no one knows."

"We can't just leave two nukes sitting out there," Woodson said, shocked.

"Why not. Come on Wood. You know they'll send a demolition team out there as soon as this whole thing cools off and either blow them or bring them back here for disposal," Gillum said.

"Bullshit," Wood retorted. "They'll sit down there until the wrong person finds them."

"Hopefully by the time they figure there was a mistake in the paperwork, we'll be long gone," Ward walked towards the shade of the hanger, helmet cradled under his arm.

"I hope so for your sake." Wood turned towards Gillum. "You can wipe the brown off your nose now. That son of a bitch doesn't even know your name. Ward there, he's one of those guys that's just putting this on his resume to run for office— take his old man's congressional seat."

"Wood, maybe that's the difference between me and you. One day he's gonna have some power. I'm making an ally, you're pissing him off."

"You think he cares about a nuke sitting on the bottom of the ocean? That thing blows, it'll kill everything that swims for miles."

1

STEVEN BECKER

A MAC TRAVIS ADVENTURE

WOOD'S
REEF

Spray coated the windshield of the trawler as it pulled up to the first buoy. The wind was rising as quickly as the barometer was falling. It wasn't forecast as a hurricane, but it was blowing thirty knots now, and that was enough to take precautions.

"Tru. First trap, a hundred feet out!" The command was barely audible over the noise of the wind and motor.

Trufante leaned his six foot plus frame away from the protection of the wheelhouse. He spotted the buoy bobbing on top of a whitecap, breathed in, and faced the inevitable spray. His knee slammed into the gunwale as the wave took the boat, and the bow fell. A stream of spray came over the side, drenching him. He extended the gaff to reach the buoy with one foot in the air, leaning over the gunwale to gain as much reach as possible. The hook grabbed the line and he pulled the gaff in until he could reach the line with his free hand. With a practiced twist he wound the line onto the pulley. The winch motor groaned as it took the load, pulling the trap off the bottom. Trufante guided the trap onto the stainless steel runners.

"This is hardly worth it, dude. There's one lobster in here. My Cajun ass should be on a barstool, not out here in this crap." He untied the knot holding the door open and extracted the lobster. "Pretty small, too."

Mac grunted. "Forget about the lobster. We need to get the traps up and stack them. This wind picks up any more, they'll fill with sand and we'll lose them."

The conversation was over, and Mac steered toward the next buoy. They worked in an uncomfortable silence for the hour it took to pull the twenty remaining traps.

"How many we got?" Mac asked as the last trap came over the side.

"Probably in the neighborhood of forty." Trufante dumped the last lobster in the cooler and closed the lid. "Can we get out of here now? You know we're the only ones crazy enough to be out here in this." He winced as a wave broke over the bow. "Storm's got a bite meaner than my grandma's Cajun pepper sticks."

"Say what you want. It's enough to keep you in beer till this blows through, and I won't have to spend a bunch of money replacing traps." Mac hit the wiper switch, and the blades dragged against the plexiglass, rubbing the dried salt before the rainwater started to dissolve it and wash it away.

———

The waves and tide were with them now. Trufante went below and came out with a beer. "Finally calm enough I can drink this instead of wear it. What's that?" He pointed toward the Seven Mile Bridge, where a piling indicated a sandbar, exposed only at low tide. Two yellow dots were visible. Mac altered his course and steered carefully toward the area, the yellow dots now growing into two people in rain slickers, frantically waving. Next to them was a boat run aground.

"Crap. Idiots."

"Yeah, you think? What the hell are they doing out here in this mess?" Trufante was close enough to see the hull now.

Mac eased his boat up to the edge of the sandbar, invisible in the storm-churned water. He studied the surface, watching the flow that would indicate the deep channel, and waited for his chance. In the meantime, he took the microphone and held it out, signaling for them to call on their radio. The man shrugged his shoulders.

"See if they need help," he told Trufante as he pulled the throttles back to neutral. Forced to make a correction by the incoming tide, he slammed the transmission back into reverse. "This tide's smoking. Hurry up."

Trufante went forward and yelled at the couple. Mac couldn't hear the conversation over the wind but had already made his decision. A nicer day, he might have passed right by knowing the tide would float the boat in an hour or two, but with this weather he knew he would have to help.

"What's the deal?" he asked Trufante as the Cajun slid behind the protection of the wheelhouse.

"Cute girl. Dude's an ass, though."

"Thanks, that wasn't quite the answer I was looking for. Think you can tell them to sit tight. We'll toss a line and pull them off. They need to stay out of the boat. This is going to be dicey. After we pull it off, we can pick them up on the beach. Take that line and toss it, tell him to tie it to the loop on the bow, not the cleat. He needs to secure it where the trailer winch hooks to. If we try and drag them off stern-first, it'll swamp. We'll have to spin it."

Trufante grabbed a line and headed toward the bow. There, he laid it on the deck and peeled off enough line to make a dozen loops, which he held in his right hand. He wound up and tossed the line, watching the wind catch and stall its progress as it unraveled. It fell into the water twenty feet short of the couple. The man yelled for him to throw again.

Trufante was about to pull the line in when he heard Mac on the hailer. "Go get it. We don't have time to be messing around, here. You have a radio? Go to channel 16."

The couple faced each other, clearly fighting. After a few

seconds, the man shook his head and waded into the water. He retrieved the line and followed Mac's instructions to tie it off.

"Get clear!" Mac shouted. He backed the boat into deeper water and turned perpendicular to the grounded boat. Both men lost their footing as the engine vibration resonated through the deck. The line came tight with a crack, increasing the stress on the engines even more. Finally, the boat started to turn on the sandbar. Mac eased on the throttle, allowing the line to go slack as he changed course. The line cracked again as it came taut, but the boat refused to move.

"What now? That thing ain't movin'." He watched as Mac backed the boat down. He started to swing the stern back and forth.

"Just got to break the suction of the sand. Just a minute." He revved the engines and steered straight.

The couple watched as the boat slid off the sandbar. The strong current grabbed it, swinging the boat dangerously close to the old span of the bridge. The man was screaming something as Mac pushed down on the throttle, gaining control of the boat.

"I'm going to put you on their boat," he said to Trufante. "Make sure it starts, and pick them up. Follow me into the gas dock at Boot Key." Mac turned the boat, allowing the current to bring the smaller boat toward his as Trufante brought in the slack line.

The boats were almost touching when Trufante vaulted over the gunwale, landing on the smaller boat. He went to the helm and started the boat. Both boats drifted together and he leaned over the bow to untie the line.

"Can't get it," he yelled at Mac. "This guy can't even tie a knot. It tightened down on itself."

"Screw it." Mac said, going for a knife. He cut the line, leaving ten feet drifting in the water. "Tell him he owes me."

Trufante reversed and nosed into the sandbar.

2

STEVEN BECKER

A MAC TRAVIS ADVENTURE
WOOD'S
REEF

THE SUN DAPPLED the surface of the calm water, slowly undulating with the tide. It had taken three days for the storm to pass, but they were finally back out on the water. Mac nodded at Trufante to drop the first trap. Mac watched, a rare smile crossing his face, as concentric rings marked the traps' point of entry.

Trufante baited the trap and slid it into the water with a practiced movement that belied its weight. Mac engaged the engine and moved toward the next spot, two hundred feet away, where they repeated the procedure. It often took years to learn the shallow Gulf waters, a desert mostly comprised of sand and turtle grass waving with the current, but there was structure and knowing the bottom features was the key. Mac had put in his time to learn the locations of the rock piles, potholes and ledges that attracted life on the otherwise-barren bottom. This was different water than the more popular Atlantic side, where the famous reef ran. Dropping five feet from the adjacent bottom, the broken rocky ledge ran for almost a quarter mile. Two hundred yards of green and blue buoys marked Mac's traps. The alternating colors bobbed in a single line parallel with the trench, dark spots against the sparkle of the late-morning sun on the water. It was a few more miles than most captains liked to run to set their traps, and past the comfort zone of the tourist boats he tried to avoid. Mac didn't care about the time and fuel. He loathed the congestion of buoys and tourists closer in. Besides, there were more lobster here.

An hour later, with all the traps soaking, he ran his hand through his receding hair and yelled out to Trufante, "Hey Tru, drop the anchor here. I want to dive and see if there's any grouper." There was a good chance there would be game fish here. They sought bait, which congregated around good bottom like this.

He went back to the transom and donned mask, fins, and a weight belt. As he went over the side, Trufante handed him the speargun. He bobbed on the surface, taking larger and deeper breaths, then pivoted at the waist and kicked through the surface. A half-dozen effortless kicks later he was at eye level with the ledge. Nothing in sight, and his lungs feeling the lack of air, he finned back up and repeated the process.

Just as he was about to dive he saw a quick glimmer of sun on glass, just east of their position. *Strange*, he thought, *you don't see many boats out here.* The boat was moving close enough that he could just make out the orange hat of the driver. "Hey Tru. Keep an eye out there." He pointed at the boat.

Mac dove again. Visibility was good, and he saw a line moving slowly over the sand as he descended. The black grouper finned in the current, waiting for prey, its checkered pattern camouflaging it from the side, though it was easily visible from above. He held his breath, holding level and just above the fish. Frozen in the water, he became a part of the landscape. The fish never knew he was there until he released the trigger and the four-foot spear shot from the gun and embedded itself behind the grouper's head. The fish tried to make a run, but Mac held the line connecting the gun and spear, looping it around his hand for leverage. He kicked to the surface and handed the line to Trufante on the transom to retrieve the fish.

"There's a couple more down there." He took back the empty

shaft, slid it into the gun, and pulled back the rubber tubing. "I'll be back."

As he dropped closer to the bottom, he began to notice a dull sheen in the sand. He wasn't sure what he was looking at, but he knew it didn't belong here. He surfaced and repeated his breathing sequence, then dove back down toward the metal object. He dusted the sand away from it, then raced for the surface, breaking through the water and yelling for Trufante to hand him a weighted buoy.

"Hit the Man Overboard button on the GPS," he yelled as he swam towards the dive platform. He grabbed the buoy from Trufante's outstretched hand and submerged again. He located the object, removed the small marker buoy clipped to his weight belt and released it. The line unwound as the small foam float ascended, leaving the small fishing weight resting on the bottom to mark the spot. He finned to the surface and climbed back to the dive platform.

Back on the boat, he adjusted the GPS to make sure the coordinates marked the buoy's spot. Right over the location, he navigated through the GPS menus, saving the waypoint. He grabbed his phone and hit the INavX GPS app and awkwardly navigated the program, tapping harder on the screen until the program finally submitted and saved the spot. Not a fan of technology, he did appreciate redundant systems. GPS numbers were irreplaceable, marking underwater features that were invisible to the naked eye. He had started putting his numbers into the iNav program which would automatically sync with his computer at home.

He knew what he'd found, and wanted to ensure he could find it again. Trufante snagged the buoy line with the gaff and wound the line around it as Mac increased speed, heading for his next trap line.

3

A MAC TRAVIS ADVENTURE
WOOD'S
REEF

THE PEARLY DEW on the ice-cold Corona bottle shimmered in the heat. It was late October, and it still got Africa hot.

They'd spent the last two hours checking their other traps, and Mac would have been heading in by now to offload his catch, but that piece of metal intrigued him. He wiped the bottle on his brow and tossed one to Trufante, then pulled the GPS coordinate up and hit the GOTO button. The course and distance came up as he throttled up, and he followed the bearing indicated on the display.

Ten minutes later he pulled up on the site. Trufante shot him a questioning look when Mac yelled to toss the anchor.

"What up, boss? Why are we back here?"

"Something down there I need to check on," Mac said, tossing him another beer to keep him distracted.

———

Mac decided on scuba diving gear this time. He geared up and with his back to the water, rolled over the side. He quickly found the metal object and released the buoy. The GPS was accurate to about thirty feet, but he needed to be right over the top of it for what he had planned.

"Pull the anchor and set the stern on top of that buoy." He pointed to the red ball bobbing off the starboard side. "Right on top. No slack in the anchor line."

Trufante gave him a questioning look, no doubt thinking his day should have been over.

"Just do it." Mac pulled himself onto the dive platform and waited for Trufante to find the mark and reset the anchor.

The current had picked up since this morning, the tide moving out swiftly, and Trufante had a hard time getting on top of the buoy. Mac's patience didn't last long. He dumped his gear, went to the bow and released the anchor line from the cleat. The line slipped through his hands as he signaled Trufante to back down on the buoy. With the line tied off again, he watched as the boat settled right over the buoy.

He grabbed the pressure washer hose and hooked the end to a quick disconnect on the transom. The pressure washer was a recent addition to the custom boat — great for a quick cleanup, though he was going to use it for something else today. He had fifty feet of hose and the bottom was thirty feet down. That gave him twenty feet for maneuvering. He geared up and was back in the water.

When he ducked back under the surface the first thing he noticed was the visibility was down to ten feet, the water full of silt picked up by the tide and his movements. A couple of hours and a tide change made all the difference in visibility. The extra weight he added took him quickly to the bottom. Kneeling in the silt, he hit the trigger on the sprayer and started washing sand away from the metal, pausing several times to allow the silt to settle. As more metal was revealed, it became evident exactly what this was. Unexploded naval ordnance was not uncommon here. But this didn't look like any ordinary bomb. Knowing he had to get it mostly exposed to break the suction with the sand, he worked his way around the object, becoming more concerned as the sand revealed an intact casing. It was old. Rust was visible on the screw heads and the dings caused by the impact.

This was far more dangerous than he'd realized. Fifty years in a saltwater environment could have eroded the skin of the bomb enough that the water pressure could puncture it causing an explosion. There was also the possibility it could have a nuclear core and allow radioactive material into the water. He calculated the odds and realized the only choice was to get the bomb out of the water. Leaving it to decay further was not an option.

Twenty minutes of blasting water against the sand revealed the full shape of the weapon—a foot-and-a-half in diameter, and over seven feet long. The bomb looked top heavy, fatter at the front, and tapering toward the end. It appeared retro — space aged—like something from a Buck Rogers movie.

He jetted two holes all the way underneath it and after removing enough material to be sure the suction of the sand would break, he surfaced.

Mac took off his gear and climbed back onboard, where he found Trufante asleep in the captain's chair. He sidestepped his crewman and headed to the crane mounted on the port side. Steel cable flew off the reel as he released the gears. One hundred feet of cable slowly sank in the green water. Next he rigged a harness from some trap line.

He geared up again, popped back into the water, and descended with the harness and winch cable trailing behind. Once at the bomb, he worked lines through the holes he had jetted and tied them off in a cradle. Checking for slack, he made a slight adjustment, and clipped the ends into the hook at the end of the winch line. He finished the rig with a rope line, which he took to the surface to be used as a tag line to control the ascent.

Back on board, he stood over Trufante, wondering if he should wake him or not. Deciding he needed the help, he leaned over and kicked him in the side.

Trufante woke with a start. Mac left him to orient himself and went to the winch.

"You good now?" Mac asked, tossing a bottle of water Trufante's way. This was going to be tricky as it was, and he would need all the faculties his crewman could muster.

"Damn near 4 o'clock, we should have been back an hour ago," Trufante whined.

Mac ignored him and moved forward to the winch. There were more important things to worry about than the time. He turned the switch on. Cable began to feed onto the roller as the slack came out of the line.

"Hold this line and stay toward the stern." Mac handed Trufante the lighter tag line.

The motor gained an octave as it felt the resistance of the weight below. The boat started to list toward port until the suction released allowing the bomb to rise in the water. It righted as cable began to wind around the winch. The motor struggled with the weight. Once confident the winch could handle the bomb Mac switched positions with Trufante, taking the tag line from him. It was more important for him to guide the bomb to the boat now.

"Bring her up easy until I tell you to stop," Mac yelled over the whine of the motor as he peered over the side of the boat, looking for the bomb to break the surface.

The tricky part would be keeping the bomb from banging the boat. He had no idea whether it was still armed and, if it were, what would set it off. It was risky enough just bringing it up, let alone slamming it against the steel hull of the trawler.

The bomb rose slowly, looking like a large shark in the water, the shape becoming more defined as the casing ascended. Mac now had the tag line in one hand, controlling the bomb, and the boat hook in the other. He called to Trufante to work the winch as if it was picking a trap out of the water. He intended to lift the bomb and swing it onto the stainless steel slides used to move the traps along the boat.

"What in the bejesus is that thing?" Trufante yelled as he saw the bomb lift from the water.

"Never mind right now!" Mac yelled back as he guided the twelve-hundred-pound cylinder onto the stainless track. "Let some slack outta the cable and hold this thing while I get something to set it on."

He handed Trufante the tag line, and ran back into the cabin to grab two cushions from the bench seat. Back on deck, he set them on the tracks and signaled for Trufante to lower the bomb. Once this was accomplished, he freed the winch hook and tied the bomb to the deck.

"What you got us into?" Trufante asked.

Mac rewarded him with a beer, and ignored the question. Checking the tie downs again, he started the engine and motioned the crewman to haul the anchor. As he turned toward home, he saw a small boat sitting motionless on the other side of the channel. It was too far to see much detail, but he noticed the bright orange color of an old Tampa Bay Buccaneers cap.

4

STEVEN BECKER

A MAC TRAVIS ADVENTURE

WOOD'S
REEF

JERRY DOANS WATCHED the entire operation through his binoculars. He was out on a scouting mission aboard his rented 22-foot center console and needed to keep an eye on his "fleet" — the handful of lobster boats that he shadowed. These were the successful lobster and crab boats, that set their traps in more secluded areas. Seclusion was important for what Jerry did.

He kept tabs on the boats to check on the location and frequency with which they pulled their traps. This knowledge was critical to his profession; he liked to dive on the traps the day before they were scheduled to be pulled, as it gave him the best chance of scoring some tails without anyone noticing the two or three he took from each trap. If all the stars lined up, he could dive on Fridays, hit the road to Miami and sell them Saturday. This conveniently had him in the city for party night, with a fist full of spiny lobster dollars. A good day could net him a cool grand.

With his binoculars, he scanned the water, looking at the boats in the distance. He wanted to get a closer look but was wary of being spotted. Travis' boat was out there, but something was unusual. Whatever they were doing over there, it was *not* lobstering, that was for sure. He finished the last of his "Big Gulp" sized rum drink and looked again, trying to make out what they had pulled up. Using the rental boat as cover, he slowly motored closer for a better look. There were rental boats all over this area, and the commercial fisherman and locals treated them like pesky mosquitoes. Using a rental gave Doans the ability to go wherever he wanted, automatically labelled an idiot tourist by the locals. He got as close as he dared to see what the boat was hauling from the bottom and sat back to watch.

It had to be worth something, he thought. Travis wouldn't waste time pulling up garbage. He continued to watch the larger boat, wondering how he could capitalize on this new-found knowledge.

The object was out of view and the other boat was underway. He refilled his drink and started figuring out how close he could follow. He wanted to know what Travis was up to.

———

Mac shielded his eyes from the glare coming off the water as he navigated the forty-two foot steel-hulled trawler through the maze of small keys and shoals scattered in his path. This was one of those places where GPS was useless. The straight line the computer and satellites would calculate always ended up grounding you in these waters, as evidenced by the propeller slashes, white in the dark turtle grass.

The trawler was making about six knots through the choppy waters, the beefed-up 760-hp diesels not needed here. This wasn't an area you could run full out. They were cruising through one of the less-travelled areas, known by the locals for good permit fishing on the right tide, but not much more. Tourists stayed away, as there were no markers except a stick with a random plastic bottle or buoy stuck on it. To the uneducated eye, there was no rhyme or reason to those, either. You never knew who set a marker or what they intended it for. It could just as easily be marking a hazard as safe passage. The red and green navigation markers liberally sprinkled through the Keys to mark the main channels were not in evidence here.

He guided the boat through mostly invisible channels, some indicated by subtle color changes, others not at all. The sun was descending toward the horizon, the air cooling slightly, as he slid up to a lone piling twenty feet from a small beach. There he found a camouflaged john boat, some traps and nets, all hidden by the mangroves growing above the water line.

"What brings you to these parts?" came a voice from the scrub.

"Need your help with something," Mac called back.

A grizzled old man walked into view. He waved his walking stick toward Mac, and Mac nodded in a greeting to his old friend.

Mac swung the stern to the pile and tied the boat off from a rear cleat. Once secure, he dropped the anchor to keep it from swinging in the current. The tide was close to its peak now, allowing the thirty-two inch draft of the trawler to swing freely inches above the sandy bottom. In a few hours it would turn, leaving the boat aground. That meant he didn't have long to talk.

"Brought me some tails, that was damn nice of you," Wood yelled.

"Yeah, I can give you some, but I need your eyes on this." He pointed to the bomb lashed to the deck.

Suddenly Wood was in the water, wading the dozen feet to the boat, his pants wet to the mid-thigh. Trufante helped him onto the dive platform and over the transom.

Mac caught the recognition in Wood's face, and knew he had brought this to the right place.

"Knew it was out there, but didn't think it would ever see the light of day," Wood murmured.

"You know what it is, then?"

"MK101-Lulu is what it is. Nuclear depth charge from back in the '60s. Kennedy's fiasco with Cuba. I know exactly what it is and how it got there. Now the question is what to do with it. That son of a bitch has eleven kilotons of nuclear meanness."

"Is it safe?" Mac asked.

"After being in that hole for fifty years, anything can happen, but in theory they're set to explode at depth. Where the hell was it?"

"Thirty-foot trench."

"Makes sense," he paused. "I gotta think about this. That son of a bitch running for President has his fingerprints on this too. You did the right thing bringing it here. Now I gotta figure out what to do about it."

"I can't take it in or leave it on the boat. Look at the thing. It's older than you. If it hasn't started leaking nuclear material already, it's bound to soon. Leaving it down there's not an option."

Wood ran his hands over the rusting rivets. "I've got some history with this. Best keep it here. You can swing around to the mangroves on the west side. There's a bar that should be showing. The water gets a little skinny there and it's hard to see unless you know it's there." He paused. "The other problem is what to do about that." He swung his head towards Trufante. "That boy's got a mouth on him that'll run from here to Key West faster than you can drive."

"I'll have to deal with that one," Mac said. "I couldn't have got it here without him."

———

Wood guided the trawler around the small island, locally known as a key — butchered vernacular of the Bahamian cay. He poled his skiff with practiced ease. Slow and strong. Mac idled behind him around the mangroves covering the seaward point of the island and cut the engine when Wood signaled.

Mac looked over at Trufante, trying to gauge the condition of his mate. He looked close enough to sober and might be useful. The men reversed the process they used to bring the bomb on board. It was soon sitting on the sandy rise. Wood pulled a machete from the skiff and handed it to the Cajun.

"This is a young man's game." He signaled for Trufante to cut some mangroves to camouflage the bomb.

Trufante snorted. "Any fool knows those are protected. You can't just cut on them."

"My island, my rules. Now start cuttin'. Cover the whole clearing with the camouflage net." Wood pointed to the ball of mesh in the bow of the john boat. "Then put the branches on it." He motioned Mac to come closer, out of hearing range.

"We're going to have to make a plan about what to do here," Wood said.

Mac slapped at the mosquitoes circling his head, wondering why they left the old man alone. "Let me get rid of that fool and come back in the morning. I'll bring some supplies for you if you need."

"What the heck?" Wood turned and shielded his weathered eyes from the setting sun, looking for the source of the barely audible engine noise.

Mac followed his gaze. A rental boat moved out of the mangroves across the way and started to pick up speed. "Fool tourists, what are they doing out here?"

5

STEVEN BECKER

A MAC TRAVIS ADVENTURE

WOOD'S REEF

THE VICE PRESIDENT leaned forward in his chair and glanced at the poll numbers his campaign manager had laid out on the antique coffee table. He rubbed his bearded face and glanced out the window of the Old Executive Office Building at 1600 Pennsylvania Ave, across the way. If these numbers held, he may just get there. The realization of his dream that had been born some fifty years ago was a week away from fruition. POTUS. President Ward—he liked the sound of it.

"They look really good, Brett."

"Yes, sir. Take a look at the battleground states. The only one in the margin of error is Florida. We need to spend some resources down there and kick it up this week."

"You're sure Ohio and Virginia are a wrap?"

"As long as there's no October surprise, I feel pretty good about it. And I don't see that coming, either. You've been sitting in this office almost two terms without a mistake. They ran you through the vetting process ten ways to Sunday before they put you on the ticket as VP eight years ago."

Joe Ward, VP, sat back and relaxed. "Anyone that climbs the

ladder from enlisted man to fighter pilot, senator, and here, has some baggage. Let's just say there may be a skeleton or two out there. They're just still in the closet. Besides, I really have not done much from here. You know the boss is all about control. Isn't it plain as day that I haven't done anything?" he asked.

"It's the vice president's job to do nothing. You've backed some good causes, kept the Senate in check, and gone to some funerals. That's a job well done for a VP. Now look at this itinerary. We'll spend a little time in the Panhandle, maybe head over to Gainesville and hit a Gators game, and then finish in South Florida. That's where the votes are. We need to get those little old ladies in Dade and Broward Counties lined up to vote for you. Pack your bags, sir. We've got less than a week, and I mean to make the most of it."

Ward could not hide the smile that was creeping across his face. After all these years playing second fiddle, starting as a junior senator, then moving up the ladder to head several prominent committees and finally vice president. He was happy, but his sixty-eight years weighed on him as he picked up the itinerary.

"I did a big chunk of my naval service at Truman in Key West. Do you think we could get any traction with the fiftieth anniversary of the Cuban Missile Crisis?"

"I'll see what I can work up. We'll need to do some focus groups and weigh the Cuban vote. I don't think there's going to be any backlash."

———

Mac turned toward port and idled into one of the canals off the main channel of Boot Key Harbor. Marathon had canals like subdivisions had roads. The boat headed into the commercial district, behind the gas docks and bars closer to the inlet. Properties here had about a hundred feet of seawall. Back yards were concrete, with scattered palm trees and shade awnings. The utilitarian yards had no lawns. Lobster and crab traps were scattered as lawn ornaments, and commercial boats lined the seawall in various states of readiness. Voices came from every third or fourth property, many slurred. Dogs barked randomly.

He coasted to a stop, turned the engine toward the dock, and put the engine in reverse, slowly moving closer to an empty spot space on the seawall.

"Not working tomorrow," Mac said as Trufante moved toward the wheel, not ready to disembark yet. "Maybe the day after. See what the weather does."

"Hook me up with some cash then." Trufante was close enough Mac could smell the beer on his breath. "Should be a little overtime for today, too."

"Here's a couple hundred." Mac pulled two bills out of his wallet and handed them to the crewman, anxious to get the man off the boat. "I don't want any drunk talk about what happened today. That stays between us, you hear me? I'll sell the catch tomorrow morning, swing by and settle up with you."

Trufante gave him the down-on-your luck, this-isn't-enough-money look. "Hey, you got more money than me."

Mac shrugged. It wasn't the first time they'd had this conversation. Trufante was under the impression that they should split 50/50, partially because he'd run his own operation in the past. "Your boat only needs a little work, and you could do your own deal." He scanned the property, settling his gaze on the group of people sitting in a rough circle under a roof overhang, cooled by a ceiling fan. "Get rid of your entourage up there. They're just drinking your beer and eating your food. Not one of them is any use to you."

"Yeah boss," Trufante mumbled. He grabbed the bills. "You know one or two of those girls up there's got her eyes on you. I could hook you up if you wanted."

"No thanks, that's trouble I don't need."

Trufante hopped over the side and gained his footing on the dock. He yelled up at the party, and then was gone into the darkness.

Mac sighed in relief — that had gone better than he expected.

Putting the boat in reverse, he cut the wheel in the opposite direction, and executed a perfect U turn. Minutes later, he was out of the canal.

———

Trufante walked up to the patio and greeted his guests, flashing his big white smile at them. He was king here — these were his people. There were three men and two women sitting around in assorted chairs, using an empty wire spool for a table. Each had a beer that did not look to be their first. He grunted a greeting as he headed for the refrigerator by the back door and, two bottles in hand, returned to settle into an empty chair.

It was an easy life hanging with his buds, drinking beer, and riding motorcycles. Katrina had forced him to make a quick move out of New Orleans. He'd been a big-time concrete contractor working on the dikes that held the Mississippi at bay ... until they didn't. Not really sure if the law was after him, he had the sense to know that he'd never get another contract. The Keys were an easy place to blend in and hang out. There were all kinds of characters here that made him seem common—except for his smile. A thousand dollars of bright white teeth, oversized for his mouth, gleamed whenever he grinned.

Though his smile showed otherwise, things were not as bright as they seemed. He couldn't afford to fix the boat and foreclosure notices sat unopened on his kitchen counter. But, you didn't need much to subsist here.

"Y'all having a good time drinking my beer," he heckled the group. "I feel like riding. Any of you sorry bastards up for Key West?"

The group was past the point of reorganizing their party an hour away. Looks were averted, and no one answered his call to action.

"Never mind then. I'll go myself. Hang out if you want, but leave a few for me." The king had to be gracious to his subjects.

———

The wind whipped his shoulder-length hair behind him. Bugs nested in the cracks of his thousand-dollar grin. He took in the view from the top of the Seven Mile Bridge and an hour later, he crossed through Boca Chica, then Stock Island, and headed toward Duval Street. This time of night, Key West was rocking. The cruise ships were gone, the families were tucking their kids into bed, and the crowd was looking for a good time.

He slid the Harley into a spot and strolled down the street. Despite his long frame, shoulder-length hair, and big white grill, he didn't attract many looks. Key West was the freak capital of the world after the sun went down ... probably before, as well.

Music came through the open shutters of the bar. He slid through the group of smokers hanging by the front door and headed in. It was close to ten on a Friday night and the bar was packed. The Turtle was more of a locals' spot than the trendier Sloppy Joe's or Hog's Breath, where the tourists hung out. That meant it was friendlier. He spied a seat down at the end of the bar and slid into it with practiced ease.

He looked both ways, scoping out the neighborhood, and caught the eye of the bartender. She came toward him, pecked him on the cheek, and placed a cold beer in front of him. He sat back and enjoyed the scene.

6

A MAC TRAVIS ADVENTURE

WOOD'S
REEF

MAC IDLED past the public mooring buoys, heading toward the maze of channels that constituted Sister Creek. He had a house on a canal off Boot Key, but he wanted no part of other people right now. The truth was, he *rarely* wanted any part of other people. They all wanted something, leaving few in his life whom he could count as friends.

Women were especially in the outlawed class. Currently he was a platinum member of the Little Rascals "He-man Women Haters Club." Not that he didn't like women—he did. But time and experience, mostly bad, had made him wary of their charms. Two divorces, both bitter, revealed too much of where the female mind could go. *Not all that interested*, was his state of mind about social entanglements.

The wake of the boat was the only movement on the water as he coasted to a stop. Ten feet from shore, he dropped anchor and let the current turn the boat so that he could set the hook in the sandy bottom. He let out some scope on the anchor line and shut down the running lights, leaving the white anchor light on top of the wheel house as the only sign he was there.

He went into the galley and poured a couple of inches of scotch from his well-hidden stash into a tumbler. The bottle remained well hidden because Trufante could smell alcohol from a distance, and had a habit of drinking anything he found. Leaving the cabin door open with only the screen to keep out bugs, he went back on deck.

The cold fronts coming from the north every week or so started at about this time of year. Late October offered the best weather of the year — it still got hot during the day, but early mornings and evenings were pleasant. The rainy season was all but over, the threat from a hurricane diminishing as the days got shorter.

The scotch began to work its magic halfway through the drink, and he felt the adrenaline of the day recede. He knew sleep would not come easily tonight, not that it usually did. The questions started to move through his mind now that it had finally shut down enough to let them work themselves out.

Nukes didn't show up every day, and now that one had, what the hell was he supposed to do about it? Truman AFB was still manned outside of Key West. Wood surely had some contacts there. The old man had run the construction on half the bridges in the lower Keys. Many of the newer spans adjacent to the old bridges had his finger-prints all over them. These same bridges had been the bulk of Mac's work life as well. Trained as a commercial diver, he'd worked for Wood in the '90s. They had built a close bond over those years. As Wood said, "Dependable help in this spit of sand is hard to find. Better you stick around." Indeed, most of the labor in the Keys came and went with seasons and storms. Mac, on the other hand, showed up one day and never left. And now he hoped to use that relationship to solve this problem.

He thought the Navy was the logical choice. After all it was theirs, but his distrust of authority and his guess that Wood knew something about it had stopped him from reporting it right away. Mac wasn't sure that the Navy wasn't the best choice after all. They'd tell them and he could wash his hands of the whole incident.

Satisfied with his solution, he drained the last finger of scotch in one swallow, as if to put the entire day in the past.

Alan Trufante was still glued to his barstool at last call, the smile from his fake choppers bigger and whiter than ever. He'd been pretty conservative on the beers, figuring he would have to drive back. Locals and experienced drinkers knew that the Keys were no place to drink and drive. The entire hundred and twenty miles of US1 was a two-lane speed trap. Big Pine Key was the worst at night, with its thirty-five-mph speed limit to protect the Key deer. It was a rare occurrence to drive the stretch of US1 from Key West to Marathon after dark and not encounter at least one cruiser. He'd been taking it easy for that very reason.

At last call, the lights turned up to full, and the bar began to empty, the bouncer calling out, "You don't have to go home, but you can't stay here."

Lisa, the barmaid came over to Trufante and took his beer off the bar. "Sorry, babe, got to dump it. You can hang out for a while if you want, but no drinks." She turned away to start her cleanup routine and Trufante admired the tight cutoff jeans barely covering her thirty-year-old bottom. Maybe he'd get some of that tonight, he thought, his grin widening.

"Got a pretty good party to hit if you want to hang out." Lisa said, cleaning the bar near him.

"Why hell yeah, little girl, don't have to be back 'till day after tomorrow. I'm up for some party. Be needin' a place to crash, though."

"No problem," she said, bumping her butt against him.

The big white smile got even bigger. Evidently she'd been thinking the same thing. "Lead on."

It was almost four when they left the bar, and Duval Street was still packed and rowdy. Drunken catcalls and hoots rang out over the cacophony of music streaming from the open shutters of most bars.

They walked several blocks to what had to be the gaudiest house on the street. It was an accomplishment to stand out in Key West, with gingerbread moldings hung heavy from most of the Victorian houses, and Caribbean colors the norm. No muted earth tones here. The lights were all on in the two-story Victorian. The house was painted purple with pink trim and the attic window glowed with a backlit stained-glass pattern of a couple embracing. The property was in a modest state of disrepair, common to the party houses. Overgrown landscape partially blocked the walk and drive almost, completely hiding a dilapidated detached garage. The white railings were streaked with rust spots from the weather eating away at the old nails.

The party was just getting going when they knocked and walked in. The host ran to the door, hands flapping, bells on his slippers ringing. "Lisa love, you made it." He kissed her on both cheeks and gave her a quick hug. "And, who's your friend?" he asked, giving Trufante's long, lean frame the once -over.

She moved closer to Trufante, as if to protect him from the onslaught she saw coming. "This is Tru. Babe, this is Behzad." She put her arm around him as she introduced him. "He's a friend from Marathon."

Behzad seemed to get the message and slid across the room to embrace several other guests.

"What the hell was that?" Trufante asked. "Never seen an Arab-looking gay dude before. I thought they whacked heads off for that."

"He calls himself Persian. I think he went to school here and stayed. He's fun, though, and just wait 'till you see the stuff he gets."

Trufante fingered the lone hundred left from what Mac had given him. He'd been saving it for just that sort of fun. Now he was looking forward to the rush soon to come.

Despite the late hour, the party was just shifting into high gear. Trufante already had a buzz on from the coke and ecstasy he'd scored from Behzad. He'd ended up in a group of half a dozen people laying lines out on a mirror, and was now kicking back and enjoying his beer as he listened to the music and chatter of the party. It was the usual

Key West mixed bag — you never knew who would show up to these parties. All kinds of folks lived in Key West, and the really interesting ones tended to work the night shift. That meant they came to parties late. He reached for the mirror and laid out the last of his coke.

He looked at his host as he handed him the mirror. Even in Key West, Behzad looked a little out of place. All fancied up, looking Middle Eastern for sure, and most certainly leaning toward boys. Trufante wondered what his story was. The curiosity ended when he took two vials from his silk pocket. He handed everyone a pill from one and tapped the other on the mirror, releasing its white powder.

Trufante, too, was feeling gracious and more than a little buzzed. He had the gift of the storyteller, and now felt he owed his host a story.

"We had a hell of a day out there. Y'all will never believe what me and Mac pulled from the bottom today." He waited until he had their attention and continued. "We were out there lobstering about twelve miles into the bayside, pulling traps, when Mac decided to dive for some grouper.

"Over the years, we've pulled up all kinds of stuff from the bottom, but nothin' like this. God damn if it wasn't a whole Navy bomb. Looked kind of weird, not like the stuff you see in the movies at all."

As he told the story, Behzad leaned closer.

STEVEN BECKER

A MAC TRAVIS ADVENTURE

WOOD'S
REEF

THE TIDE HAD JUST STARTED to rise when he pulled anchor and got underway. The trawler moved through the maze of mangrove-lined channels, Mac's hand on the wheel, steering from memory, as it retraced its course back to the bay side. Once under the Seven Mile Bridge, he headed east toward the fish market to unload his catch.

After an easy run through the bay waters, Wood's place came up on the horizon. Mac pulled up to the single piling he had tied up to the day before and secured the boat. He scanned the shoreline and called out for Wood. Seeing no sign of him, he hopped over the side of the boat and waded ashore.

There was a well-disguised trail off the beach, where a mangrove branch dragged across the opening acted as a gate. Mac removed the branch and followed the trail inland. It was a small atoll, roughly a hundred yards by fifty — close to the size of a football field, but only half of it was dry. He slapped mosquitoes from his face and neck as he worked his way past the mangrove swamps on his left, wondering how Wood could live among these creatures in peace. For Mac, mosquitoes were the biggest downside of the Keys, besides the tourists.

The trail followed a serpentine path for a hundred feet before he reached the clearing where Wood lived. The site was carefully crafted, allowing the maximum use of space with minimum visibility. The small house was elevated ten feet above the sand below. This served several purposes: it allowed the breeze to reach the shuttered windows and porches, as well as keeping the mosquitoes below. It would take a major hurricane packing a direct hit, with the moon and tides in perfect alignment to create a storm surge big enough to reach the living quarters. The main roof was made of woven palm fronds, with a steep pitch to shed water. The porch faced southwest, with solar collectors on it for power and open cisterns for water. The house was accessed by stairs leading to the porch. Once inside, the finishes and craftsmanship belied the location. Mahogany flooring and wainscot, with built-in bookcases and hand-plastered walls, provided an old-world feel below the palm frond ceiling.

Though rustic in outward appearance, the house was also in excellent repair. Put this up on the Internet with a few good pictures, and this place would rent out as a vacation dream spot. Then the renters would see where it was and back out.

Mac saw no sign of his old boss. He climbed the stairs and sat down in one of the chairs on the deck to wait.

Half an hour later, he heard the sound of a small outboard motor pulling up to the beach. He went to the shore and watched as Wood gunned the engine, gaining just the right amount of speed before hitting the kill switch and tilting the motor out of the water before the propeller hit bottom. He aimed for the two trenches cut into the beach. Close to the high water mark, an old truck axle with mismatched tires stood waiting. The boat came to a rest with the bow a foot from the axle.

"Get the tide right and I can hit that thing right on," Wood muttered.

He hopped over the side of the skiff and headed toward the mangroves, where the tracks disappeared, moving several branches out of the way to reveal a small clearing just large enough for the boat. At its end, anchored in a large concrete block, was a winch. He put it in free spool and dragged the cable to the boat.

Mac knew the drill, and went to help. As he turned the crank on the winch, the boat slid easily onto the axle and moved along the tracks toward the clearing. The mangrove branches were replaced, effectively screening the craft from sight, and the two men headed up the path toward the house, Wood carrying an old milk crate he'd taken from the boat.

He dumped the contents of the crate onto a fish cleaning table adjacent to a small shack that served as a storage shed. Stone crab claws gleamed in the sunlight. He went inside and returned a few minutes later with a large propane burner and pot. Mac filled the pot with water from a hand pump. "Haven't used this sucker since the season ended last March."

"Nice catch. All's I've heard are dismal reports since the season opened last week," Mac said. "Damned jewfish eat those things whole. Idiots in Tallahassee have no idea what they did when they protected them."

"I've got a couple of secret spots where I can usually pull some out. The pots have been soaking extra, since the season opened, 'cause of that storm."

They watched the boiling water change the crabs' color from dark brown to bright red, and Mac's mouth started to water at the thought of them. He was a lobster fisherman. Which meant, of course, that he preferred the taste of crab. "What are we going to do about the bomb?" he asked.

"I couldn't sleep last night, thinking about that. It can't stay here. Too much risk of someone spotting it. I've been thinking of the best way to sink Joe Ward's campaign and dispose of the beast at the same time. I keep coming back to the Navy. Loose lips sink ships and there're a lot of those around there. Especially the base commander. Fellow named Jim Gillum. Remember him from that bridge deal down by Sigsbee Key?"

"That jackass? He couldn't manage a peanut stand."

"Word's bound to go running to Ward now that this is out in the open. I'd like to see that son of a bitch run scared. At the same time, maybe the demolitions unit down in Boca Chica can deal with the nuclear core."

"Yeah, I don't know about your deal with Gillum and Ward. I'm more concerned about that thing ruining the ecosystem than taking down a Navy captain and a presidential candidate," Mac said. "You seem to know more about this than you're letting on. Is that it?"

"Like I said yesterday, me and that bomb got some history." He turned off the propane burner. "I think we ought to take a ride down to Boca Chica. But first we're gonna eat."

A MAC TRAVIS ADVENTURE
WOOD'S REEF

Mac watched Wood from the driver's seat as the uniformed guard gave the old man a cockeyed look. He didn't get many folks drive up in an old pickup, rusted out from the harsh climate, and ask for the Base Commander by name, Mac thought.

"I asked you to call up Captain Gillum, son," Wood repeated.

"I heard you the first time, mister. What business should I say you're here on?"

"All you need to do is tell him Wood is here."

The man looked hesitantly at his partner. Tourists asked directions throughthe windows of late-model rental cars, but not often did an '80s pickup with what looked like two fishermen ask to see the base's commander. Keys residents were notorious for avoiding authority.

"I'll call up for you, but this better not be some kind of hoax." He returned to the guard station and picked up the handset.

Several minutes later, the gate swung open and the soldier waved the old truck through. "That boy sure changed his tune once he talked to your friend," Mac said.

"Never mind about that. Best you keep to yourself here. Me and the Captain go way back, and it hasn't always been good."

They pulled up at a cinderblock building left over from the 1960s, recently painted yellow, its green metal roof dulled from the topical sun. As they were getting out of the truck, they were greeted by a small-framed man in uniform, with a captain's insignia on his lapels.

"Don't know whether to be happy to see you or scared stiff," the officer said, extending his hand to Wood.

"You can decide after we have a little chat, Jim. God, man you look pale," Wood replied, any friendliness hidden by his tone of voice. "You remember Mac Travis from that Sigsbee causeway job we did."

Jim Gillum walked toward the driver's door and shook Mac's hand. "Come on in, then. We can talk in my office." He held the door open for the two men and followed them in.

"It secure in there?" Wood asked.

"It's a Navy base, Wood. It's secure."

"All right then. Just be sure it is."

"What's so important you have to visit me? I don't expect it's a social call. I haven't seen or heard from you in twenty years. Last time was when we titled that piece of sand to you."

"I would've been happy if that was the last time, too," Wood said. "Saved your career, that deal. If that was the last time I had to be here, that would have been fine with me."

Mac wondered if this was really a good idea. They walked into the sparsely decorated office and sat in the chairs facing the desk.

"Coffee, anything I can get you?" Gillum asked grudgingly.

"Cut the crap. You know I'm not here to reminisce about the old days." Wood leaned forward, elbows on the desk. "My boy here found a Lulu."

Jim Gillum sat back in shock. "What are you talking about?"

"You know what we did, you lying piece of crap. You were the Aviation Ordnanceman, for Christ's sake."

"There was all kinds of stuff going on back then. There was more ordnance coming in and out of here than we could keep track of. Thankfully, that was before computers, and those records are gone."

"It's the Navy. Nothing's gone," Wood replied. "They're in a storage building somewhere, catalogued in some arcane system that nobody remembers anymore. But they're not gone."

"All right, so you found a Lulu. And you came to me. Does that mean you're going to trust me with this?"

"Trust you, trust the Navy. No, I don't think so. Last time I trusted you, I had to bail your ass out of trouble. I don't trust you … but I need you."

Mac sat erect in the chair ready to interrupt the conversation. He was unsure if Wood really had a plan or if he was just here to throw the past in the Captain's face. He wasn't into politics and had no feelings about Joe Ward. What he wanted was the bomb disarmed and the nuclear core properly disposed of. If it blew or leaked into the pristine waters, the Keys would be ruined.

Gillum looked over at Mac, evidently hoping for a more civil response. "Care to tell me what happened?" He took out a pad and pencil.

"Jesus man, put that away. This is what you Navy boys call 'ears only.' No way we're going to leave a record of this."

Gillum put down the pencil and looked at Mac to begin. Mac relayed the story, up until the disposition of the bomb, where Wood quickly cut him off.

"Well, where is it now?" Gillum asked.

"That's gonna stay what we call 'classified' until I know what you have in mind," Wood said.

Gillum took a long time to respond. "Defuse and dispose. We have an Army underwater demolition team based here. We can set it up like a training exercise. No one else needs to know anything."

"Who are you protecting? Yourself and your pension or Joe Ward? You're both guilty. This needs to be out in the open. I'm sure this isn't the only thing Ward has done. Striped marlin don't lose their stripes. They light up like neon and get more visible when they're stressed. How do you think he's gonna do as President if he couldn't make the right choice then, or come clean since?"

The men were startled when Mac spoke, so focused on their past they forgot he was there. "That thing's fifty years old. What if it blows? We may have damaged it by moving it."

"It's not going to blow. The controls were simple in those days. Heck, there weren't even circuit boards then. Just snip a couple of wires and it's done. Then they can disassemble and dispose of the core. We can scatter the rest of the parts." Gillum said.

"It ain't that easy and you know it." Wood gave the Captain a hard look. "We're going to do this together, me, you and Mac. You have access to the bomb specs and wiring diagrams and I don't. That stuff is probably still classified. It's sure as hell not on the internet."

"I don't know if I can get access to that information without setting off an investigation."

Wood's temper was up now. "Figure it out. This could be a career wrecker for you, not to mention that ass running for President. You're about to retire with a pretty nice pension, and I'd hate for something like this to come along and take all those dreams of yours away."

Gillum paused for a moment, took a deep breath, and then nodded. "There're some numbers I need off the unit. Should be a series of four or five numbers stamped into the tail section. Get those for me and I'll see what I can do."

STEVEN BECKER

A MAC TRAVIS ADVENTURE

WOOD'S
REEF

MAC AND WOOD were staring at the bomb, looking for the numbers Gillum had asked for. Mac scraped at the area near the tail, trying to uncover the serial numbers now covered with barnacles. Wood kneeled in the sand near the nose, looking the casing over, studying the access panel.

"You know, I could probably dissect this sucker without the schematic. We're talking the '60s here. How complicated could it be?" Wood asked himself out loud.

"That could go badly. Remember the old spy movies. Clip the wrong wire and boom," Mac said.

A distant buzz caused them to look up at the same time, searching for the source of the outboard engine that seemed to be closing in.

———

It was well into the afternoon when Jerry arrived at the dock. His head still hurt from a long night partying, but he had work to do. He sensed a payday. The boat's motor fired up and he waited for his handheld GPS to display the coordinates from yesterday. He entered these into the boat's built-in unit and pushed down on the throttle. An arrow on the screen showed the fastest route to the destination. Head banging, he set the course, passing over several shallow sand bars without knowing it.

The boat leveled off and started moving at an easy twenty knots, the ride smooth, the seas flat. Jerry was feeling better; the wind on his face, blowing through his hair, helped clear his head. Five miles from the dock, he saw birds standing in the water and veered around them. Once past, he resumed his heading.

He approached the island at full speed, the late afternoon sun hiding the bottom and shoals from view. The water was clear, but the direction of the sun disguised the features and color changes. Still traveling at twenty knots, the propeller suddenly hit a rock, the impact tearing the steering wheel from his hands. The boat spun out of control and turned ninety degrees. It was airborne and running straight toward the mangroves when it touched down, smashing into the sandbar.

———

Wood's legs were underneath the beached hull.

"What the hell you think you're doing?" Mac screamed at the intruder.

The man was trying to reassemble himself, checking for damage. The adage that drunks land well must be in play today, for despite being airborne for thirty feet, he seemed unhurt.

"Aren't you supposed to mark low water?" he responded, playing the victim.

"It's my island, my rules. I want folks around here, I'll put out a welcome mat of green and red markers clear back to Marathon. Turns out I don't want guests." Wood spat out in pain, then settled back in the sand.

Wood tried to move, grunting in pain, the white sand now red below him. Mac tried to move the hull, but it was too heavy.

The intruder, finally waking to the reality of what happened, noticed the old man's condition. He moved cautiously to the hull and studied the situation.

"Goddam' if you ain't some city fool. What are you doin' out here anyway?" Wood snarled.

Mac stepped between them, forcing the stranger back. He watched the intruder, following his gaze as it moved over to the camouflage netting, it's end lifted off the sections of the bomb they had been working on. He could clearly see the nose and tail fin, and recognition was evident in the eyes of the stranger.

Wood noted his gaze as well. "Nothin' there you need to worry about."

"You. Come with me." Mac pointed at the man. He had no intention of leaving him there alone with Wood. They set off towards the interior of the island. Both men struggled as they forced their way through the mangroves, clearing a path with their hands as they went.

They were back a few minutes later with supplies. Mac set the pry bar into the sand and tried to lever the hull up. But the more pressure he placed on the bar, the deeper into the sand it sank. He yelled over at the stranger. "Put that bottle down and get me some of that driftwood over there."

Several minutes passed as they dug out some sand and created a driftwood platform for the pry bar to rest on. Mac lifted again, and the boat moved slightly. A little more, and he ordered the stranger to place a larger piece of driftwood between the hull and the sand. As soon as the pressure was off his legs, Wood used his arms to extricate himself. He took inventory of himself and looked at the man in disgust.

"This ain't good." Wood said.

Mac looked down at the sliver of fiberglass from the broken hull embedded in Wood's side. The piece stuck out several inches. There was no telling how far it had gone in, but from the look of the blood pooling in the sand it was deep.

"Can you walk?" Mac asked Wood. He turned to the man. "Help bandage him up." Not really sure what to do, but knowing he had to stop the bleeding Mac opened the first aid kit. He ripped Wood's shirt away, exposing the wound. "This is going to have to come out. Give me that bottle."

The guy picked up the bottle, took a slug, then handed it to Wood.

"What the hell? Are *you* hurt?" Mac yelled as Wood winced in pain. He grabbed the bottle and poured tequila on the wound. "Get a bandage ready and some tape. This is going to be ugly. Don't know how much it's gonna bleed."

Mac grabbed the fiberglass chunk and yanked. Wood passed out when it left his body, a steady stream of blood pulsing from the wound. Mac watched the other man puke into the sand as he tried to apply pressure to the wound.

He waited for the man to recover. "Think you can hold this on here before passing out? I'm gonna bring the boat around. We need to get him emergency treatment and fast. It'll take half the time for me to bring him in than having to wait for a boat or chopper to come out and get him." Mac set off down the path.

What seemed like hours later, but was only several minutes, Mac pulled the trawler into view. The man was still holding the bandage, soaked with blood, a panicked look on his face, the empty bottle of tequila at his side.

"How 'bout we change that out for a clean one? That tequila was supposed to be for this, not for you."

"It was. If not for that bottle, I would be passed out on the ground right next to him and he'd be dead. I'm not good with blood."

Mac ignored this bit of idiocy and taped the new bandage to the wound. The blood had stopped pumping, but the pad was soaked through again. This was bad. They needed a hospital.

"We've got to move him. If he loses too much more blood, he'll go into shock."

Mac waded out to the boat he had anchored as close to shore as possible. The shallow water extended a hundred feet until it was deep enough for the boat to rest. He eyed a paddleboard strapped down on top of the cabin. Removing the tie downs, he tossed it into the water, aiming it toward the beach, and walked the board toward shore. The two men dragged Wood onto the board and guided it back to the trawler, where they lifted him onto the dive platform. Mac made him as comfortable as possible and set off for Marathon.

STEVEN BECKER

A MAC TRAVIS ADVENTURE
WOOD'S
REEF

MAC HAD DROPPED Wood at the dock and handed him, unconscious, to the waiting EMTs who had treated him for shock and re-bandaged the wound in the ambulance on the short trip to Fishermen's Hospital. They parked under the overhang at the emergency room entrance and now Wood's gurney was being wheeled into the emergency room entrance.

Unnoticed, Jerry Doans had slithered away from the boat as soon as they reached the dock. He had no intention of talking to the authorities. His clothes were tattered and wet, his face dirty, hair unkempt. There was no way he was going to get a ride anywhere like this, either, so he started walking. He quickly covered the mile back to US1 and collapsed on a bus bench, thankful that it provided some shade. Dehydrated from the tequila and slightly delirious from the entire incident, his most rational thought was to get himself cleaned up and head to the closest bar.

He took inventory. The first thing he noticed was that his phone was gone. In his front pocket was the handheld GPS, screen smashed. With only a few soggy dollars in his pocket, he was now a man with a plan. He got off the bench and headed north on US1 to find a gas station. When he got there, the clerk made quick change of his dollars, just to get him out of the store, and pointed him in the direction of one of the few remaining pay phones in the civilized world.

He had no idea of his friend's phone number, now lost in the contact list on his phone; and with the phone book long gone, he dialed information. It took a dozen rings for the man to answer, and fifteen minutes later an old Toyota Corolla to pull up.

————

Mac looked around for the guy who'd hit Wood, but he was gone. Thinking he probably took off as soon as they'd hit dry ground, he put that on the back burner and thought about the call he had to make.

He'd decided to walk the mile from the hospital back to the boat ramp at 33rd Street where the EMTs had met his boat. Once there he fired up the engines and headed West towards the Seven Mile Bridge. He steered through the old and new bridge sections, aiming between the second and third power pole, then headed past several markers before changing course to the east.

He steered by instinct into the Knights Key channel and entered Boot Harbor, thinking about Mel. He knew from Wood's sporadic conversations with her, that his daughter was living somewhere around DC, but he had no direct number to reach her. Slowing to idle speed, he rehearsed the conversation he was about to have in his head. He turned the boat into the canal backing on his house and tied up at the dock. Inside, he fired up his laptop and started searching.

They hadn't spoken in years, but he had to break that silence now.

He pulled up the Davies and Associates website, and called the general information number, half-hoping someone would be working this late, the other half-hoping that he would get a reprieve until morning. It had been a hard day, and he wasn't sure he was ready for this. After talking to several of her coworkers, he finally found someone who was willing to give him her cell number.

He took a deep breath and dialed.

"Melanie Woodson," came the slightly out-of-breath answer.

"Mel, this is Mac down in Marathon." The nervousness turned to a queasy feeling. The pregnant pause was unbearable, but he gathered his courage and continued. "Listen, your dad's been in an accident. He's in surgery right now at Fishermen's Hospital."

The silence continued, then finally broke. "And why are you calling? I knew when I saw the Keys area code that this was trouble."

Mac ignored the hostility. "Do you even care about him? He's hurt, Mel."

"Of course I do. Tell me what happened."

Mac told her about the boat accident, and she sighed.

"I'm sorry I snapped at you, Mac. I'll get the next flight down there. Probably won't be 'till morning now, but I'll be there."

"Thanks, Mel, I know he'd appreciate you being here."

STEVEN BECKER

A MAC TRAVIS ADVENTURE

WOOD'S
REEF

BEHZAD WOKE TO A DISASTER. The sun was already well on its way to the western horizon, and he lay in bed wondering first, who was next to him, and second, what had happened the night before. He watched the sun disappear below the third-floor roofline of the house next door before he finally gained his feet, his corpulent belly hanging over the silk pants he'd worn for the party. There was something about the sun going down that made his hangover better.

He walked by the coffee maker and over to the half-empty bottle of wine on the counter. Too late for coffee, he thought. A glass of wine in his hand, he sat down at the kitchen counter and tried to piece together what had happened the night before. There was something he needed to remember. He hated it when his memory eluded him, and it was happening more frequently of late. Making no association with his lifestyle, he assumed it was his thirty-year-old body decaying. He had no idea how older people dealt with life.

Fortunately, his background and training all but eliminated aging from his worries. He was bred to be a martyr. Just not until he was fifty, he hoped — life was fun now, even if Allah didn't approve. Sent to the US by his parents to get an American university education, he was befriended by two groups at college, both Middle Eastern. The first group were the reborn Muslims — reborn to live like Americans. They saw beyond the strict laws with which they'd been brought up. So they weren't always about enlightenment; in fact, most of the time they were just about the fun and the girls. The second group were the fundamental Islamists, who hated everything American, more now that they lived amongst them.

Most Middle Eastern foreign students arrived naive, with heavily accented but passable English. They quickly fell in with one of those two groups, but Behzad had fallen for both. He'd quickly learned that the strict Islamic laws weren't for him. The American lifestyle was more appealing. But, without intending to, he fell for a member of the fundamentalist group. The fun lovers were tolerant of his fundamental lover, because they were enlightened now and thought tolerance was cool. Ibrahim, his lover, was high up in the fundamentalist group and circulated the lie that Behzad hung out with the other group to gain converts. Sexual mores in the Islamic community were hard to understand from a Western point of view. Homosexuality, although a quick path to hell, was rampant.

Behzad was fearful. He was terrified of not going to Paradise, though he didn't have the backbone to adhere to the moral codes necessary for getting there. Many practitioners of Islam hedged their bets, much like the death bed confessions of Catholics.

His answer was martyrdom at fifty - maybe earlier. Why not call it quits when he envisioned himself too old to party like a rock star? He saw no life after fifty, why not call it good and go to Paradise? The only praying he did was that the seventy-two virgins promised in Heaven were boys. Thoughts of the virgins and paradise faded as fragments of the night tried to re-form in his mind. Lubricated by the wine, his memory started to return and he recalled something about a bomb. He topped off his glass and moved over to his computer, suddenly thinking about Ibrahim. The two men had not been in touch for years, as Behzad's lifestyle and Ibrahim's fundamentalism had driven a wedge between them. The passion had fizzled with time and distance.

The last method of contact they had used to protect Ibrahim's identity had been through an anonymous email account. Although it had become commonplace in real life as well as novels, this setup was virtually undetectable. He logged into the old Hotmail account and entered their shared password. The home screen came up showing no messages. Behzad navigated to the draft window and started typing. When he was done, he saved the draft and logged off.

———

Mel was back under the barbell. Her compact 5'3" frame easily handled the weight. Abs tightened and defined, the weight went overhead, her butt and legs tight. She did a few quick presses and dropped the bar after the last one, the bumper plates bouncing on the floor. A few breaths later she grabbed the kettle bell. Fifteen swings later, it was back to the bar. After five rounds of this, breath came in gulps and sweat pooled on the floor. Grabbing her phone she stopped the stopwatch, recorded the time and went to the main screen. A text message displayed her flight times.

It was quiet in the yellow Jeep. Now, finally alone, it hit her that her dad was in the hospital. Tears flowed down her face as the memories of their relationship overwhelmed her. It was she, mad at him for living on that island like a hermit, and he, mad at her chosen career as an ACLU lawyer. Stubbornness ran deep in the Woodson gene pool, and neither would allow the other their own point of view. He had remarried shortly after her mother's premature death, to a mean, self-centered woman who drove a wedge between them any time she could. She'd married her career, something he never understood. The train wreck of their pasts haunted her on the short ride back to her Georgetown apartment.

Home-making was a clear second to her career, and her apartment was in its usual state of flux. She pushed aside the pile of clothes on the closet floor, pulled out her suitcase, and began throwing clothes into it. Bag packed and ready to go, she checked her email and laid out the next day's work for her team. Exhausted, and with a 6 am flight, she was in bed before ten. She tossed and turned 'till midnight, when her pulsing muscles and adrenaline buzz finally wore off and allowed her sleep.

STEVEN BECKER

A MAC TRAVIS ADVENTURE
WOOD'S
REEF

HAPPY HOUR WAS in full swing when Jerry Doans slid onto the bar stool. He'd grabbed a quick shower and change of clothes, gorged on water, and headed directly to the upholstered seat in his favorite bar. The first shot and beer settled his nerves, but he kept glancing at the door, fearing some official would walk in looking for him. His description must have been issued to law enforcement, even if they didn't know his name. If the police were on their game, they had followed his trail back to the boat rental outfit. They had copies of his driver's license and credit card, required for the rental. It was only a matter of time.

The day had been a disaster, and he'd gotten nothing out of it. The wrecked rental boat he could walk away from. But the old man in the hospital could land him in big trouble. He knew the younger guy from poaching his traps. Suddenly unsure whether that knowledge was reciprocal he jumped every time the door opened.

This time, the guy that walked in didn't look like a cop. He had shoulder-length blonde hair and a smile that could light up a dark cavern. He slid onto the barstool next to Jerry, nodded to his new neighbor, and ordered a beer.

He watched as the barmaid approached the guy with the teeth. She lifted her chest, pushing it towards him. And that pissed off Jerry Doans. He'd had a crush on her for months now, and she wouldn't give him the time of day. He didn't understand it. He was better dressed, better looking, and didn't have that ridiculous Cadillac grill for a smile.

For her part, Annie had that look that identifies long-time Keys residents, especially those running toward middle age. It was the *au natural*, been-in-the-sun-too-long, no-makeup, no-time-to-do-my-hair look. On some it made them look worn out, but on Annie it worked.

Every time she came toward this end of the bar, she leaned over and had a quick, whispered conversation with his neighbor. Yeah, she was courteous to him, checking on his drink and giving a quick smile ... clearly working for tips. But not giving him anywhere near the attention the other guy was getting.

Jerry, ever the salesman, ego in hand, had to get into the conversation. He waited for Annie to move to the other end of the bar, then turned to the guy. "What's the secret with getting the ladies?"

The guy's smile dimmed. "What? Me and her, we're just old friends."

"That's not how I'm reading it. I can see how she looks at you, and it's more than friendly. I'd take a piece of that if I could."

"Easy there, partner." The guy turned toward him, scowling. "You don't need to be talkin' that way. She ain't gonna have any interest in you. Besides, you look like some insurance salesman come down from Miami, looking for some action. Anyone from around here can read that a mile away."

Jerry looked into his drink. "That bad? I've been hanging around here long enough, thought I'd be fitting in."

"I'm not one to start givin' advice, but you reek of a scam. I don't know if it's what you've just done or what you're about to do, but my radar's flashing red alert."

"No scam, friend. You're right, I'm from up north. Tampa, not Miami, for what it's worth. I wholesale all the t-shirts and shells to the tourist traps." He recited his well-rehearsed cover story, wondering if it would work. He'd tried others, but it was never a good idea to mention anything having to do with real estate, the water, fishing, or boats to the locals. They inevitably knew more than he did.

The other guy relaxed. "That's a large step up from insurance sales." The grin was back. "You want to get on with the locals, you got to chill a little. This may only be a few hours from Tampa, but it's a whole different attitude. These folks here don't care what you're made of, just how you act. We all got some baggage or history. That's why we're here. Just lose that chip on your shoulder and loosen up. It's all about a no-pressure, see-what-happens kind of 'tude."

"I'll have to work on that. Maybe try some meditation or something. I can run a little to the high-strung side."

The guy laughed, showing the biggest set of teeth he had ever seen. "Tell you what, you work on that meditation thing and I'll introduce you to Annie."

"I'd appreciate that. I've kind of had a crush on her since I've been coming in here. She just ignores me, though."

They sipped their drinks, watching Annie as she worked her way toward them. "Name's Trufante, folks call me Tru." He said extending his hand. "Maybe lose a little of the 'tude, chill a bit. You'd fit in better. "

"How's this?" Jerry put on his sunglasses and hat. "Name's Jerry. Buy you a beer?"

———

Trufante did a double take, racking his brain for where he'd seen this guy before. Those glasses might have blended in with the people up north, but they sure looked Hollywood here. Said something like *Roxy* on the jeweled side bars. The hat was an old Tampa Bay Bucs hat, in their infamous bright orange from the early years. Something about it was nagging at him, though he couldn't figure out exactly what it was.

"Sure, I'll take a beer. 'Preciate it. I got to go check in with some-one, see if I've got to work tomorrow. Can't hear in here, I'll be right back," Trufante said, in answer to the stranger's question.

Doans nodded and called the unimpressed barmaid over. Trufante went to the door and stepped outside into the cooling night. He pulled out his cell phone as he walked to the end of the building, out of earshot of the smokers near the entrance.

Mac answered on the third ring. "Hey, you alive? Thought I would have heard from you by now. Looking to work?"

"Yeah, I'm good. Listen, that boat that was out by Wood's place yesterday, I think the guy running it is sitting next to me at the bar."

"That was a long way off. You sure you'd recognize him?"

"It's not him as much as what he was wearing. That old orange Bucs hat and those glasses — I could see them from a mile away. Pretty sure it's him," Trufante said.

There was a pause, then, "Where are you? He must have seen something the other day. Might have been him that crashed on Wood's place and tore up the old man. He's in surgery right now down at Fishermen's," Mac said.

"No shit. I'm at Annie's place, hanging out with him. He's trying to get some tips on picking her up. Good luck there, doesn't seem to get it that she plays for the other team."

"Can you keep him there for half an hour? I'm on my way."

Trufante coughed, rethinking the situation. "Hold on, what do you have in mind? I don't want no trouble in her bar."

"No, I'll call you when I get there. We'll figure something out."

Trufante walked back into the bar. He slithered sideways, working his way through the building crowd. Back on his bar stool he took a sip of the beer the stranger had bought him.

Twenty minutes later, beers empty, Trufante watched as Doans pulled his money off the bar, left a modest tip and pocketed the cash. "Thanks for the advice, but she's not interested. I think I'll move on and see what else I can dig up."

Trufante paused, his mind obviously struggling for an excuse. "At least let me return the favor and buy you a beer," he finally said.

"Thanks, but no thanks. I'm out of here."

Trufante was getting nervous. He would be pretty conspicuous trying to follow him on his Harley and Mac wasn't here yet. "You a gambling man?"

"I've been known to take a bet," Doans eyed him with renewed interest. "What do you have in mind?"

"I got a secret that'll tell you what's up with that barmaid you're hot after. A game of eight ball for the info. I win, it'll cost you another beer."

Jerry had to know. It wasn't a maybe — he needed this information to soothe his bruised ego. "I'm in."

13

STEVEN BECKER

A MAC TRAVIS ADVENTURE

WOOD'S
REEF

"Look at you, designer jeans, button-down shirt, and dress shoes — really? You want to fit in around here, the whole look's gonna have to change." Trufante sent the cue ball toward the pyramid. The balls connected and the chain reaction sent them to all corners of the table, dropping two of them.

"Looks like you've played this game before." Doans took his turn after Trufante missed.

"Not my first rodeo," Trufante responded. He evaluated the play of his opponent, not sure if he was worth the effort. It would take a couple of hours and a dozen games to get any real money out of the guy, and all indications were that he didn't have much. He decided to play him along until Mac showed, and call it a tactical loss. If their paths crossed again, he could pick up the hustle where he left off. Besides, it would be fun to break it to him that Annie was gay.

They traded shots, each sinking a ball, then missing.

He looked nervously at his watch, waiting for Mac to call. There were only three balls left on the table. He juiced his next shot with a little too much spin and it careened off the corner of the pocket and bounced away.

"Looks like it's not my night," he said as he watched Doans clear the table.

"So what's the big secret about the girl?"

Trufante leaned toward him and whispered in his ear. The stranger reared back angrily.

"You son of a bitch. Why couldn't you just tell me straight up?"

Surprised by the reaction, Trufante started to walk away. As Doans grabbed his shoulder, his phone rang. Hoping it was Mac waiting outside the bar, he yanked the hand away and started pushing Doans in the direction of the door.

"What're you pushing me for? You wanna mix it up?" Doans was too far gone to stop now. He picked up a pool cue and smacked Trufante in the head.

———

Mac entered the bar just in time to see the first strike. He shoved through the crowd, but could only watch as Trufante fell, smacking his head on a table. People moved out of his way, sensing his urgency as he dragged Trufante to the side and faced the assailant.

"Annie, call the sheriff!" he yelled over the hushed crowd. He turned on the man, giving him a quick backhand strike to the face, followed by a side kick. The man staggered backward toward the wall. The guy got up, grabbed a bottle off the closest table, and went after Mac.

A group of men now surrounded the two men.

Mac easily dodged the strike. His furor increasing when he recognized the man. Mac blocked upward and landed a fist, knuckles extended to the throat. Doans fell backward, and was caught by two of the onlookers.

"Hundred apiece if you get me out of here," Doans said to the men.

They put him down and went after Mac. He blocked the first strike, pivoted and blocked the next from behind. He turned again and landed a quick jab to the first man's face. But the movement gave the man from behind time to recover. He grabbed Mac in a bear hug, waiting for his buddy to attack from the front. Mac put all he had into an elbow to the man's gut, then grabbed his head with both hands, and flipped him over his shoulder.

The first man started to back away, but tripped over Doans' body, still sprawled on the floor. Mac turned to assess the situation and saw Jules, the sheriff, enter the bar. The crowd deferred to her uniform allowing her to approach the men.

"Easy there, cowboy," Jules said to the larger man on the floor as she zip-tied his hands behind his back. "Stand down, Mac," she said as she approached the other man and quickly zip-tied him as well. "I know these two. Give me a hand getting them to the car and I'll get your statement."

————

Doans slithered across the floor, out of sight of the sheriff. He moved to a corner of the bar, got up, and started to make for the door. He waited until the sheriff left the bar, escorting the first man to her cruiser. As soon as she turned away, he left the bar and moved toward the dock behind it. In seconds, he was away from the lights and out of sight.

He moved carefully, staying in the shadows. Confident that the man from the island had recognized him, he wanted to get out of here as soon as possible. Not sure if the dock dead ended he started looking for a hiding place. Towards the end, in the shadow was a docked boat. It looked more like a dive charter than a fishing boat. Jerry hopped over the transom and hid.

————

Mac helped Jules escort the men out of the bar. A minute later, Trufante staggered out of the door, weaving toward them.

"Where'd the son of a bitch go?"

"We got them both right here," Jules said, pointing to the two men in the back seat of the car.

"Don't know who those guys are, but they ain't our boy."

"What boy is that?" Jules asked.

"The sorry MF that ran Wood over and put him in the hospital this afternoon."

"He can't have gotten far. Take the dock, Mac. I'll take the street," Jules said as she called for backup.

———

Mac started down the dock with Trufante several steps behind. The first few slips were well lit. Charter boats, their cleaned and polished teak and stainless shining in the glow cast from the floodlights on their flybridges. Mac moved quickly past them. No place to hide there.

The dock ran parallel to the street, and the further from the bar he walked, the darker it got. Lights were spaced every twenty feet showing the walkway but they left much of the dock in shadows. Mac cautiously checked each boat for movement as he passed. He was about halfway down the dock when he spotted something moving in the cockpit of a dive boat.

"Hey," Trufante yelled.

Mac's instincts directed him to stay low. He recognized the man as he emerged from the shadow of the transom, speargun in hand, and he dove as the man braced his elbows on the boat and aimed.

Mac went down prone on the dock. He heard a scream behind him and watched the spear embed itself into Trufante's leg. Looking up from his friend, he saw the man jump onto the dock and move quickly away from the parking lot.

Mac chased him to the end of the dock. He stopped short as the man dove into the water, disappearing in the darkness. His quarry lost, he went back to the injured Cajun.

"You all right?"

"Son of a bitch." Trufante tried to move. Finally, he was able to get to his feet with Mac's help, but movement was awkward with the spear sticking out of his leg.

Mac shook his head, placed an arm under Trufante's shoulder, and took the weight off the injured leg. Slowly they made their way back to the bar. Mac fumed as they walked. Having hurt two of his friends, Mac would have to watch his back now that the guy knew he was onto him. Cornered animals were unpredictable.

14

"WOULD one of you two tell me what the hell is going on here?" Jules asked as she wheeled Trufante into the emergency room. She had called for backup to take the two thugs to the station, and was now wheeling Trufante, leg extended, spear standing straight out from his leg. Shot at close range, the barb had traveled deep into the leg, making a quick removal impossible. She'd cut off a large piece of it with bolt cutters from the trunk of the police cruiser, leaving about a foot still extending from his leg, the barb deep in muscle.

"Don't give me that bar fight crap. Maybe you," she looked back at Trufante, "But Mac here is not one to get mixed up in this kind of thing. Now, give it to me straight."

Trufante winced in pain. "That guy I was after, we think he was the one that crashed his boat at Wood's place."

"Good of you assholes to take the law into your own hands. That's what we need here — vigilantes, avenging all kinds of shit."

"We were just trying to scope the dude out. Then we were going to call you," Trufante said. "Didn't want no trouble. The guy just comes in the bar and sits down next to me. I recognized his hat. Knew he was the one watching the other day when we were with Wood. So I called Mac."

"There's this piece of paper called a police report." She turned on Mac. "You may want to consider filling one out next time." She turned to Trufante, "I have half a mind to take you in for obstruction of justice. I'll let him suffer the pain as his punishment." She thought back to the look on his face when she had cut the spear.

The ER nurse took control of the wheelchair and pushed Trufante through the double doors, leaving Mac and Jules behind, effectively ending the conversation.

————

Behzad checked his email, not sure if he was hoping for an answer or not. Thoughts of martyrdom aside, he liked his life, and figured he would for the next ten years or so ... until the inevitable decay of old age set in. The screen answered him with a new message in the draft folder. He opened the message and realized his life was about to take a turn.

My brother in God. So good of you to contact me. I had feared you left our cause. But now I am assured that you will indeed seek paradise. Pick me up at Miami Int Airport tomorrow morning. American flight 745 arrives 8:15.

Behzad entered the flight info in his phone and deleted the message. He glanced at the time on his screen and realized he would need to leave now; the drive, including the inevitable rush hour traffic in Miami, would take over four hours. He would have liked the convenience of meeting Ibrahim at Key West Airport, but knew security in the smaller airports was tighter. He and his friend would stand a better chance of being noticed here than in the turmoil of Miami International. All the same, he loathed venturing off his island.

With his schedule now defined, he decided to make a productive night out of it and see if he could move some product to friends in

Miami before the pickup. Business would shut down with Ibrahim here and the dealer that had fronted him the product was not likely to care about his guest. He went upstairs to his closet, cleared the top shelf, and removed the false panel disguised as a piece of wallboard. Inside the compartment was his scale and stash. He weighed some of the product, placed it into four small scraps of magazine paper which he folded into envelopes. These went carefully into a baggie which, he carefully sucked the air out before sealing it. Looking at what was left, he decided he might get lucky and move it all and shoved it into a separate baggie. Product in hand he replaced the panel and went to shower.

An hour later, he was cruising through Marathon, thankful for what looked like a bar fight with two police cruisers in attendance. That would occupy all the cops between here and Islamorada, which lay forty-five minutes closer to his goal. Comforted that there would be no speed traps to impede his progress, he stepped on the gas.

An hour and a half later, he felt fatigue set in on the lonely stretch of road connecting Key Largo to Florida City. The anxiety of driving US1 at night through the Keys left his adrenaline waning. Needing a bump, he pulled over on the shoulder, turned on the interior light, and pulled the baggie out of his pants. He hadn't intended to dip in, but he never did. Last night's party had cost him a big chunk of the profits from this last shipment. If he could move the rest tonight, he might just get out intact, able to pay off the Mexican. But he needed to actually get to Miami, and for that he needed to stay awake.

He opened the larger baggie and dipped in his pinkie nail. The nail was left long and manicured for just this purpose. He loaded it with white powder and inhaled, then sat back and waited for the rush. Eyes closed, he heard the boom of a loud subwoofer from a passing car. He failed to notice that the sound didn't fade, and opened his eyes to a tapping on the windows. The barrel of a gun was motioning for him to roll the window down. If the gun didn't scare him, the figure wielding it did. A shirtless six-foot Haitian, bandana pulled over his face, scar across his right eye and trucker's hat cocked on his shaved head, looked down at him.

Not realizing the baggie was still open on his lap, he rolled down the window.

"This a dangerous piece of road here, man." The accent was hard to decipher, but the meaning was not. The Haitian held him in place with one hand and checked out the baggie with the other. "What we got in the bag there?" he asked as he removed a switchblade from his pocket and lifted the bag off Behzad's lap with the tip of the blade.

Behzad almost peed himself when the gunman turned back to his own car and mimicked a throat-slicing motion with his gun hand. The music and lights went off immediately, and two men exited the car. mosquitoes made the only noise now as they zeroed in on the only fresh meat for miles. One man came around to the driver's side, the other stood behind the car.

"Pop the trunk, turn off the lights, and get out of the car," the first man said as he stepped back to allow the door to open. "What you shaking for? We're not going to hurt you." He clocked him on the head with the gun.

Behzad was slow to move as he recovered consciousness. He sat up carefully, one hand on his head where the gun had struck him. Acknowledging this as his only injury, he got to his feet and took inventory. He was alone on the warm asphalt. His car was gone. They had checked his pockets and taken his wallet, but hadn't checked deep enough to uncover the second baggie that was carefully placed in his underwear. If that was his silver lining, it wasn't much of one. The baggie they took had most of his product in it.

Scenarios of how to cope with this disaster swarmed through his mind like snakes in a pit. He sat down on the desolate stretch of road to the mainland, swatting at the mosquitoes feasting on his neck, and extended his thumb out to every passing vehicle, hoping for a ride. The accelerated martyrdom scenario was starting to appeal to him over what Cesar, his Mexican supplier, would do to him. His knowledge about the bomb was the last card left in his hand. He hoped that in return for his help finding the bomb, Ibrahim would make his problems disappear.

15

STEVEN BECKER

A MAC TRAVIS ADVENTURE

WOOD'S
REEF

BEHZAD SAT by the side of the road, staring into the black water of Lake Surprise. Intermittent lights from the vehicles entering and leaving the main route in and out of the Keys illuminated the two-lane stretch of road. Most of the traffic at this time of night were big rigs hauling goods down US 1 to Key West, or returning empty.

He had no idea what to do. No way to reach Miami to pick up Ibrahim or even a phone to call. The loss of the cocaine weighed heavily on his thoughts. "Run and hide" seemed like a really good option. All he had was the baggie in his pants, a few hundred worth, if he could avoid temptation and sell it. Not very likely, since he'd started to dip in already, and was tempted to take another bump to change his head. And why not? What was he going to do, walk to Miami? No money, no phone, no car, and stranded on one very lonely and often-dangerous stretch of road ... his options were few.

He was due to make a payment in two days and his supplier would be unforgiving if he didn't. He skirted the edge of the supplier's patience in good times. He came up with their money, but never the whole amount when promised. It was no secret he used too much product, but he moved a lot, so they tolerated him. He had no cash, but the Mexicans fronted him the drugs on credit. The volume and higher price they garnered made the risk worthwhile. Particularly because they took lives when the payment wasn't right. Which was what worried him now. Risk management in the drug world was a little different than on Wall Street.

The adrenaline from the carjacking and robbery was waning; in contrast, his paranoia, elevated by the coke, was peaking. Every sound reminded him that he was alone and defenseless. A splash caused him to jump. There was no telling what inhabited these dark, brackish waters. Looking back to the pitch-black water, he wasn't sure if the bulge in the water was an alligator or a figment of his imagination. His solution was to reach into his pants to pull out the baggie. He dipped his nail twice and leaned back, waiting for the powder to perform its magic.

Slightly restored, he got to his feet and decided the only way out was north. Ibrahim seemed his only hope. Knowledge of the bomb had to be worth something to him. He thought about the money he needed to pay back for the drugs—surely a pittance for a high-level terrorist. The question was how to get him to help. He moved slowly down the shoulder of the road, weaving slightly, thinking martyrdom was going to come a little early.

———

Jerry Doans, head on a swivel, cruised north on US1. He cleared Key Largo, ever vigilant for State Troopers. He imagined the scene in the courtroom as the charges were read: poaching, reckless endangerment and maybe manslaughter if the old man died. It was late, going on four in the morning, but it was still hot out. He turned the AC to high and opened the windows, hoping the cold air mixing with the humid night would keep him awake. He had to shut the windows, as the combination of refrigeration and humidity quickly created its own weather system, fogging up the entire car. The closer he got to the Dade County line, the better he felt. With any luck, the Monroe County sheriff hadn't identified him yet, and he could blend into Miami or cross over to Ft Myers and lay low for a while. His Keys career was likely over for now, so he was already thinking about his next move.

The fog was clearing in the cab when he thought he saw a lone figure with his thumb out by the side of the road. He thought about speeding up to pass, but the road was narrow here. Water butted up to both sides of the highway as it ran like a land bridge. If he didn't stop he might hit the man. Not wanting to add vehicular homicide to the list of charges, he slowed down and stopped on the shoulder, waiting for the figure to move toward the truck.

The stranger leaned into the vehicle from the passenger side. "Need a ride or something?" Doans asked.

"Please, I got carjacked by some freakin' Haitians. I'm stuck out here," the man answered.

"No problem. Hop in, I'm heading to Miami," Doans said, hoping the good samaritan act would change his karma.

"Miami's good. I was heading to the airport to pick up a friend."

"I'm good with that," he said. "I can drop you there."

They drove in silence and Jerry started to nod off. The car started to swerve, the buzz of the tires hitting the centerline bumpers startled him awake.

"I could give you a little bump, if you want."

"Really? That would be cool." Doans felt that karma swing. Pretty impressive that he'd managed to hook up with someone who had that sort of thing available. And was willing to share.

"Name's Behzad," he started to get chatty as he got more wired. "What kind of business are you in? You a fisherman or something, with all those coolers in the back?"

"Kind of a part-time thing. I do a lot of real estate work. Financing, repos, flips, that kind of thing. Always looking for something new. Thinking about heading over to Naples or Ft Myers and try my luck there. It's about run out down here."

Their friendship solidified with another dip in the bag. "Yeah, I think I'm in the same boat. My Key West days look numbered. Those Haitians took my stash and I can't go back without a fistful of dollars for the supplier." Behzad loved the old movie clichés.

"Maybe we can help each other out," Doans probed.

STEVEN BECKER

A MAC TRAVIS ADVENTURE

WOOD'S REEF

Mac sat in the waiting room, slumped in a chair, eyes closed, when Mel came storming in. She took one look at him and thumped him in the chest with both hands.

"Where's my dad?"

Mac opened his eyes. "Good to see you too. He's in intensive care. They say he's still critical but stable right now."

A nurse turned the corner, and glanced at Mel. "Can I help you with something, ma'am?"

"My dad, Bill Woodson. He just had surgery. Is there a doctor or someone I can talk to?"

"Give me a minute and I'll see what I can do. Are you two alright?" She looked at Mac for an answer.

"Yeah, thanks, we're good." He wasn't really sure if that was the case. Their relationship was uneasy on a good day. They'd known each other for years. Eight years older, he'd first been a big brother and later a crush. Mel had been incensed when he married when she was sixteen. Her feelings weren't on his radar. An unhappy teenager, stuck without a mom in a place she didn't want to be, she used Mac's marriage as another excuse to turn against anything to do with the

Keys. He'd noticed her as something different after his divorce, but the years of bitterness had taken their toll. The rage had subsided slightly, and Mel set her sleek frame into a chair. "Start talking, Mac. I want it all."

Mac recounted the events of the last two days. He started with the discovery of the bomb, the encounter with the Navy Captain and finally the crash. He watched her face as he spoke, hoping for some indication of sympathy, but got a stone cold-stare instead. He saw the imminent explosion coming before she opened her mouth.

"Did you have to get him involved? Couldn't you handle it yourself? He's seventy if you haven't forgotten."

"He was in the service when the Cuban Missile Crisis was going on. The piece we picked up sure looked like it was from that era. How was I supposed to know some idiot would be following us?"

"That's the trouble with you, Mac. You don't think things through, or realize how your actions affect other people."

"Enough of the holier-than-thou crap, Mel. You're a lawyer. You comment on stuff after it's happened. You live your life in hindsight."

"Oh, big talk from the only guy who didn't get hurt." She pushed him again.

Mac told her about the skirmish outside the bar. Her eyes narrowed, not with the comfort that he hoped, but rather with scrutiny.

"You know they have police for that, don't you? Trufante is sitting next to the guy that almost killed my Dad and he calls you?"

"Yeah, I already got the speech from Jules."

"She's probably the best thing that's happened to this rock since I left."

"Your patience for all things Keys related is duly noted. How was your flight?" he asked, hoping to defuse her.

The nurse came around the corner, saving him. "The surgeon will meet you outside his room. I don't know if you'll be allowed to see him yet, but the doctor will fill you in."

"Thanks," Mel said as she took off down the corridor.

"Can we just bury the hatchet for your dad's sake? You know he means a lot to me." He took off after her.

"You can come, but there's nothing you can do or say to undo this."

————

They arrived at the door to Wood's room, and Mel looked through the observation glass at her father. The surgeon approached and she turned away from the window, a lone tear in her eye. "Hello, I'm Melanie, Wood's daughter," she said.

The surgeon glanced at Mac and, not receiving an introduction, went on. "He's doing alright. We've got him stable, but only time is going to tell how he pulls through this."

"What's wrong?" Mel asked. "I just got here and I'm a little short on details," she said, casting a burning glance at Mac.

"Lacerated liver. He took a chunk of fiberglass deep in his side. It's going to be touch and go for a few days. Then it's up him to let it heal. In someone his age, especially with a little wear and tear, the liver doesn't always recover well."

"Is there anything I can do?" she asked emphasizing the 'I.'

"Like I said, we need some time to see how he's going to pull through."

"Thanks Dr. Hanson," she said, catching his name tag as she gave him a long look.

The doctor walked away, and she walked back over to the observation window. Wood was on his back, with a breathing tube in his mouth. He looked peaceful, but the IV drip was a clear signal it was drug induced. "Dammit, Mac, what am I supposed to do now? I can't just sit here and watch him."

"No, that's not what he would want," Mac answered. "Look. You might not like this, but I'm right in the middle of this. Let Jules find the guy that ran the boat up on him." He paused, steadying himself to make his case. "We went and saw this Navy captain yesterday. Wood didn't trust him with the disposition of the bomb, and the guy gave me the creeps, too. He's playing a bigger game. You want to hang with me, maybe we can figure out what's so dammed important about this bomb." He glanced at Wood, "He said something about Joe Ward, the VP, being involved. I don't care much about that angle as just making sure the damn thing doesn't go off.

"What's Ward got to do with this?"

He repeated as much as he remembered of Wood's rant.

'That could be as big as the actual bomb exploding. Do you have any idea what would happen to the election if this got out? There are already accusations of him covering up things. He's been able to get past all the scandals so far, but this is big. You may have the key to deciding an election and the future of the country here."

Mac nodded, eyes down. He'd readily admit he had no political interests. "How 'bout we just defuse the thing, then figure out what to do about Joe Ward."

"Oh, the locals will love watching the two of us run around together again. It's been a few years, but they have long memories here."

"How 'bout we declare a truce and get some breakfast?" Mac asked as he walked toward the exit.

Mel took another look at Wood and followed him.

17

STEVEN BECKER

THE NAVY ZODIAC bounced in the building chop, heading north through Florida Bay. Four bright orange life jackets bobbed with each wave, and the knuckles of Jim Gillum's right hand were turning white as he grabbed the rub rail. He fought the nausea as he tried to read the chart in his left hand.

"Where to, sir?" the man at the wheel asked.

"Give me a minute, sailor. It's been years since I've been here."

"Sure thing, sir," he replied as he backed off the throttle.

Gillum studied the map. They'd been running in a basic search course — circles expanding from a central point he thought was the location of Wood's island. Each circle grew larger and more distorted as the breadth of the search increased, the boat constantly swerving as it was forced to avoid countless submerged obstacles. He hoped the bomb was on the island. It was the only lead he had.

It was close to twenty years ago that they had reached their settlement and Gillum still got nervous thinking about it. Skeletons hung in his closet like clothes on a sales rack. Wood had gotten his contractor's license and started his business in the late 1960s as an engineer and contractor. He quickly built a reputation for performing on jobs and successfully built many of the Navy projects in the 1970s and 1980s. Gillum had oversight of many of these jobs, although the men had minimal contact.

The Navy, always on a tight schedule, had been pressuring Gillum to get a fill section of Dredgers Key Road leading to the Sigsbee Key housing annex repaired. Gillum had been the second in command then, with eyes to the future. He was an administrator, not a sailor, garnering the contempt of many. Too lazy to search for competitive bids, he had contacted Wood for the work. Although their relationship was contemptuous, Gillum knew the man was competent. He put aside his feelings and awarded him the job.

Wood had discovered some artifacts while excavating the failed fill section of the causeway. What he showed Gillum wasn't much, just some stone tools and bowls left above the high tide line long ago, probably buried by years of storms and erosion. Although good for publicity, finding relics on a construction site was bad for business. Every find needed to be reported to the State Archeologists Office, and then all manner of administrators descended on the site, stopping all work. This could often go on for years until they were satisfied. None of this was good for Gillum's schedule.

He got to Wood before he reported it, and played his best card. It was rumored that Wood had homesteaded an island out in the bay and Gillum confronted Wood about the legality of his retreat, thinly veiling the offer to make it legal if the relics disappeared. Or turn him in if they didn't.

Wood had been at the bridge building and engineering game for twenty-five years at that point, and was pretty much checked out of it. He was looking at retirement, and loathed the bureaucratic crap that was starting to pile up in the construction industry. He'd seen it coming as early as the seventies, with licensing and stricter codes, but Hurricane Andrew in 1992 had pushed it over the top. Everything was blamed on the builders, and the bureaucrats seized power, for the public's good. A contractor's job turned into paper pushing and satisfying inspectors, rather than building. Wood knew the relics he found had no significance, and had no qualms about burying them again and moving on. His only terms were that Gillum would leave his island alone, and that he would make it legal.

Gillum was able to work some channels and generate a ninety-nine year lease in exchange for the maintenance of the island and his silence.

———

They sat across from each other, each leaning backward, creating as much space as possible between them. The Stuffed Pig was starting to empty from the breakfast rush, so they had the place mostly to themselves. They sipped coffee, and dodged the old questions both of them weren't sure if they wanted to ask. Menus open in front of them, they looked warily at each other. Mel tried to avert her eyes but couldn't. He was still the picture in her mind of who she wanted to be with. Never in a relationship for long, she had drifted from partner to partner, not wanting to get involved. She saw in Mac something the Ivy League city guys who pursued her didn't have: competence. They might have been good lawyers, but they had no life skills. She tried to look away again.

"I thought we had a truce. Come on, for your dad's sake."

"We do. I'm not yelling at you, am I?"

"You're freezing me with that look, and you know it."

"Warming up to you is going to take some work."

"Let's get some food and figure out what to do. Just back off a little. Give the DC high-altitude lawyer thing a rest for a while. Look around — it's the Keys, relax."

"Relax? My dad's in the ICU and I'm stuck here with you. I grew up here. I don't have to work to fit in."

"Mel? Is that you?" the waitress asked as she approached for their order. "I heard about your dad. Hope he's ok."

"Good to see you, Sherrie," Mel answered, trying to look sincere, not sure if it was working.

They ordered, then waited in silence for their food. Mel was thankful it arrived quickly, but she was too preoccupied to eat. Finally, they pushed aside their plates, both realizing it was time to talk.

"I want to go out to Dad's place and see what the hell you found. If all this is related to the bomb, and it appears that way, we need to figure out what you have and what to do with it. This guy that ran him over and shot Tru—he keeps popping up. Too many coincidences. I've been thinking about what to do with the Joe Ward connection too. I can't let him get away with this, as much for dad as doing the right thing. I'm pretty much on his side of the aisle but don't trust him. He's got a reputation for having his own version of the truth." She knew her brain was starting to spin out of control with all the possibilities, but Mac brought her back to earth - something else she liked about him.

"I'm good with that. Let me get the check and we can head out there. Might be a little bumpy this morning," Mac said, looking out the window at the flag now extended from the wind.

18

A SMALL WAVE crashed across the bow as the helmsman turned into a larger circle, trying to buy some time for Gillum to give him direction.

"Idle for a moment, I think I've got it now."

The helmsman handed the wheel over to a crewman and moved next to the commander. Gillum pointed out the island and surrounding shoals.

"We don't want to run up on it. Stay off to the west about a mile, and we'll launch the Wasp." His hand came to rest on the large box behind him.

"Yes, sir. It's going to be hard to operate the drone circling in open water. There's a cove on the lee of the island here," he said, pointing to an adjacent key on the map.

"That'll work, son. Let's head over there, set up and see if we can find the bomb."

Fifteen minutes of wet spray and pounding later, the helmsman eased back on the throttle and the Zodiac coasted into the cove. With the anchor dropped, the Zodiac sat motionless. Thankful for the break from the open water, Gillum reached behind him, grabbed the waterproof case, and opened it on the seat next to him. The Aqua Wasp looked like a kid's toy plane: a three-foot wingspan with a propeller for propulsion. But it was far from a toy. At a cost in the tens of thousands, the drone was the newest in high tech. Battlefield deployable with a small console for a controller, the Wasp's batteries allowed forty minutes of flight time with a precision camera controlled by a joy stick.

It was a risk, but one he had to take. Gillum knew the consequences if he were caught. He remembered something about Wood's daughter being a lawyer, and suspected she would end his career in a heartbeat. He couldn't hide behind the Navy if this got out. He deemed it worth the risk, and the drone was the perfect way to see if the bomb was there.

The first mate cocked the drone and threw it out like a football pass. The propeller kicked in and the third man, a remote pilot specialist, took control.

Gillum sat next to the pilot, concentrating on the small monitor.

"I want you to take her over the island on a basic search grid."

"What are we looking for, sir?"

"I'll know it when I see it. It's an old munition. About seven foot six inches long and three feet in diameter."

"That's pretty big. The optics should be able to see that, but we'll have to lower to fifty feet."

"Let's keep it up high until we see something. Then we can drop and get a better shot."

The wind picked up as Gillum stared intently at the monitor, the island centered in the camera, hoping this worked. Recovering the bomb and helping out Ward would put another feather in his cap. Maybe give enough push for a promotion before he retired. Certainly it would get him out of here and into an easy job in DC. The last thing he needed was Wood or his sidekick fouling things up.

————

They were as far apart as the small wheel house of Mac's boat would allow. The boat cut through the chop, spray splashing the deck behind them. The bay side didn't often have the big waves that the ocean side had, but could be uncomfortable with the wind-blown chop, especially when the tide ran against it.

"It'll be easier on the way back. We'll have the wind at our back then," Mac said.

Mel gave him a 'whatever' look and returned her concentration to her phone. Both thumbs blazing, her head bobbing with the boat, she'd hardly looked up since they left the dock.

Mac tried to ignore her as he steered the familiar course. His thoughts drifted back to the period after his divorce. He'd seen her with Wood shortly after he'd separated from his wife. She looked and acted different than the teenager he'd remembered. She'd grown into the woman he should have married. Strong and confident, much like her dad, though she'd never admit it.

He navigated the familiar route, slower than usual as the waves began to increase. Finally, they coasted up to the piling. He couldn't help but watch her as she went forward and tied the boat off with practiced ease, her silence causing an anxiety he rarely felt.

"Still good on a boat. Most would have puked three times already, just staring at that thing," Mac observed.

"Never mind what I'm good at." Mel jumped over the side and waded ashore. "Coming?"

He followed her onto the beach, and they walked the path to the clearing the house was set in, thankful now for the breeze that kept the mosquitoes down. "I still don't get the appeal of this place," she said, looking around. "Modern fish camp decor, mosquitoes, battery power, and pump your own water."

Mac decided against a rebuttal. He guided her towards the path he'd travelled the other day when he came back for the first aid kit. With a machete taken from the side of the shed he slashed down evenly on both sides widening the trail, barely breaking a sweat as they approached the clearing. "There it is." He directed her towards the bomb and away from the wreckage of the boat that had hit Wood. It almost looked like a movie set. The boat was fully on the beach, intact except for the crushed section of the bow where it had made impact.

"Okay, let's have a look."

As they were about to remove the camouflage from the bomb, Mac heard the whine of a small engine. "Get down and leave that net alone," he said, scanning the area for the source of the sound.

"What now? There's nobody around for miles."

Just then, Mac squinted into the sun and saw what he thought was the profile of a man-o'-war in the sun. The frigate birds were common here, useful for spotting fish, and an experienced fisherman could see one from a distance. They flew with the wind and coasted against it, using the air currents to save energy. But this bird was flying a straight line into the wind, without showing the grace common to bird. His eyes followed it, realizing that it wasn't a bird after all.

"What the hell is that thing?" He pushed Mel deeper into the mangroves.

She gave him a look and then followed his gaze. "I don't know what you're looking at."

"It's no bird." He pointed toward the dot on the horizon clearly moving toward them.

She saw it now, and stared at it, following its movements. It was about fifty yards away now. "I recognize that. It's a drone. Someone else wants to know what you have."

"How do you know so much about drones?" he asked.

"Long story, but it's something I'm working on."

———

It was becoming harder for Gillum to see the terrain. The wind was bouncing the Wasp around, making the image fuzzy. He was having a hard time keeping his stomach in place and watching the display at the same time. Something on the screen caught his attention.

"Can't you do anything about this?" he asked the crewman operating the joystick. "It's all fuzzy. The image is jumping around. Between that and the seas, I can't see much."

"I can take her down lower. It's the only way to get a clearer shot."

"It looks like something's going on there now. Can't tell for sure with the turbulence."

"This kind of weather and that small drone, there's not much we can do. I can make a few more passes and record it on the hard drive. It'll be easier to analyze it on land with a bigger monitor."

Gillum was all for getting off the water. "One thing first. Do a flyover of that boat and see if there's a name, or at least get the registration number off the bow."

The pilot moved the drone across the island and out over the water. He turned it and flew close to the boat, capturing the image.

"Got it, sir."

"Great. Let's get out of here," Gillum commanded the helmsman.

———

"It's gone," Mac said, standing up.

"Stay down. Let's make sure it's not coming back." They were pushed against each other in a clump of mangroves.

"Something's not right here. Surveillance drones are not supposed to be spying on US soil, and especially not US citizens." She moved away.

Her look was enough to quiet him. "Drones are a hot topic right now. It's too easy for the government to spy on its own people with those things."

"Right. For once we agree."

He scanned the sky for the drone again, wondering what was going on. Who had access to a drone like that, and why were they looking at Wood's island? He knew the answer: The bomb. He just didn't want to accept it.

After giving it a few minutes, he removed the camouflage from the bomb.

"That's the weirdest thing I ever saw," Mel said, looking at it. She took her phone out and started shooting pictures of it from all angles.

"Any identifying marks on it?" She walked around the cylinder. I see the old Navy markings, but not much else. There's got to be something else we're not seeing."

"By the tail fin. I saw some numbers."

She zoomed in on the tail, shooting a closeup of the two rows of numbers and letters etched into the metal.

"There's no cell service at this resort, is there?" she asked, glancing at her phone for coverage.

He shook his head. "No, have to head back to my place if you want to use your cell."

"Oh, be still my heart, an invitation to your place."

STEVEN BECKER

A MAC TRAVIS ADVENTURE
WOOD'S
REEF

BEHZAD LEANED FORWARD as the passengers exited the terminal. This was the third time they'd circled the arriving flights area. Each loop took fifteen minutes, and Doans was getting anxious. They hadn't dipped back into the baggie since they hit the mainland over an hour ago. Both men were coming down, and the law enforcement presence was not making things easier.

Doans was getting agitated with the traffic, clearly overtired from the last few days. "Gimme another bump and I'll hang out and wait with you."

Behzad took out the bag and held it low. Doans watched the traffic for a break, ducked down and inhaled. "Thank you, my friend. I lost my phone so I won't get his call. If we can circle a few more times, I'll make it worth your while," Behzad said.

———

Ibrahim finally appeared. He had lingered in the area on the gate side of security where there was free WIFI access. With several email accounts to check, the anonymous Internet the airport provided was the perfect spot.

"There he is." Behzad pointed to the middle-aged businessman.

Doans pulled up to the curb. Behzad got out and signaled the man. He looked more like an attorney than a friend of the guy he'd just spent two hours snorting coke with.

The man came forward, and he and Behzad embraced quickly, looking like brothers to anyone watching. They walked to the car.

"Ibrahim, this is Jerry. He gave me a ride after I had some trouble last night," Behzad said.

"Always trouble, little one." Ibrahim used the term with condescension.

"Not so. I pulled over to rest for a few minutes and was mugged and car jacked by some Haitian gangsters. It could have happened to anyone."

"And this kind stranger just picked you up in the middle of the night and agreed to not only drive you to Miami, but pick me up as well." The skepticism was evident in his voice.

"I was cruising up US1, getting out of town for a while, when I saw your friend on the side of the road. I was tired and figured some company would be good, and he was clearly in need of assistance." Doans came to Behzad's aid. Ibrahim looked at Doans. Not believing in coincidences had kept him alive and undiscovered. This was clearly a red flag.

"Anyway, had some domestic trouble in Marathon and figured the ride and change of scenery would help clear my head."

"We both thank you for your kind assistance," Ibrahim said. He noticed that both men were wiping their noses, and wondered what Behzad was up to. Now that he had been seen, he had to assess this American — and quickly. He knew that neither he or Behzad by themselves would trigger any red flags. Neither looked like a terrorist — they were both clean shaven and had adopted American personas.

———

Doans saw the sign for the airport exit. "I should probably drop you guys off at a rental car place or somewhere." He was starting to get uncomfortable around this stranger. Maybe a trace of paranoia from the drugs or maybe it was just obvious, but this guy was clearly treating him with suspicion. After years of living on the edge, Jerry's radar was up and working non-stop, looking for people to steer clear of. This guy was a big red blip on the screen.

"Please, allow me to buy you a meal in thanks for saving my friend here," Ibrahim offered. Doans got the feeling he was being sized up.

"I could do that, and take a break from driving," Doans said, never one to turn down a free lunch.

He exited the airport, heading west on the 836. After merging south on the Florida Turnpike, he exited at the first sign of food. "Waffle House okay?"

———

They were seated in a booth, drinking coffee, waiting for their food. Ibrahim had been asking all kinds of questions, and though he might intend for it to be a pleasant conversation, it clearly felt like an interrogation to Jerry Doans. He wondered what this guy was after when the questions started focusing on Marathon.

"I thought you said you were from Key West." He looked at Behzad.

Ibrahim answered for him, the previously chatty Behzad being extremely quiet and deferential since Ibrahim arrived.

"We have a business opportunity in Marathon," Ibrahim continued probing. He had ascertained from the questions that Doans was definitely not what the Americans called a "hard-working citizen." Still, if he could help them in Marathon, he might be worth keeping around. "Do you know the waters around the area?" he asked.

"Pretty well," Doans replied.

Ibrahim was eating now, focused on his food. Behzad and Doans were pushing the food around their plates, still wired from the coke and now the coffee. Each took a small bite now and then for appearances, but neither was interested. He wondered again what was going on here.

Ibrahim finished eating and looked up from his plate, his mind made up. "We could use a man of your knowledge and position to help us in our venture. There will, of course, be a reward for this." He offered the bait to Doans, knowing full well that the compensation would be a trip to the other side of paradise. He'd made his decision and felt that he could trust him as long as he thought there was something in it for him. Greedy Americans.

20

STEVEN BECKER

A MAC TRAVIS ADVENTURE

WOOD'S
REEF

GILLUM WONDERED why the image on the screen was making him as seasick as the actual boat ride. The video from the F470 inflatable was bouncing up and down following the rhythm of the sea. He'd been going back and forth through the drone's video for the last hour, the bourbon almost gone from his tumbler.

The picture's definition was amazing; the level of detail taken from the drone could show a bead of sweat on a hermit crab on a beach. But the image was erratic. He slowed down the video, working it one frame at a time. That helped, but would take forever. The island, with the exception of a clearing where the house and an outbuilding were located, was densely covered in mangroves. He was looking for shapes and lines, indicating something outside of nature, but to see anything in the tangled brush was close to impossible. He got up and refilled his glass.

Into the third hour, and the third inch of bourbon, he saw something out of place. The drone's camera was focused on the area where Mac Travis and the unidentified girl were walking. He moved the mouse and enlarged the foliage nearby. *That has to be it,* he thought. It took a few minutes, but he started to pick out the dissimilarities between the camouflage netting and the native flora. He zoomed in further and saw what looked like a glimmer of metal reflecting in the sun.

He leaned back in his chair, working on inch number four, and trying to figure out what to do next. The obvious choice would be to send a special ops team to the island and just take it back. One problem was that he didn't have the authority for what would need to be a classified mission. The other was that he didn't want the publicity of the bomb being found to trigger the obvious question of why it was there in the first place—and who knew about it. Wood was right. The Navy kept records for everything. Although it was buried deep, there was always a chance someone would find it. That would ruin his career and destroy the Vice President.

There were only two other men alive who knew what originally happened to the bomb. Ward probably hadn't thought about it in fifty years and Wood was in the hospital. The carefully guarded secret was now sitting on a beach instead of hidden under Florida Bay. Add in the handful of locals that knew as well, and the group was too big for a secret like this to remain intact. It was time to let Joe Ward know. He had the most to lose, let him make the call. The problem now was how to get a message to him. They hadn't spoken since 1963, when he'd been transferred after the missile crisis ended.

Gillum leaned forward and opened his web browser. He searched several web sites but none revealed a phone number. The closest he could get was to send a message to the Vice President on the White House web page. He tried other searches, but every path ended on the same page. He began to fill out the form, hoping to include something that would force whatever intern or aid that was responsible for monitoring the site to pass it up the chain of command.

As he came to the subject line he wrote: *Message from old Navy buddy*. He hoped that would at least get the contents read. In the message section he wrote:

We served together during the Cuban Missile Crisis in Key West.

I was wondering if you remember that pilot that came in light. I was working with him that day. Something has come up and I need to reach you about the pilot.

He clicked the box asking for a response, and closed the browser. It was a long shot, but hopefully the message would reach the VP.

———

Minutes later, the message appeared on the intern's monitor. Max VanDoren was just finishing for the day. It was almost 8pm, but that was what it took to intern — do whatever they said and hope for the job offer or at least a good recommendation at the end of the term. One of his responsibilities was to monitor the messages on the VP's White House web page. It was actually an interesting part of his job, better than filing and research. The comments seemed to change with the wind. Some days it was a rage against the administration or rants against the VP, other days it offered praise. Max charted the comments on a spreadsheet aimed at tracking which way the political flag was blowing. As the election neared, the comments had become more polarizing.

Scrolling through each comment, he deleted as he went, answering each query when called for. He had some latitude in answering the messages, and a blurry line defined what needed to be passed higher up. The message in front of him was one of those. The mention of the VP's naval career and a direct reference to an incident flagged the message to go higher up. The check box for an answer was highlighted, indicating that the author hoped to hear back. He typed in his best robot: *This message will be passed to the Vice President.*

A copy of the message in his hand, he took the elevator from the basement of the Naval Observatory up to daylight. He followed the ornate corridor to the chief of staff's office.

"Sir, got a minute?"

Dick Watson looked up from the pile of papers on his desk. No computer monitor was evident; the chief was strictly old school. "What is it?"

"This message came in on the comment page of the boss's White House page." He handed the paper over.

The older man glanced at the note. "I'll pass this along. We were just talking about the boss's service during the Cuban Missile Crisis this morning. Do we know who this guy is, or how to get a hold of him?"

"Just the basics from the form. Name, address, email."

"In the future, you get something like this, why don't you save us all some time and find out what you can about who sent it. Check the name, run the address, let's see if this is real."

Max took the scolding in stride and headed back down to the dungeon.

————

Watson had the phone in his hand the minute the aide was out of hearing range. The Vice President's personal secretary picked up on the second ring.

"Yes, sir." She knew who it was from the caller ID.

"Is the boss around?"

"No, he's shaking hands and kissing babies. In the middle of a fundraiser. Want me to pass along a message?"

"Slip him a note with the name Jim Gillum and Cuban Missile Crisis on it. See what his reaction is."

————

The aide wrote the note out on an index card and went to the VP's table, and discreetly handed over the note. Ward glanced at it and quickly.

"Would y'all excuse me for just a second?" he said while getting up. The southern accent was for the direct benefit of the Georgians sharing the table.

He exited the banquet room, the aide in tow, glancing once again at the note. Panic cracked his voice. "Get Dick on the phone."

She pressed the chief of staff's private number and handed him the phone.

The VP started pacing, waiting for an answer. Finally Watson picked up on the other end.

"Where did this come from?" Ward asked.

"It came through the form on the White House web page. I wasn't sure if I should bother you, but we were talking about making an appearance down there the other day."

"You did the right thing. Do we have a number for this guy? I vaguely remember something about this," he lied.

"Working on that right now. We have an email, but should have a phone number momentarily."

"Get it to me as soon as possible. And Dick, let's keep this quiet in case it's some crackpot."

"No problem, boss. We'll get you the number as soon as we have it."

Ward handed the phone back to the aide. He wiped his brow and tried to breathe deeply. Relax. He hoped Watson would not question the immediacy and secrecy he was asking for.

21

MEL WAS BACK on her phone, thumbs jamming away on the keyboard. As Mac had predicted, the ride was smooth. She glanced over at Mac as he shook his head watching as she navigated the tiny screen. Basically a Luddite, he didn't get it at all.

"You know your messages can wait untill we get back," he said.

"You know that thing's a nuke, don't you?" She glanced up from her Wikipedia screen. "The amount of military-related information on Wikipedia is astounding."

"How did you figure that out off that thing?" he asked.

"Duh, run a search on the picture and bam, instant results." She decided it may be a good idea to tone it down a little. "Although the Internet is not the source of all knowledge, it can be useful. What we have here is a MK 101 Lulu. A 11-kiloton bomb used from 1958 to 1971. I wonder what it's doing here?"

"That's what he called it — a goddamn Lulu." Mac gazed over the salt-crusted windshield. "From World War II through Vietnam there's all kinds of unexploded ordnance in these waters. The armed forces didn't have the oversight that they do now. There were huge swaths of land and water they were allowed to use for training missions and testing. Some are marked as munitions dumps on charts, others are unaccounted for. All kinds of stuff was coming in and out of here during those couple of months."

"Surely even the Navy wouldn't leave a nuke out there," Mel said, "I know dad's skeptical of the government's ability to do anything. I am too for that matter." The only thing they were good at was fighting her lawsuits, she thought.

"The last storm must have shifted things around down there. I've dived on that ledge dozens of times and have never seen it."

"The drone we saw," she said slowly, starting to put things together. "You and Dad talked to someone he knew at the Naval station. I bet they're after it. It had to be them."

"I don't know why he wouldn't just turn it over. You know how he is with authority, but it seems like there's more to it. His contempt for the Navy guy and Ward was evident. Just kept muttering to himself on the way back about sinking both of them."

"Yeah, he's used to keeping himself company on that island. Must have some great conversations with himself."

They shared a small moment of brevity, both processing the information available.

"What if Ward, Gillum and Wood were the only ones that know it was a nuke? That would explain a lot—the secrecy and distrust. Gillum and Ward would be ruined if the truth came out that they had covered it up. Wood just needed the proof to do it. That explains why he wanted to see Gillum. He had no intention of turning it over. He wanted to let him know he had it."

"I'm thinking we have two options. We either have to tell them where it is, provided they didn't see it from the drone, or put it somewhere they won't find it," Mel said, back in lawyer mode.

"If Wood doesn't trust the Navy, I'd say he has good reason. I know he can be an ornery old coot, but he's got good sense. I've never known him to be paranoid." He thought for a minute. "There's some nuclear waste facilities I know about. A lot of compaction testing equipment has nuclear cores. We had to service and disable a few of them. I can look up what we did with the core material. Maybe we can divide it up so no one gets suspicious. Aside from the primer, which I can probably disable, the rest is just a hunk of metal. We can take it and dump it somewhere deep."

"I'm with you, except that we don't know how stable it is," she said. "The last thing we want is for that thing to blow while you're messing with it and take half the Keys with it."

"What about the Navy?" he asked.

"They're not just going to go away," she said. "I have a mind to go down there and confront them about that drone anyway. Spying on US citizens is not cool. I can turn this into a Federal suit, get the kind of attention this whole drone thing deserves. I can go down there and record the whole thing on my phone. Maybe get some kind of confession out of him."

Mac choked. "We've got a live nuke out there and you're worried about a case? Come on, girl, get some perspective."

The ringtone from her phone halted the conversation. "Local number, maybe it's the hospital," she murmured, glancing at it.

She answered, listened, and asked a few questions. Then she hung up and sat back in relief. "He's awake and asking to get out of there. That means he's okay. We need to head over there before he causes any trouble. You know how he can get."

22

THE TROPICAL HUMIDITY was taking a toll on Mel. She was acclimated to DC's high humidity, but the Keys raised the bar on that index and she was thankful as the automatic door opened, letting out a hint of the air conditioning about to encompass them as they entered the hospital. She looked at Mac, who was not even sweating.

"Let me see him alone for a minute." She went for the door. His eyes opened as she entered. A faint smile showed on his face.

"Mel." His voice was raspy from the ventilator.

"Dad, don't talk, it's okay." She took his hand.

They sat in silence for a few minutes, neither knowing how to go from there. There had been a glint of happiness when they first saw each other, but as the minutes passed, the old uneasiness returned.

Finally Mac entered and broke the silence for them. "How are you feeling? Glad to see you're still tough as nails."

Wood gave them a thumbs up. "My side hurts like hell, but I'm ready to get rid of this." He looked at the IV.

Mel gave him a disapproving look. "You are going to do what the doctor says, exactly. You're not going to pull your usual crap and decide for yourself. Do you have any idea how serious this is?"

"Good to see you too." He looked at Mel. "That damn fool doctor won't give me a direct answer if it would save his own life."

She teared up, "I'm sorry. I was really scared you weren't going to pull out of it. I'll find the doctor and use my lawyer skills on him."

"Why don't you just smile and look nice? May get you further than that lawyer crap."

The automatic closer slammed the door behind her as she left.

———

Mac looked at Wood, trying to evaluate his condition. "You clear headed enough to talk about the bomb?"

"Yeah, can't feel half my body, but I hear you."

"Mel and I were out at your place to check on the camo job and make sure everything was ok. We heard some kind of buzzing and saw this model-airplane-size drone cruising around. I think it was taking pictures."

"Goddamn Navy. They can't just spy on me like that. Sounds like old Gillum took the bait for sure."

Mac's brow furrowed, his suspicions confirmed. "Don't worry about that. The lawyer is all over it. Why don't we just give it to them?"

"Can't trust 'em," he said as he pushed the button on the remote, releasing another dose of pain killer into his system. His eyes drooped.

Mac was about to probe further when Wood's head fell to the side. The monitor by the bed continued as before, easing his fears, but he sat and wondered why holding on to this bomb was so important to his friend.

Mel sat back in the chair next to the bed. "The nurse says the doctor will be up here in a few."

"Great. I'm going to get some coffee. You want anything?"

"Something stronger would be good, but coffee will work for now.

I'll wait up here and see what the doctor says." She pulled out her phone and started pecking at the keyboard.

———

Mel was lost in her phone when the door opened. She looked up and felt naked. The doctor was looking right at her, not your usual "say hello" look, this was definitely an "I'm interested" look. Her hair was a mess, still blown from the boat ride, and salt rims were forming in all the wrong place on her t-shirt. What little makeup remained was from yesterday. She got the feeling he really didn't care, but still felt awkward.

He gave her an approving nod and walked over to the computer monitor, with the chart in his hand.

"He looks stable. Really good, actually, for his age and what he went through. Name's Dan."

"Mel," she replied pulling her hand through her hair. "He's pretty darn tough." She glanced first at her father and then at Dan. She tilted her head without even thinking about it. "What can we expect from here?"

He picked up on her body language, and smiled. "Well, you can expect a dinner invitation. He can expect some serious recuperation time. His internal injuries should heal by themselves, as long as he doesn't get an infection. We're pumping enough antibiotics into him for a large elephant. The bigger problem is the stitches healing. I don't know him, but a lot of folks have warned me that he may not be an ideal patient."

Mel laughed and tilted her head again. "That's my dad."

"The stitches — staples, actually — are in a bad place. Forty-eight from his side around his back. He needs to stay immobile for a week to ten days, allow the wound to heal."

She ignored his first remark about dinner and got to business. "That's not going to be easy with him. Can't you just drug him for a couple of weeks?"

Dan laughed. "That would be the easy way. We can probably release him in a day or two. You'll just have to keep an eye on him. Is there somewhere he can stay and not get in trouble?"

Mel grimaced, thinking she would have to forfeit the next week of her life fighting with her father. She looked back at the doctor, then, thinking that it might not be so bad.

Mac walked in then, doing a juggling act with the door handle and coffee as Mel replied.

"We can put him up at Mac's. That might give us a couple of dinners."

Mac spilled coffee on his shorts.

23

Vice President Joe Ward held a drink in one hand and the phone in the other. He was kicking back in his suite in Atlanta, winding down from the fundraiser.

"Go through this sequence once more for me, Dick."

"An intern came up to my office a couple of hours ago with a printout from your White House web page. It implied that the author served with you in Key West at the Naval Air Station during the Cuban Missile Crisis. That's pretty much it. Said something about remembering a pilot coming in light, whatever that means.

"We figured we ought to at least run the guy's name by you and see if it meant anything. Turns out this Jim Gillum is actually Captain Jim Gillum, commander of the Key West Naval Station. So what's the connection here?"

Ward took his time responding. He thought back to the early 1960s, when he was stationed there. The name didn't ring any bells, though the reference to coming in light sure did. In his mind, he reconstructed the landing where light on fuel, he'd jettisoned the wrong bombs. There were two men on the ground involved; this must be one of them. But what did it mean now? Did this guy just want to make some points, remind the future President that he had old friends with secrets?

"I'm not really sure what this is about. Could just be some guy I may or may not have known, trying to hitch his star to mine. We still talking about a campaign stop down there next week?"

"I think we should. Florida is looking good, but not secure. I think some time there would be well spent. I'm not sure how we should play the Missile Crisis thing, though. Cubans will line up to vote for you if you hit on it, but we better float some trial balloons and see how the blue hairs are going to react. Those folks are the ones that are going to win this for you."

"You do that. Maybe contact this guy and keep him in the loop. Heck, maybe I ought to call myself. I'm trying to remember who he is, but I guess it doesn't really matter. At least I'll get a vote for the phone call. I'm not polling too high with the military. Get his number for me."

"I'll get Stacy to look up the commander's number at the base for you."

But Ward wasn't sure he wanted this to go through the base switchboard. He didn't want a record of the call. "Why don't you have her call down there and get his cell number? You can probably get through now. I'll call him tonight."

———

Stacy Green was nothing if not efficient. She handled all communications for the VP, and within minutes of receiving the order from the Chief of Staff she was on the phone with Key West. It only took a few well-constructed sentences, and she had the cell phone as well as the home phone number of the commander. She handed a piece of paper to Ward.

He excused her with a glance, picked up his cell phone and dialed the home number.

Gillum picked up on the fourth ring. "This is Jim Gillum," the sleepy voice slurred.

"Jim Gillum, if it isn't you, and you probably thought I wouldn't remember you after all these years." Ward used his best campaigning voice.

Gillum was startled awake. "Mr. Vice President, it's been a long time. You're right, I wasn't sure if you'd remember me or not, and I had no idea how to get a hold of you. I'm glad you called, sir, something's come up from our past that I think you need to know about."

"Your message mentioned something about coming in light. If I remember that reference, you're talking about that incident that happened down in Key West?"

"Yes, sir. I thought that was over and done with. We'd never have to think about it again," Gillum said.

"Has something come up?" the Vice President asked.

"Do you remember that third guy on our team? Name of Woodson? He's been down here in the Keys, building bridges since he retired from the Navy in the early 70s. I've had several run-ins with him. He's always been a little bit difficult to work with. Now it seems that a buddy of his was diving out on the Gulf side and found it."

"Well, what's the problem, then, Jim? You're commander of the naval base down there. Can't you just put together an operation and go get it?"

"It's not quite that easy, sir," Gillum said. "If I authorize a mission, it'll have to be open book, and everyone will know about it. Not really a big deal — recovering munitions, even this kind, is a good thing. What I'm worried about is if someone started digging around about how it got there. Congressional hearings have happened over less. Your name's bound to come up and I don't have the authority to authorize a classified mission. I would never think to bother you if I could handle this myself."

"This puts us in a bind, then. We've only got about a week until the election, and everything I'm doing is under a microscope right now. There's no way I can authorize anything without the press and my competition looking over my shoulder. Isn't there any way we can just make this go away until after the election?"

"Too many people know, and half of them have their own agendas that don't align with ours. I don't want to make this a bigger deal than it is, but the nature of the item is going to raise eyebrows. If it wasn't for Wood, there'd be no problem putting this on ice. But he's a loose cannon, and there are several other people down here that know about it, including a person we suspect to be his daughter. She's a lawyer. Some kind of activist. Could be more trouble than he is."

The Vice President sat back in his chair and started reviewing his options. Best case was this would go away until he was firmly in office. Second best was to find the bomb and dispose of it, but that would leave a trail.

"I've got an idea sir," Gillum said after a moment.

"Run with it. I need the plausible deniability — no details. I trust you, Jim."

"Thank you, sir, I won't let you down."

24

JIM GILLUM WAS UP EARLY, his second cup of coffee just starting to make a dent in his hangover. The four inches of liquor last night had his head pounding. He had a lot to think about and he replayed the conversation with the Vice President from the night before. There was no mistaking the tone — if he succeeded in making this go away, he could write his own ticket. There were several juicy postings in the Pentagon he'd had his eye on for years, and any one of them would make the remaining years before his retirement easy, as well as give a nice boost to his pension.

The promise made last night had been empty. He had no idea how to get the bomb and dispose of it without a paper trail. The Navy loved paperwork — there were records for every roll of toilet paper requisitioned and every PT session conducted here over the last fifty years. Using Wood was out of the question. There was no way that ornery old man was going to help him with anything. He started thinking about the other two from the video, the guy that came to his office with Wood a couple of days earlier, and the girl that was with him on the island — Wood's daughter. They both obviously knew where the bomb was, and where it came from. If there was some way to get to the guy, that might be the answer. With a little patriotic pressure maybe he would cooperate. A plan started forming in his mind. He picked up the phone and asked the secretary to connect him to the Master at Arms.

"Chief Petty Officer Garrett."

"This is Captain Gillum. I need to arrange for an officer and a vehicle to go with me to Marathon and remand someone."

"Yes, sir. We'll need to fill out some paperwork, but we can do that when we get back. I'd be happy to go with you myself. When would you like to leave?"

"Thank you for your cooperation. I'd like to leave as soon as possible."

"I'll fuel a vehicle and pick you up in ten minutes."

Gillum hung up, still fretting about the paperwork trail. He'd have to make a decision on the fly about CPO Garrett. Mingling with base personnel was not his thing. He didn't know more than the names of most of his command, and had no idea who he could trust to keep this quiet; he knew his plan skirted the edges of the law, possibly crossing into the wrong side.

———

Gillum was consulting the papers in his lap — printouts from the Internet. The men had been quiet during the hour-long ride. Gillum obsessed with his own thoughts and Garrett only speaking when spoken to. Once over the Seven Mile Bridge, he directed Garrett to turn right after 15th Street.

"Dammit, that was the turn." Gillum exploded.

"Sorry, I need a little more notice." Garrett pulled into the next street and executed a three point turn. Back out in traffic, he waited patiently in the left turn lane for several cars to pass and he turned.

They drove slowly to the end of the street checking numbers on the mailboxes as they went. They reached the last house and pulled into the driveway. It was more of a commercial area than a residential one — mostly small, commercial buildings backing up to a canal. Commercial fishing vessels and construction barges were moored in front of most of the buildings. Stacks of traps, lines, and buoys were scattered throughout.

"You think we might need some backup? Is this guy going to be any kind of trouble?" Garrett asked.

They got out of the car and walked toward the door. Gillum was sweating heavily, nervous about how this could go wrong. His hand shook as he reached for the holster.

"Just side arms should be fine. I don't believe he'll be armed." His voice cracked.

———

Mel answered the door, drenched in sweat and breathing hard. The two men had been pounding on it for several minutes and were clearly impatient. They pushed past her, weapons drawn, scanning the interior. The first floor was mostly open space, divided into a workshop, with a small gym area off in the corner. Stairs led up to a living area. It was actually the old exterior of the house. Mac had added an atrium on the front, enlarging and connecting the downstairs space to the living quarters above.

"US Navy. I'm Captain Gillum. This here's Garrett. Where's Mac Travis?" The older man asked.

She looked him over, worrying about the shaking hand holding the weapon. "Do you guys have some kind of a warrant? You can't come in here with guns drawn, tidy whities in a bunch. I want to see a warrant right now or I'll have your butts in court this afternoon. And that's no idle threat. There is nothing I would like better than to see you two squirm in front of a local civilian judge. I don't think they take kindly to a couple of Navy goons ignoring civilian civil rights." She played on the man's nervousness.

"Just tell us where he is, ma'am," The younger man said. He

looked more confident—like he was used to doing this. "We've got a warrant to take him in for questioning."

"I'd like to see that warrant right now, please. And those guns had better find their holsters. This'll look great in the papers," Mel snapped back.

Gillum holstered his weapon, motioning for Garrett to do the same. He dodged the question. "Let's just make this easy, ma'am. Tell us where he is, we'll take him down to Key West to answer some questions, and he'll be back by dinner."

"You guys think you can just barge into a private home, grab a citizen and take him down to Key West to answer some questions," she said sarcastically. "We'll see what the ACLU says about this. What is this, Nazi freakin' Germany?"

Gillum was turning red, clearly flustered now. "This is a matter of national security. I am well within my rights to detain and question a civilian that has knowledge."

Mel noticed his agitation. "This wouldn't have anything to do with that drone that we saw yesterday, spying on us out at Wood's Island, would it?"

"Ma'am, you're welcome to come with us if you like, but one way or another we're taking him to Key West."

"What's all the commotion down there, Mel?" Mac asked from the balcony overlooking the main floor.

"These Navy boys have some kind of a wild idea they can haul you down to Key West for questioning."

Mac moved down the stairs. "I suppose there wouldn't be any harm in me going down there to answer a few questions for you. Can I have a word with Mel in private before we go?"

Without waiting for an answer, Mac grabbed Mel's arm and took her off to the side. "What the hell? They can't just detain me, can they?"

"Not legally," she said. "I've thrown out every threat I have. I think you're going to have to go along. I'll get to a judge and clear this up."

"We need to get going, Travis," Gillum said.

Mac whispered to Mel, "Follow my lead, we're going to head for the boat."

"Just a minute," Mac said to the Navy men. "I've got to shut down the boat and close up here." He headed out the rollup door and onto the gravel path leading to the dock without waiting for an answer. "Mel, let me show you how to switch the shore power."

She got the message and caught up to him, the Navy men followed behind. Just as she was clear of the door, Mac turned and pulled the rollup door down as fast as he could. "Make a run for the boat!"

They sprinted for the dock. Mel, exhausted from her workout tripped on the transition from the concrete path to the wood dock. Mac grabbed her, looking over his shoulder at the men coming through the door. He pushed her forward. "Jump on and start her. I'll get the lines."

Mac jumped on the boat just as the Navy men hit the concrete. Garrett was in front, Gillum trailing behind. Lines hit the dock and the engines started. Mac looked back from the bow, a smile on his face as the boat moved away from the dock.

"Stop that boat!" Gillum yelled.

Garrett was running through his neighbors' yard, gun drawn, Gillum following. Mac took the wheel from Mel. The boat had been docked with the bow towards the back of the canal. Mac had to spin the boat before he could move into the main channel. This gave Garrett enough time to pull even with the boat.

Mac watched as Garrett stopped to pick up an anchor, shaped like a grappling hook, from a neighbor's dock. With the hook in his right hand, he quickly coiled a half dozen turns of the line in his left hand, then threw the hook and watched it land on the deck of the boat. Grabbing the bitter end, he tied it to a cleat on the neighbor's dock. With a snap, it came taut and jerked the boat.

Mac had the boat turned and was moving toward the end of the docks lining his street, about to gun the motors when something hit the transom. He had to think, quickly evaluating the damage before it happened. Something had to give. The hook was either going to take the transom off the boat or tear the dock off. He grabbed a knife from the console and dropped the boat into neutral, ready to cut the line, but there was too much tension on the line. Cutting it now would make the recoil as dangerous as a gunshot. The transom started to creak, forcing Mac back to the controls. He slammed the controls down. The line sagged slightly as the boat reversed its forward progress, churning up water as the propeller reversed.

He handed the knife to Mel. "Cut the line, quick!"

Gillum had caught up to Garrett. Both men had their weapons drawn. The boat was drifting backward now, bringing them into range.

"That's enough," Garrett said. "Hands up and cut the engine." He waited as the boat died in the water, Mac seeing no choice but to comply. "Now move to the stern." He pulled the boat back to the dock with the grappling hook, motioning for Gillum to secure the boat as he kept the crew in his sight.

Mac and Mel were on the dock, hands still over their heads as Garrett reached for his handcuffs.

"Just Travis. I don't want the headache of detaining a woman - especially that one," Gillum said.

Garrett had Mac cuffed and was walking him around the side of the building toward their car before Mel could catch her breath.

"I'll be down there as soon as I can and get you out!" she yelled after him.

25

A MAC TRAVIS ADVENTURE

WOOD'S
REEF

THE LAST TRAFFIC light going southbound in Florida City, the last bastion of civilization before the half-hour ride to Key Largo, turned green. Doans reluctantly hit the gas pedal. He had eyed every convenience store, hoping for an excuse to pull over and get a beer. His head was hurting after being up all night partying with Behzad. A beer would take the edge off, but there was no stopping now as they passed the last store. The ride from Miami had been quiet, with Behzad unconscious and snoring in the back seat. Ibrahim sat stiffly in the front, looking straight ahead as if in a trance. Doans tried to concentrate on the road and how much money he could extort from these men. He smelled a score.

"So this is what the Florida Keys look like," Ibrahim said.

"Not quite yet, we just left Florida City. We'll be heading into the Keys shortly. So, what kind of an opportunity do you have in mind? You never got specific back at the restaurant."

"We are looking for someone to head a salvage operation. There is a rumor that something of value has been brought up near Marathon. It is important to our organization to get our hands on it, and worth a good payday to you if you will assist us."

Doans adjusted the air-conditioning vent, forcing the cold air to blow directly on his face in an effort to clear the cobwebs from his head. This couldn't be a coincidence, he thought. There is no way two Middle-Eastern-looking guys are after a shipwreck or something. It's got a be the bomb he'd seen on the island and it had to be something special if these guys were after it. That would explain why it was hidden. He was starting to get excited now. He finally had some leverage on something somebody else wanted. This could be a big payday.

"Exactly what kind of salvage operation do you have in mind?" he asked.

"We need to reach an agreement about this, and your silence before I can disclose any details."

"Well, at some point you have to trust me. I've got a pretty good idea what you're looking for, and I think I know where it is. So, now to the real question. What kind of compensation do you have in mind?"

Doans drove on, watching Ibrahim from the corner of his eye. He was back into reality now, a calculating look on his face.

"We would be willing to pay you five thousand dollars per day plus expenses to recover the object."

"Can we please stop referring to this as the object? It's a goddamn bomb, excuse me Allah. You know it and I know it and it's not much of my business to care what you are going to do with it. I would say that five grand a day is not quite enough for this kind of intelligence. Without me you're back to the drawing board. You don't even have a place to start. Good luck trying to find a charter boat or anything else in Marathon looking like two rug salesmen."

Ibrahim was fuming at the infidel's rudeness. He tried to control his emotions, knowing that he would make him pay when this was over. "We are not set on that number. We are willing to negotiate. What do you have in mind?"

"I will recover the object and handle the expenses for a fat hundred." Doans said.

"For that kind of money, my friend and I will stay in the hotel room. You will have to organize and staff the operation by yourself. We have no desire to be visible."

"So, we have a deal, then. I'll require half up front and the balance when I deliver the bomb."

"We will give you twenty-five up front and the balance upon delivery. That is more than enough to cover all your expenses, and leaves enough to keep you honest."

"Done."

"When we get to Marathon, we will rent a hotel room. I will pay you the deposit. We will expect delivery of the bomb in forty-eight hours. I will arrange a drop-off point to expedite transport of the item."

Jerry Doans sat back and tried to focus on the road. Yes, the money would solve all his problems. And so what if these guys had a bomb? That wasn't *his* problem.

———

Trufante had become a celebrity in the hospital. He knew every nurse's name, and they knew his. A cute blonde was wheeling him around. He had talked, or rather charmed her into taking him to Wood's room, and he asked the nurse to push him inside. Wood leaned up in bed, his lips curling into a small smile as he viewed the man in the wheelchair.

"Well goddamn if it ain't Alan Trufante."

"Wood, you old bastard. I heard you were in here. Y'all doing all right?"

"Yeah, I've been better. My damn side hurts, and they got me on some drugs that can't hardly let me think straight, but other than that I'm good. What are you doing in a wheelchair?"

"Some son of bitch shot me with a spear gun. Can you believe it? First this guy smacked me upside the head with a pool cue. Then me, Mac, and the sheriff start chasing after him. Cornered the sucker on a charter boat and the dude shoots me with a spear gun in the freakin' leg."

Wood laughed so hard he started to cough. Pain lines replaced the smile. "That can only happen to you, son, no one else could even make that up."

"Be that as it may, being rolled around this hospital in a wheel-chair has its perks." He looked up at the nurse, smiling.

"Ma'am, you think you could leave us alone for a few minutes?" he asked, winking at her. "I've got some private business with your patient here. I promise I won't hurt him." Wood said.

The nurse smiled at him, patted Trufante on the shoulder, and left the room.

When the door closed, Wood focused on the Cajun. His tall frame in the wheelchair looked cartoonish, his knees almost in his chest. "You 'bout ready to get out of this institution? Mac's in trouble, and we're gonna help."

"Don't know if I'm quite ready to get out of here yet." Trufante glanced out the window to the nurse. "They're taking good care of me, man. That's Sue. I think she's sweet on me. Ain't no beer, though. I've been trying to talk one of the girls into smuggling some in for me, but no luck."

"Oh, cut that crap out. You can come visit anytime you want," Wood said.

"Well what exactly do you have in mind?"

Wood looked around, just to make sure no one could hear what he was about to say. "We need to deal with that bomb."

"Well what about Mac? Why don't you just get him to dump it?"

"While you were in here partying it up with all the nurses, the Navy's taken Mac and put him in the brig. I'm working out a plan of how to deal with the damn thing."

"If it'll help Mac out, no problem. When are they going to release you?"

"Hell if I know. The two of us are walking out of here. I've had enough of these doctors and nurses and all their crap. Come back here about eleven, when they change over to the night shift, and we'll get the hell out of here."

26

A MAC TRAVIS ADVENTURE

WOOD'S
REEF

"I'M GOING to have to file a report on this." Garrett stood in Gillum's office.

"I'll take care of the paperwork." Gillum said.

"I'm a little worried about what just went on up there. You just took someone into custody without probable cause. And there was a witness. Someone who knew what she was talking about."

Mac was a few doors down, locked in an empty conference room. He had been cooperative on the drive down to Key West, but Gillum knew that was probably not going to last.

"Forget the probable cause, we've got resisting arrest now. There *will* be no paperwork. I have orders from high up in Washington to handle this in any way I see fit. I'm the commanding officer here. You can take that as a direct order."

"Sir, sorry, with all due respect, I understand your order."

"You are dismissed now."

"Yes, sir."

Garrett turned on his heels and walked out of the room. Gillum started pacing around his office. Almost two hours later, and he was still pumped up from the arrest. The first step in his plan had gone off with complications, but at least they'd arrested Mac. He knew men like Garrett, and ultimately he would follow orders and not be a problem. From now on, he would just have to handle this himself. The real question was what to do with his prisoner. He needed the bomb. The spotlight was on him after his talk with Joe Ward. He had to do it without the use of the forces under his command. Involvement from anyone else at the Naval base would surely be noticed. There could also be no paper trail. His best chance at getting rid of the bomb was using the guy that found it in the first place.

———

He left his office and walked down the hall to the room where Mac was being held, pulled the key from his pocket and opened the door. Mac squirmed in the chair, the handcuffs on his wrists limiting his movement.

"There is no need for all that," Gillum said. "You're not going anywhere until I say so. Anything but full cooperation and I'll bring in that girlfriend of yours as well."

"You have no reason to be holding me."

"I have every reason to be holding you. I have authorization from Washington. If you cooperate, you can walk away from this and go back to whatever it was you were doing."

"What exactly do you want from me?"

"We're aware of the bomb you discovered. We also know where the bomb currently is."

"If you know so much, what do you need me for?"

"The bomb is sitting on private property. I can't authorize a mission without getting Wood's approval," he lied. "The powers that be are also reluctant for any publicity concerning this."

"So this is going to be a cover-up."

"We're not trying to cover anything up. If word gets out about this, there will be general panic. More people are likely to get hurt, and more property damaged, than if we can work something out."

"And my involvement would be ..."

"You would be doing your country a service if you would work with us and recover the bomb. It's been down there for fifty years. There's no reason to start a panic. We need to keep it quiet. The newspapers get a hold of this it'll just make people worry."

"And this whole thing goes away if I help you out? I appreciate you want to defuse it, but I trust Wood's judgement and he has no confidence in you."

"Yeah, we have some history. But you know how stubborn he can be. Just understand how high up these orders come from. It's not really that hard, Mr. Travis. Just do what we ask and your girl and Wood will be fine."

"First of all, she's Wood's daughter. Second, she's not my freaking girlfriend. And third, I bet you didn't know that she's a lawyer. She saw that drone you guys were flying over Wood's Island and wasn't happy about it. If I were you, I wouldn't mess with that one."

"She's a goddamn lawyer?" Gillum said, flustered by the new information. "Well that doesn't change anything. You want to leave her out of this, that's fine. But in exchange for that, you need to do what I'm asking."

"That girl can take care of herself. I'd be worried if I was you. As far as I'm concerned, you can get a court order or whatever you need and take a bomb squad out there and do this properly."

Gillum reached in his back pocket and removed his cell phone. He made a show of dialing the number for the Master of Arms and started talking, shielding the screen with his hand. "I have a prisoner to be placed in holding."

"What the hell are you doing?" Mac snapped.

"Mac Travis, you are now being held as an enemy combatant." Gillum played his bluff. "Based on the information this office has obtained, you will be detained and await a military tribunal."

"You can't do that!"

"Yes, I can. You are in possession of a nuclear weapon, and know the whereabouts of several others. You are unwilling to cooperate with this office and the recovery of those devices."

"Slow down there, Captain," Mac said. "Did you say there's more than one bomb?"

"I did some research," Gillum said, not wanting to let on his first-hand knowledge. "There appears to be another bomb missing from that mission."

"So *that's* what this is about. If it was just the one sitting there, you'd have no problem calling and having someone defuse it. But now you need *me*, because I know where it came from. You think I can lead you to the other!"

"Are you going to cooperate, or do I need to see that you get put on the ghost ship anchored off Guantánamo Bay? Awaiting a military tribunal is a lot different than being locked up as a citizen in this country. There are no rights of *habeas corpus*. You don't get your phone call, and we can disappear you for as long as we need to. I can put you someplace that girl will never find you."

"Go ahead and lock me up. You have no idea what you've unleashed." Mac squirmed in his chair, not sure if he made the right decision.

27

TRUFANTE PUSHED THE WHEELCHAIR, moving as fast as his injured leg would allow. He probably should have been in a wheelchair as well, but a couple of Vicodin had solved that problem. Wood remained stoic as the chair hit a bump on the sidewalk. Once they had gotten off their floor, the escape had been easy. Wood had been moved from the ICU unit to a semi-private room earlier in the day, and the other bed had been empty, so Trufante had moved in. Getting him out of bed and into the wheelchair had been the biggest problem they'd faced so far. They'd dodged a few preoccupied doctors and nurses in the halls and elevator. Without the scrutiny of the ICU folks, it had been pretty easy.

"Where to now, boss?" Trufante asked.

"Let's get the hell out of here. Figure out some way to get us over to Mac's place. We can figure out what to do from there."

"We got no transport, man. I came over here in the sheriff's SUV. You came in here on a stretcher."

Suddenly a nurse came around the corner. "What are you two doing out here?" she asked.

"Just getting some air, hon." Trufante racked his brain for her name, but the drugs must be dimming his memory. She was way too attractive to forget her name. Then his eyes focused on her name tag. *Sue*. His grin eased her caution.

"He's supposed to be on bed rest and you should probably be in a wheel chair, not pushing one."

"Now, Sue, I gotta be straight with you. We gotta get outta here. I can't get into all the details now, but it's important. A friend of ours is in deep trouble and we've got to help him out."

"That's all good, but you're in no condition to help anyone out." She glanced at Wood, who appeared to be asleep in the chair. "And look at him, he just got out of the ICU this morning. He should be in bed."

"He's okay, just gave him a few of those pills you gave me for the ride. I'll make sure he rests."

She sighed. "Well, there's nothing I can do to keep you here. They call it checking out against medical advice. If you want to go, then you can." She appraised the odd couple. "I could lose my job, giving you those extra pills, and you could have killed him. You don't know what else he's on. These aren't recreational chemicals here."

Trufante started pushing the chair, trying to get the conversation to move around the corner, where they were less likely to be overheard. "I do appreciate everything you've done for me here." He gave her the big smile, teeth gleaming. "I really do, but we gotta do this. If there was any other way ..."

"You know, if you're stuck on discharging yourselves, least I can do is keep an eye on you." She winked at him. "I've got a couple of days off."

Trufante's brain was only moving at half-speed, churning for an answer. He was trying to balance what he knew he had to do for his friend against what he wanted to do. From somewhere deep within his head, the answer came that he could have both.

"I've half a mind to take you up on that. I gotta warn you though, there's a high degree of danger here."

"Danger, yeah I'm in for some excitement."

Wood stirred. "What the hell are we still doing here? And who the hell is she?"

"Settle down, I've just recruited some help."

Wood looked the girl up from top to bottom and made his decision. "Well, she damn sure looks like she'll be more help than you."

———

Mel had just finished working out when the door opened. She'd done a hard twenty-minute circuit of pull-ups, push-ups, and squats. Now she was on her back trying to recover her breath. The second workout today was bound to hurt, but it was her way to control anxiety and get her mind in the right place. It was late, and there was nothing she could do about Mac until the morning. She'd put feelers out to her boss, some contacts in the legal community, and anyone else she could think of that might be able to help. She hoped the workout would burn off some of the anxiety she was dealing with. Take the edge off, and maybe let her sleep.

She was also dodging her emotions, not wanting to face the feelings she'd felt when Mac was led away. Deep inside her she knew her teenage crush was not realistic. He'd always been like a brother to her. For the first time in years she evaluated her feelings with a rational mind instead of using pure emotion. She was always more rational than emotional and never understood why she had spurned his advances after his divorce. It just happened.

The sound of the front door opening snapped her back to the present. She hopped to her feet, leaving a sweat angel behind on the ground. A shotgun leaned up against the bench press rack, keeping her company. After this morning she had decided to keep it close. She picked it up and chambered a round, hoping the unmistakable sound of the gun cocking would be heard by the intruders. Maintaining a firing stance, she approached the door, weaving back and forth through the furniture, trying to keep out of sight and obtain cover at the same time. As she approached the door, she saw three figures enter, one in a wheelchair. She worked her way closer until she could see.

"Dad?"

"You can put the gun down and relax, it's just us."

"What are you doing out of the hospital? You don't look like you're in any kind of condition to be out on your own yet."

"I tried to take them back." The woman in the scrubs said. "I did what I could, but these two are so stubborn that there's no stopping them. I figured the best I could do was to stay with them and keep an eye on him. That way if something went wrong I could help."

"I certainly appreciate that," Mel said, noticing how the woman leaned toward Trufante. She turned to her dad. "So would you like to explain to me what's going on here? And what is Alan Trufante doing with you? And Christ, he's hurt too."

"Well maybe if we could all get comfortable ... I could sure lie down and have a drink. Help get me settled in and we'll talk about it."

"I don't see you getting up the stairs. Mac's office is over there. It's got a couch. That'll have to do." The group moved toward the room. It took all of them to get him onto the couch. Wood finally relaxed and Trufante settled back into the wheelchair.

"Okay, Dad, start talking."

"I could sure use a drink. Those pain pills have about worn off."

Trufante started a stiff-legged attempt at the stairs in search of some alcohol, but Mel stopped him abruptly. "Negative. There's no drinking for sure, and no pain pills until the nurse here tells me it's okay. Now, why are you here?" She picked up her phone and started to dial. "Never mind. I'll just call the hospital and tell them to come pick you two up."

"Now settle down, Mel. Truth is, we heard that Mac was in trouble, and there's nothing we could do to help him sitting in that damned place. We need to make a plan and get him out of there, and then deal with our other problem. I'll be fine. My partner over here just has a small leg wound."

Mel turned toward the nurse. "Can he do any damage to himself here?"

"Not if he stays put. I can't say for sure, but a patient can discharge himself with any condition at any time. I think the best we can do is just keep an eye on them. They'll be safer with us watching them than if we let them go back and they check themselves out again. I can go back tomorrow and get some antibiotics and pain pills."

"All right, you guys can stay here tonight and we'll see how things are in the morning. For now, I have to get a shower and some sleep." Mel headed off to the shower.

28

JERRY DOANS SAT at the hotel desk, a piece of stationery in front of him. He'd started a list of items he'd need to recover the bomb. At the top of the list was a boat. That might be a problem. After wrecking the last one, he knew his driver's license picture would be in every boat rental place from Key Largo to Key West. He'd need to get around that to make this work. He had thought about letting Behzad or the other guy rent one for him, but those two looked more like they ought to be renting a camel than a boat. Their appearance and lack of any kind of boating skills would send a red flag to the top of the pole.

If he wanted to pull this off, he'd have to leave them out of it. He actually had no intention of letting them get their hands on the bomb. He wasn't sure how, but somehow, he was going to get his money and give them a worthless piece of metal.

"I'm going to need that twenty five grand right about now." He held up the list. "I've got things I need to buy."

Ibrahim looked at him suspiciously. "Yes, we have a deal." He reached under the bed and pulled out his suitcase. He opened it and withdrew five bundles of hundreds. He set the money on the desk next to Jerry. "Here is your money, infidel. Now, I want to see some results. We will be watching you."

Jerry pulled the money toward him. "You can watch me all you want, but if I see you, that means that somebody else might see you too. I've got this figured out. Don't blow it. You just make sure you have the rest of the money when I deliver." He lifted his shirt and stuck the bundles side by side into the waistband of his pants. "I'm outa here."

———

The bar was about three-quarters full when Jerry entered. The bartender came and he ordered a shot of tequila and a beer. He needed something to steady his nerves. The shot went down before his butt hit the stool. Deep in thought, trying to figure out how to get a boat, he felt a hand grab his shoulder. He turned and saw a pretty face attached to the hand.

"Now, you take it really easy. You're going to get off that chair and follow me out of here. I don't want to have to cuff you in here and cause a scene. Understand?" The sheriff squeezed a little harder. She grabbed his free arm and locked it behind his back before Jerry knew what was going on.

The bar door slammed behind them as the sheriff guided Jerry to the cruiser. "You're the guy from the other night. I've been looking for you." She spun him around and frisked him, pulling the bundles of cash from his pants. In one swift move, he was cuffed and in the back of the car. "That's an awful lot of cash to be carrying around."

"As far as I know, there's no law against carrying cash. I don't even know what you're talking about, I haven't been around here for a week."

"We'll head down to the station. You can go ahead and try to prove that. Until then, I'll hold onto this cash," she said, laying the cash on the front seat.

Doans slumped into the back seat, trying to figure a way out of this mess. There were a handful of people at the bar the other night that could identify him. So she was right — he wasn't going to be able to get out of that particular fight. Now, his cash in the sheriff's hands and his freedom in jeopardy, he needed to reformulate his plan. If there was one thing he knew, it was that plans sometimes needed to change in the middle of an operation. As they pulled up to the sheriff's station, he eyed the thirty-foot boat sitting on a trailer, his brain starting to click into gear.

Jules walked him in the side door of the station. Doans knew he needed to avoid being booked. There would be no way out then. "I have some information that you might want to hear."

"The only information I want to hear out of you is a confession for putting Wood in the hospital, shooting Trufante with the spear gun and starting that bar fight the other night."

"No, you got me all wrong. I've got a hot lead on some terrorists."

He saw the disbelief in her eyes. But he knew even the remote possibility that he had any information, no matter how insignificant, could undo her career if one of the federal bureaus found out she had ignored a potential lead.

"This better be good, or it'll come back on you." She led Doans down the hallway. He grinned as they passed the rooms for mug shots and fingerprints. She led him to an interrogation room, opened the door and pushed him in. "I'll be right back. Maybe you ought to reflect on what you intend to say. False reports of terrorist threats could land you in trouble with the feds." Doans was placed into the seat facing the mirror, and handcuffed to a steel loop on the desk. Jules went out to start the mandatory recording equipment and let the prisoner sweat for a few minutes, or maybe as long as it took her to eat dinner.

Doans was used to this kind of pressure. He knew the sheriff was putting him on ice, and would leave him for a while. The solitude of the interrogation room for an hour or so was sometimes enough to break a prisoner by itself. Doans got as comfortable in the chair as his restraints allowed, closed his eyes, and was asleep in five minutes.

"The son of a bitch is still asleep," Heather said.

"Must be drugs or something. He didn't seem under the influence when I brought him in," the sheriff said. "Make sure the recorder is working. I'm going in."

Heather checked the equipment and nodded.

Jules strolled into the room and banged her hand against the table, waking Doans. Then she pulled out the vacant chair and sat. "You said you've got information. Let's have it. And it better be good, or you can spend the night in the drunk tank."

"Now, is that any way to treat the guy that's going to get you promoted?"

She ignored him. "Start talking."

"Well, it started like this," Doans said, his voice raspy. "You know I could really use a drink. You got any Coke?" He laughed.

The sheriff hit the table with her hand. "You can toy with some, but not me. You have five minutes. Speak. There's a couple of mean-looking dudes, all inked up, in lockup. They'd love a roommate."

"Well, you know, there's a bomb out there. There's a couple of guys that know where it is and a couple of terrorists looking for it. I kinda got dragged into this mess. I'm just trying to help out here. I'll admit this may have gotten a little out of hand." Doans gave his twisted, abridged version.

"Out of hand, is that what you call it? I got a friend of mine in the hospital 'cause of you, and another guy had a spear sticking out of his leg, never mind about the bar fight. And now there are terrorists here?"

"Well, things didn't go quite as I planned. The cash was a down payment on me delivering the bomb to the terrorists. Now, of course, I have no intention of doing that. I was gonna get the FBI, or whatever bureau is in charge now, involved, but thought a little cash wouldn't hurt. Now, I'm here, so it's your lucky day."

"You're a freakin' moron. Tell me where the terrorists are and I'll get the Feds to pick them up. You think the bomb is out at that island where you crashed? Is that what you were doing out there?"

"That's where it is. I had to make sure before I went to the authorities."

"I'm going to put you in custody and see what the Feds want to do."

STEVEN BECKER

A MAC TRAVIS ADVENTURE

WOOD'S
REEF

Behzad watched Ibrahim roll out his prayer rug and wondered if he should grab a towel from the bathroom and start acting the part. The sun was rising and Ibrahim was on his knees, facing east and chanting the first of the five daily prayers. Behzad had not practiced his religion in years. He had more fear than love for Allah. Like the followers of many religions, the masses of Islam did as little as they could, just enough to stay out of God's dog house. People did their own cost/benefit analysis of how much effort they should put into their practice, and in most cases it wasn't much. This was especially true for Behzad.

"You really should begin your practice again, my friend." Ibrahim finished and rolled up his rug. He stood and rubbed his knees. Ten minutes was a long time to be kneeling. He'd done the 5 or 6 minutes of compulsory prayers and added in another 5 minutes for a Sunnah, asking the prophet for guidance in their endeavor.

Behzad had escaped to the bathroom during the prayer. He exited now, toothbrush in his mouth, and shrugged his shoulders, feigning that he could not respond. He went back in and finished his toilette.

———

The sun was climbing in the sky, reflecting off the water as they headed over the Seven Mile Bridge toward Key West.

The minivan kept them at a distance from the cab driver, but they chose to speak in hushed tones. "What a glorious bridge to blow up," Ibrahim said.

"It would not have the effect worthy of the effort. Have you thought about what we are to do with the bomb?"

"I have some ideas in mind. I think Key West would be the best target. We could obliterate the entire island, erasing the den of iniquity off the face of the world."

Behzad was reluctant to admit this was a good idea for a symbolic target. With a population of close to twenty thousand people, plus tourists, it was an ambitious goal. Many were his friends, though, and their innocence in this made him sad.

Ibrahim noticed. "They are infidels. All of them. There is one solitary mosque on the entire island. We will visit there today. Maybe the leaders will be sympathetic to our cause. Are you familiar with it?"

"Yes, brother, I know where it is located." He failed to tell Ibrahim that it was only a few blocks from Duval Street, center of the Key West party scene. He passed it all the time. But like a library, knowing where it was and actually entering were two different things. They crossed bridge after bridge as they made their way closer to the southernmost point in the US. "We should go to your house first. We need to sit down, call some truck rental places, and see if the Imam of the mosque is there."

Behzad tapped his foot incessantly. Unable to sit still, his paranoia increasing as the numbers on the mile marker numbers decreased towards zero—the end of the road. The ridicule he would face if Ibrahim discovered any more about his lifestyle was not going to be pleasant. In fact, he'd do anything to keep his friend *out* of his house. "Let me have your phone. I can start working on it on the way."

"I am wary of using a cell phone. The NSA is listening. A land line, they need a warrant to listen to. No, we will wait and use the phone at your house."

———

They pulled up to the purple house with turquoise trim and paid the driver. Behzad was so worried about Ibrahim that he failed to notice the other van parked across the street. They walked past the over-grown hibiscus lining the walk. Just as Behzad was about to enter the house, he looked up and saw both doors open on the van. Two men jumped out and ran toward the house. He panicked, losing precious seconds working the key in the lock. Finally the cylinder turned and the door pushed open. Ibrahim darted in first, and Behzad followed. He started to shut the door when a booted foot blocked its path. Behzad tried to slam the door again, with no luck. The second man kicked the door and both men entered, guns drawn.

"Behzad, you freaking fag. You disappeared on me. Haven't answered your phone in days. You know, someone less trusting than me might start to wonder if we were really friends after all." With the gun still pointed at them, the man waved them toward the kitchen and closed the door.

"What is the meaning of this? You know these men, Behzad?" Ibrahim lagged behind until he felt the butt of a gun land a blow to his head. He staggered forward into the kitchen.

"Just a misunderstanding, my friend. A small debt."

"If you think ten grand is small, that's up to you. Where's our money?"

Behzad looked at Ibrahim for help. "I have your cash in the car." Ibrahim came to his rescue.

Behzad breathed a sigh of relief.

The smaller man grabbed him by the elbow and walked him

toward the door. "Just play it cool and nobody needs to get hurt." He put the gun back in the holster clipped to the small of his back.

Cesar waited until the door closed before he backhanded Behzad across the face. Behzad fell from the chair and curled into a fetal position, trying to protect himself from the steel-toed cowboy boots slamming into his kidneys.

"That is the last time we are going to front you anything. He better have all my money," the man said.

Behzad worked to get to his knees. "He's got it."

The door slammed, and this time the Mexican staggered in first. Ibrahim had the gun pointed at his head. "Both of you, against the wall there. Behzad, get off the floor and get his gun."

Behzad struggled to his feet and took the offered gun from Cesar. Ibrahim motioned both men into chairs.

"Find something to tie them up."

Behzad thought for a moment and went upstairs. He came back down with two pairs of handcuffs. The locks clicked and the drug dealers were secured to the chairs.

"I'll not ask what this is about now," Ibrahim said. "Allah will want a full explanation at the gates of Paradise. Handcuffs and gangsters? Behzad, old friend, what have you been doing?"

Behzad glanced at the gun in his hand, wondering if this would be a good time to use it, either on himself or Ibrahim.

He quickly recovered his composure. "We have the guns now. It's all good. The plan is still on track."

Ibrahim stuffed a dish rag into the smaller man's mouth.

"You think you need to fear Allah, Behzad? It is Cesar who will be coming for you." Ibrahim forced the second towel into Cesar's mouth, ending the threat.

JOE WARD REACHED for the coffee pot on the sidebar of the breakfast buffet. This was his third cup this morning. He hadn't slept well
last night, and probably wouldn't until the election was over on Tuesday. The room was a standard-issue hotel conference room, crowded
with name-tagged guests. The names on the tags spoke to the cost of
the fundraiser. For a thousand a plate you got a name tag. For ten, the
candidate was required to know your name.

Ward pressed the flesh, shaking hands and patting backs as he
made his way through the crowd. He worked his way toward the back
corner of the room, where Gary Hawkins was standing, deep in
conversation with another man. Hawkins, now a professor at Georgia
Tech, had been the nuclear advisor to the President for the last few
years. He was just the man to give some enlightenment to the Vice
President. For better or worse, he needed to know more about this
bomb.

He sidled up to the advisor. "Hello, Gary. Good of you to come."
He turned to the other man. "Good to meet you, I've heard a lot
about you and want to thank you for your support." He shook his
hand, too anxious to take the time to read the name tag. "I have a

favor, though. Do you think I could have a private moment with Gary? I'd appreciate it."

The man walked away.

"Got a minute, Gary? I need to pick your brain on something."

"Sure, Mr. Vice President, what can I help you with?"

"Please, we've known each other long enough. Call me Joe." Ward placed a hand on the man's back and guided him out of hearing range of the adjacent guests.

"Tell me, what do you know about the old MK101 Lulu?"

"What's brought that up? Those bombs have been extinct since the late 1960s."

Ward had thought this through while he tossed and turned last night, and was ready with an answer. "I was stationed in Key West during the Cuban Missile Crisis and handled a lot of armament, including those. I'm heading to South Florida from here to try and wrap this thing up, and thought bringing up my old service and emphasizing the nuclear threat that Kennedy averted would help out. It's the fiftieth anniversary. Maybe help with the Cuban vote, too."

Hawkins didn't take long to comb through his memory for the specs on the bomb. "The Lulu was a nuclear depth bomb. Made sense that you used them back then. They were mostly deployed against submarines from planes. It's got a pretty big blast, with an eleven kiloton warhead. That's just shy of the size of Little Boy, the bomb dropped on Hiroshima. A lot more efficient, though. The bombs were detonated with a barometric pressure trigger. You would set it to the depth you wanted and it would blow. The only thing is if one of these accidentally dropped from a ship, it would still go off. They fixed that after a while, having the pilot activate a second trigger from the cockpit after it was released."

"Sounds like a good thing they're obsolete."

"Why the interest in the Lulu?"

"Oh, that." Ward searched for an answer. "I've got a picture of me with one of those. They think I'm soft on the armed forces down there. Nothing like posing with a nuke to disarm that view."

Hawkins laughed. "Well, good luck to you."

"One more question, just curious, how would you disarm one of those suckers?"

"Aside from the barometric trigger, there's a python primer. The primer is an explosive that is heat detonated when the depth is reached. This reaction triggers the fission in the bomb. Just remove the primer and the bomb is safe. Planning a demonstration?" Hawkins kidded.

Ward ignored the comment and shook hands. He continued pressing the flesh as he made his way back through the crowd, moving toward his travel secretary. He caught a glimpse of her and moved in that direction. About a hundred handshakes later, he was by her side. She saw the boss coming and quickly ended her conversation.

"What's up, boss?"

"You still have the number for that guy I called last night? You know, the guy at the Naval station down in Key West?"

"Sure." She glanced at her phone and scrolled through the call history. "Right here."

"Can I use that and call him?"

———

Gillum answered on the second ring. The number showed as restricted on his cell phone. Ordinarily he wouldn't answer, but things were far from the usual. "Gillum here."

"Jim, it's Joe Ward. Listen, I figured what to do with that thing. I need it. Locate it, secure it, and get it on a truck to Miami. Be safe, but don't make a spectacle out of it. I'm doing a rally there this weekend and it would make a great backdrop. Hell, we'll just call it a stage prop."

"That's a live bomb, sir."

"Here's the thing, Jim. If it appears in public like this, then no one will think it was ever lost. No one will ask where it came from.

They'll assume it's been in storage and came from somewhere safe, and that it's going right back there. It'll go back with you. No questions asked. And Jim, you know what this means to me."

"Yes sir, we'll be there. But you remember there's another bomb."

"Do what you can about that one. Just handle it. It'll look even better with two."

STEVEN BECKER

A MAC TRAVIS ADVENTURE

WOOD'S
REEF

I T T O O K Mac several minutes to orient himself. He woke in the conference room, his arms cramped from sleeping bent over on the desk. He got up and started moving around the room. By the phone was a note: *Dial extension 223 when you are ready to talk.* He needed to clear his head and evaluate his options before calling.

Mel came first to his mind. She'd obviously had no luck or he would have been able to at least talk to her. It was Saturday morning and there wasn't a courthouse she could get in to help him until Monday morning. Wood and Trufante would be no help in the hospital. It was clear that Gillum wasn't going to let him walk out of here. If the Captain was willing to take the chance of detaining him overnight, he would no doubt follow through on his other threats. The only alternative remaining was to make a deal. He would just have to stay fluid as things progressed, waiting for an opening to take over the situation.

He dialed the number and waited while the phone rang. His annoyance increased with each ring, the feeling he was just stuck here gnawing at him. The phone his only lifeline.

It was still ringing when the door opened. He wondered if

Gillum had intentionally ignored the call, hoping to gain even more of an advantage over him.

"Ready to have a chat now?"

"Yeah, we can talk. What do you want from me?"

"Just a little guided trip. We go get your boat and pick up a couple of bombs. Deliver them to our truck, and we're done."

"Oh, that's all?"

"Considering the situation you're in, I think that's a hell of a deal."

"What happens when we're done?"

"Everyone goes about their lives like nothing happened. I take the bombs and dispose of them properly, you walk away."

"My other options aren't looking so good," he said, thinking for a moment. "That's what you want, and I walk away, no collateral damage to Wood or Mel, and you've got a deal."

"I knew you'd come around." Gillum walked around the desk and unlocked the handcuffs. "Just one thing, though. You pull any crap and there's a ghost ship off Guantanamo you can spend a few years on. We understand each other?"

"Yes, but we're going to need some help."

"I'm your help. Take it or leave it."

Mac appraised Gillum, thinking he looked more like a CPA than a Captain. "I need a bathroom and some food. Then let's do it."

———

Jules had slept little. She had been up most of the night waiting for the Feds to call. What a crock, she thought. She had called Homeland Security and the FBI, following every protocol she knew, but there was little interest from the minions forced to answer late-night phone calls. Now she sat up on the couch and rubbed her eyes, hoping the douche bag in custody had slept worse than she had. She'd left instructions for Doans' overnight stay, saying he was to be given a private cell and bathroom. The prisoner was treated better than the sheriff would have liked, but if this was for real, and the Feds got involved, Doans was sure to let them know every detail of his incarceration. The last thing she needed in a laid-back spot like this was an alphabet agency looking over her shoulder.

Her eyes started to focus as she emerged from her office. After a quick trip to the restroom to freshen up, she felt human again. In the lobby, the officer at the desk indicated that no calls had come in. She had done her duty and reported the threat, but this was her town. Distressed, but not surprised by the inaction of the federal agencies, she would do what was necessary to mitigate the threat and take responsibility for what went on here. A terrorist plot was NOT going off in Monroe County on her watch. She called down to lock-up and asked for the prisoner to be brought back up to the interrogation room.

———

"Here's the deal." Jules made sure the cup was close enough for Doans to smell the rich coffee, but not taste it. "The Feds don't seem to care about you. No one has even called back. That's what they think of your half-baked ploy to get out of jail."

"I can see why they're not reacting. A threat reported from a guy about to be locked up is surely suspect. But what I'm telling you is real. Go check it out yourself. The rag heads are staying at the Tropical Inn, down the street from the Turtle Hospital."

"I have nothing to hold them on besides your word, and that, like you said, is suspect."

"I'm just saying, a good investigator would check out the lead. Talk to the staff, they'll tell you about those two dudes. At least you'll know I'm not lying."

"None of this is going to stop me from prosecuting you."

"Maybe you ought to think about what I may or may not have done. I'm not admitting to anything here. Just saying, running a boat aground around here happens all the time. I'm sorry someone got hurt, but it was an accident. A little scuff up in a bar won't even be worth a court date, and shooting that guy in the leg was purely self-defense. He was after me, I had no choice."

She sat back and processed his line of thinking. She hated to admit it, but unless she could prove willful negligence, which was near impossible, the douche would probably walk. Probation, at the most. She grunted and accepted the reality of the courts, be it right or not.

"I'll tell you what I'm gonna do. You'll be arrested for disorderly conduct. I'll leave the boat crash and the spear gun incident out for now, but if this terrorist thing doesn't pan out, I'll go after you for that too. We'll check out your claims, and if you're on the level, you can probably walk with probation. If this is a crock, just to get out of these charges, I'll be handpicking your cellmate for the next few years." She watched him, knowing the hook was set.

"Deal."

———

The motel clerk had just started her shift when the sheriff walked into the lobby. Jules was not in the mood for small talk.

"I'm looking for a couple of Middle-Eastern-looking guys. May have checked in last night."

The clerk answered that she hadn't seen anyone looking like terrorists, but had just come on duty. She scanned the records from the night shift and noticed that two rooms were checked into overnight. One occupied by a couple from Fort Lauderdale, the other rented by a single male. The man had paid in cash and presented an ID with the name of James Wells. Didn't sound like a terrorist, but she was here anyway, Jules thought. May as well look around.

She got the room number from the clerk and walked around the corner, counting down the numbers as she went. The cleaning cart was parked right in front of Unit 16. She knocked on the jamb of the open door and stepped into the room. The maid was in the bathroom, so she cleared her throat and called out a greeting. A head timidly peeked around the corner and nodded at the sheriff. She took this as an OK to look around. Careful not to disturb anything, she looked through the personal objects scattered around the room. It looked like one man, but the bed had two depressions - both sides had been exited.

She checked the bathroom next and confirmed that there was only one toothbrush. Interesting. About to leave, she looked under the bed. A rolled-up prayer rug and a bag were set neatly next to each other. With no warrant, she could only observe, but it did help her confirm Doans' story. She opened the bag and stared at the bundles of cash. Quickly she put both items back under the bed and left the room as she had found it.

32

MAC'S PLACE WAS QUIET. Sue and Trufante were gone, apparently shacked up at his place. Wood was finally asleep. He'd had an uncomfortable night until she caved in and made him a cocktail of Scotch, pain killers, and some Advil PM, just for a kicker. She could hear him snoring through the open door of Mac's office.

Not a word from Mac, and her efforts to contact him had failed. The operator at the Naval base had refused to connect her to anyone in charge and she doubted her messages were even being passed on. True to her nature, she was relentless until the Petty Officer on duty, his name written down and underlined a dozen times on the yellow pad in front of her, once for each call, had finally told her he would have the police after her for harassment. He was clear that there were no prisoners at the Naval base. The detention center there had been mothballed years ago.

She turned to the computer and scanned her email. A couple of work-related notes, but nothing positive from her inquiries about Mac. She had received a note from an old colleague, saying that this sounded like a personal matter. He was clear that the ACLU would not get involved in personal issues. If there was a broach in civil liberties, she could file papers later and he would review it. Saturday morning was not a good time for lawyers. Nothing could be done without getting a judge off the golf course, or in the Keys, off his boat. Anything other than a child abduction was going to wait until Monday, and more than likely Monday afternoon.

Once in a while, her profession frustrated her, and this was one of those times. The law was the law for better or worse, kind of like a marriage. Her unshakable beliefs allowed her to apply it in black or white terms. She had no problems representing a Greenpeace activist, an illegal immigrant, or a housewife in Montana if the law had been violated. She knew most attorneys saw the law on a sliding grey scale applied to each case depending on its variables, and most often their fee. With her background, it was hard to make the kind of friends that could help her now. Her affiliation with the ACLU and currently Davies and Associates often hurt her more than helped. Once more, she thought about her future. What these people never got was that no matter how sensational the case, it could happen to them. Maybe not tomorrow, but the ever-increasing reach of the government into private citizens' lives was happening, one baby step at a time.

She went over to the kitchen and started some breakfast. Surprised by the selection in the pantry and refrigerator, she placed the ingredients for a frittata on the counter. Diced onions and garlic were tossed into a cast iron skillet, butter already melted on the bottom. While the onions became translucent, she chopped a sweet potato and a couple of zucchini. Next she diced some bacon and cooked it in the microwave. As the ingredients cooked, she reflected on Mac.

She'd known him since she was in high school. Eight years older than her, he had been working for her dad. They'd been buddies. He'd taken her fishing and crabbing and even taught her to drive when she became frustrated with her dad. Mac became a crush as she matured. She wouldn't admit to herself that he was too old for anything to come of it. As she progressed through college and her political views changed, she started to resent her dad and anything attached to him. This meant Mac as well. Yes, her views in those years had been a little idealistic, or as she reflected — maybe a lot. She'd protested everything from Iraq to the rights of immigrants. But as the years went by, her views softened. She had gained some perspective and started to understand, although she hadn't yet acknowledged the merit of her father's arguments. She'd come back several times more from guilt than want. She'd seen Mac again after his divorce, even felt some empathy, but couldn't muster the courage to comfort him.

The years had paved a path of bitterness between them that had never been reconciled. Communicating feelings, especially when it came to apologizing, was not a Woodson trait. She felt badly about everything left unsaid. Although she and Mac now shared a libertarian viewpoint, she came at it from the left, and he from the right.

She took her frustration out on the eggs, beating them into submission, then adding them to the mix with the cooked bacon. Mac again occupied her thoughts as the dish cooked. She wanted to deny the attraction, but couldn't. She had noticed the look on his face when the doctor had asked her out, and had to admit it made her feel good. And again how alone she felt when the Navy men had taken him into custody.

The eggs were firm on the bottom and crusting on the side when she placed the pan under the broiler to finish it off.

————

Trufante and Sue were heading up the stairs and surprised her as she took her pan out of the oven. She'd been deep in thought and didn't hear the doorbell, if they even rang it.

"Still got my timing," Trufante said as he limped into the room, his grin large. Sue trailed close behind, smiling as well, both of them fresh from the shower. "Smells good. Old man never said you could cook."

"That's cold. There's a lot about me you don't know."

Wood stood at the bottom of the stairs and yelled up. "Take it to go. We gotta get a move on. Y'all are having a party up there while Mac's missing and no one's watching my place."

Trufante opened the door. "Wood, you old bastard. I knew they couldn't keep you down."

Wood grimaced in pain as he started to head up the stairs. He only got a few steps up when Sue intercepted him and walked him back down. She sat him in the office chair and started examining him.

"You look pretty good," she said. "Let me check the wound."

He got up and lifted the bottom of his t-shirt, revealing the criss-cross of staples.

"Where's the dressing? You have any idea how susceptible to infection that is right now?"

"Don't worry about me, sister. It's not infected. I looked in the mirror. Can't reach around too well, though. I'd appreciate it if you'd bandage it back up for me. But first, do me a favor and get my daughter and that Cajun boyfriend of yours down here. We need to make a plan."

Sue called upstairs and ordered him onto the couch. Turning the deck light to illuminate the wound, she examined it for signs of infection. Satisfied for the moment that it was okay, she started to clean the area around the incision. After applying antibiotic cream, she was just starting to tape the bandages in place when Mel and Trufante entered the room.

Wood stood and examined Sue's work. He gave a quick nod to her and began. "We need to head out now. That sorry ass Vice President has a surprise coming."

"You're not going for a boat ride like that. Look out there." Mel turned to the open garage door overlooking the canal. "The flags are almost straight out. I haven't been around here for a while, but I bet that still means it's bumpy as hell out there."

"Bumpy, my ass," Trufante said. "It's damned nautical. This here's sitting on the porch, beer-drinking weather."

"No matter, you candy ass. We're going on the bay side. That wind is out of the south. We'll be in the lee of it."

Mel looked at Sue, knowing where this was going. "How much can he really do?"

"Well, I'm not a doctor and I can't give —"

Mel cut her off. "Nobody's gonna sue you, least of all him. That's Mr. Personal Responsibility there."

"If the stitches open, it's gonna be ugly. If he gets banged around and hits that spot it could do internal damage. If nothing else, it's gonna hurt."

"See that? I'm good. Let's go." Wood stood and headed out the door. He hobbled down to Mac's boat and struggled over the side, making sure to turn his face away from the group to conceal his pain.

"There's no stopping him," Mel said, hands on hips, shaking her head. "I'll go fix him some food and pack some stuff. Tru, get the boat ready. Sue, would you come along and keep an eye on the two cripples?"

The engines started, and Wood called out, "Get a move on, girl. I'm in no mood."

"You'll wait for me or I'll swim out there and kick your old ass."

Wood gave her a grin. *That's my girl.*

33

GARRETT SCANNED the CNIC Inspector General's website. He'd never even considered filing a complaint before, but what he had just witnessed might change that. Key West Naval Air Station was a conglomeration of many departments, several of them belonging to other branches of the military. As Master of Arms, the Navy's military police, he was responsible for base security. Jim Gillum had been entrenched as base commander long before the twenty-eight-year-old Petty Officer had been assigned there. He knew the man's reputation for total conformity, not even getting close to grey areas. Command ineffectiveness was the term often used to describe the many career men with long-term postings and no hope for promotion. They were all over the military, and usually had these types of base assignments.

The call from Gillum had been interesting, to say the least. The only time he'd ever had contact with his base commander was for a review or recommendation of one of his subordinates. The red flags were up like hurricane warnings as soon as he'd taken the call. He'd had no choice but to comply with a direct order from his commander, but what he'd witnessed in Marathon could not be ignored.

As Master of Arms, he was confident in his knowledge of Naval law, and detaining an American citizen on American soil was not included in the *you can do this* chapter. In fact, the U.S. armed forces were prohibited from Naval operations on U.S. soil. The abduction and restraint of an American citizen could not go unreported, no matter what the Base Commander said.

The website listed the contact information, easier to access here than the dozen binders he had to constantly update resting on a shelf behind his desk. He wasn't sure whether to be worried about filing the report. The Navy was supposed to protect whistle blowers, but they also had an old boys network that ran deep. If this report fell into the wrong hands his career would be over. Feeling he had to do the right thing, hand trembling slightly, he clicked on the email link and quickly closed the screen as someone entered the office. A few minutes later he reopened it. The pause had instilled doubt and he knew his future was uncertain if he hit the submit button.

What if it happened to someone I knew was the final rationalization for hitting send. Once the email was gone into the vapor of the internet, he sat back and breathed deeply. For better or worse, he'd just done something that could not be undone. A moment later, the screen flashed with an incoming message. He opened it, expecting an auto-response that his message had been received and would be reviewed in due course. It was not. The message asked for an immediate phone call.

He went off base to make the call, not wanting any chance of being overheard. Pacing the sidewalk off US1, he dialed the number. Again he pondered his future and wondering if this was the right move — but it was too late. He had to follow through with the complaint now, or they could investigate him.

"Bill Gordon."

"Yes sir, this is Petty Officer Garrett in Key West. Sir, you requested that I call."

"Yes, Petty Officer, thank you. Are you in a place we can talk freely?"

"Yes, sir, I am off base."

"Please describe the incident and surrounding circumstances to the best of your recollection."

Garrett went on to describe Gillum's actions on the Marathon trip. Gordon allowed him to finish before asking questions. The tone of Gordon's voice became more serious as the conversation developed and the question and answer session, became an interrogation. He paused abruptly when Garrett mentioned that he had overheard something about a bomb.

Then, Gordon changed direction. "Tell me exactly what you heard."

Garrett recounted the conversation he'd overheard, and finally Gordon answered. "As I see it, you witnessed not only the illegal detention of an American citizen, but the cover-up of a potential threat on our soil."

Stunned that the cover-up of the operation was more damning than the detention, Garrett waited for Gordon to continue.

"You did the right thing, Petty Officer. I'll take it from here and make sure you're protected. Please leave me a number where I can reach you."

Garrett gave him his cell number and disconnected.

————

Gordon set the phone down, grabbed his notes, and went next door to his CO where he laid out the situation. When he finished, the men just looked at each other.

After a long minute, the Commanding Officer started, "What a mess. Arresting a captain and base commander is going to ruffle some feathers somewhere. I've got a buddy down there that runs the Underwater Training School for the Army. They're housed in the same base. Let me try him and see what's going on down there." He picked up his phone and dialed. The conversation was short and one-sided. Gordon listened in as he explained the situation. Finally he sighed and put the phone down.

"Looks like our boy is a career guy, going nowhere. He does squat — neither good or bad." He looked at his computer screen. "Gillum's record is clean as a whistle. He's been based on or near that station since the '60s. Saw active duty during the Cuban Missile Crisis. After that, strictly a desk jockey." He sat back, silent for a minute. "Arresting him is bound to end up in the press, and we don't need that. Why don't you head down there and have a chat with the guy? He's been serving almost fifty years. Maybe he just needs to go out to pasture. Email me a summary, will you?" he ordered.

Gordon went back to his office. The evidence clearly suggested that Gillum was on some kind of rogue mission, trying to recover a bomb. Interesting, he'd just read that Ward had served in Key West as well. Intrigued at the long shot that there might be a connection, he pulled up the VP's record and compared it to Gillum's. Looking even further, he noted that Gillum was in armaments and Ward had been a pilot in the same division during the Cuban Missile Crisis.

Although, not a fan of the Vice President, along with most of the military, he tried to remain impartial and give the man the benefit of the doubt. He considered both sides, but had a job to do.

34

THE WEEKLY CABINET meeting was underway when Vice President Ward walked in, late as usual. He took his seat and opened the folder laid out in front of him. But it didn't matter. The President, soon to be a lame duck, was strictly in legacy building mode. He'd been that way for months now. His recent motto, coined by Ward, was *Don't screw it up.* Avoid a crisis, delay any hearings, and hope nothing new surfaced in the world at large in the next few months. And God forbid, no press conferences.

Ward was not opposed to this. He'd actually helped author it. Anything attached to the current administration, especially if it were bad, was bound to reflect on him as well. With only days left in his campaign, he needed clear skies and following seas. He remembered the term from his Navy days. A smooth ride, no mistakes until Tuesday and, if the polls held up, he'd be president.

The meetings were getting shorter and shorter as the election neared. Decisions were put on the back burner for the next administration to handle. One by one, the cabinet members and their aides exited the room, leaving the President and Vice President alone.

"How's the campaign shaping up, Joe?" the President asked. "I've been looking at the polls, and it looks like you're pretty solid. Lock up Florida and you're going to be sitting in my chair."

"I'm headed down there now." Ward skipped the usual ass kissing formalities — he was near exhaustion. "A stop in Tampa and then it's all about Dade and Broward Counties."

The current President had raised the height of the bar for future elections. He was an experienced and formidable politician. His campaign strategies would be in text books. "You've got a great team behind you." He'd assembled the team for himself four years ago, and knew they were the best. Ward winning this campaign would be another feather in his legacy cap. It made him happy that the VP was clearly riding the President's coat tails. "What can I do to help you?"

The offer, although phrased as a question, was really not. The President's ego would not permit him to sit on the sidelines and watch his underling win without his face prominently in the foreground.

"What do you have in mind?" Ward knew the rules as well. Unlike some past presidents, whose appearances were liabilities to the candidates, the President was popular and would be an asset.

"Why don't we tag team Florida? If we're both out there, the press will have to cover both of us. That means your opponent will get less coverage. We'll be front and center — right where you need to be. Then we can meet up on Sunday and do some kind of church thing for the conservatives."

Ward had to admit that the man was a master. "Great. I was going to do a rally Saturday afternoon in Miami. Focus on the anniversary of the Cuban Missile Crisis. Tossing Kennedy's name out there never hurt anyone."

"Done. I'll be there. Then we can go to church on Sunday. That'll be a great photo op of us walking out of church together."

The two men clasped hands, then collected their things and headed out.

"One more thing, Joe. Honor the veterans. It's close to Veteran's

Day. Bringing in some military for the rally will make it more colorful."

"I've got some ideas on that, sir."

————

Back in his office across the street in the Old Executive Office Building, Ward sat across from his campaign manager.

"We need a good spot for this rally." Ward focused on the man working his iPad, his mind racing through ideas.

"I'm checking out some spots right now. I'm thinking something close to Homestead, just south of Miami, would be good. We don't have enough notice to reserve a big-time venue. The security alone would be impossible to arrange. Homestead Air Force Base may be too military looking for us, but Bayfront Park looks better. It's close to the base. They can set up the security for the President quickly, and there will be plenty of uniforms from the base around for show."

"Sounds good, let's do it. We ought to add some Navy men to the mix. I've got a buddy who's the captain of the Naval station in Key West. I want him in a prominent place."

"Got it. Get me his contact info and I'll set it up."

Ward hit the intercom button on his phone and called for his aide, who walked in, phone to her ear as usual. She made eye contact and hung up. "Sir?"

"You guys need to make some arrangements. I'll leave you to it." As an afterthought, he asked for her phone.

He stepped out of the office and dialed Gillum's number. There was static as he answered.

"Jim, you there?" Ward asked, trying to break through the static.

"On the road, sir. Going to take care of our problem right now."

"Good. I need you in Homestead tomorrow afternoon. Bring it with you."

"Shouldn't be a problem."

"Make sure. I'm counting on you."

STEVEN BECKER

A MAC TRAVIS ADVENTURE

WOOD'S REEF

"What up, Behzad? What brings you to my humble business?"

Behzad cringed as they walked in the door of the U-Haul dealer. Nothing was going his way today — some kind of karma, he guessed. The clerk, a customer of his, was Key West cool, surely violating the dress code; U-Haul uniform shirt untucked, short sleeves rolled up showing some ink, a few too many buttons undone to reveal nothing anyone really wanted to see. He had enough hair gel in his spikes to reflect the fluorescent lighting. The mandatory earrings and nose ring adorned his freshly shaved face. All in all, it couldn't be worse.

"You sure are well known here, Behzad."

He ignored the comment. Cesar and now this dude, whose name eluded him. His associations were not looking good to the intolerant Ibrahim. He thought about buying a prayer rug and getting tight with Allah, just to make up for it.

"We need to rent a truck," Ibrahim said.

"That's what we do. Hey Behzad, that was some party the other night."

"Enough. We need a truck," Ibrahim said.

"What's up with your friend? It's the Keys, man, chillax."

Sweat broke out on Behzad's face. He leaned over the counter and whispered to the man, "I'll make it worth your while if you help my friend out here."

The clerk was all business now. "What size truck, and for how long? I'll hook you up with our best deal."

"Thank you," Ibrahim said.

"Something like that." He pointed outside. "That will work. We need it for several days."

"No problem, you can have that one. I'll give it to you for a week at a special rate." He winked at Behzad, who felt like he was about to throw up.

"Very well. Any problem if we pay in cash?"

"No, cash is good. Just can't insure it." The clerk looked proud of himself. "Give me a grand for the deposit and I'll refund the difference when you bring it back."

Ibrahim counted out ten hundred dollar bills from his pocket.

The clerk grabbed the money and handed over the keys. "Take care of that truck now, you didn't buy any insurance. No hazardous materials." He winked at Behzad again.

———

"You don't look so well," Ibrahim said as Behzad pulled out of the lot.

"I'm just not used to driving a truck."

"First the drug dealers, now this man; you sure it's not your associations here? You have some interesting friends."

"Key West is an interesting place." Behzad rolled down the window and slid toward the door, trying to put as much space as possible between him and Ibrahim. The thought of opening the door and bailing onto the street began to cross his mind. The last thing he had wanted when he contacted Ibrahim was for his life to be under a fundamentalist microscope. Meeting his associates and seeing how he lived was not part of the plan.

The tension mounted as they drove in silence, retracing their route from this morning. As they neared Marathon, Ibrahim appeared anxious.

"The infidel, we have not heard from him. I don't trust him. Do you suppose he just took our money?"

Behzad was thankful for a distraction from his thoughts. "You're right, he should have called and checked in by now." His brain churned, working out the best way to find him. "He needs a boat. We could check the boat rentals and ramps."

"There're boat rentals and ramps every ten feet around here," Ibrahim said, glancing at either side of the road. They were just passing a sign for a boat ramp at 33rd Street. "We might as well start there."

"It's a shot in the dark. He could be anywhere." Behzad was not sure how he wanted this to play out. His system was strung out from too much partying and not enough sleep and he'd finished his stash in the restroom at the truck rental, leaving a small pile for the clerk. He should have left him more, but greed overtook him. The road to paradise was paved with potholes.

"We need to start somewhere. He's either going to buy the cheapest boat he can, or rent one. He said that he wrecked a rental boat last week, so I don't think he can rent another. We've got nothing to lose."

36

STEVEN BECKER

A MAC TRAVIS ADVENTURE
WOOD'S
REEF

THEY WERE BACK in the interrogation room. Doans had a bag of fast food in front of him. "I guess you found something."

"I confirmed part of your story. They were gone, though," Jules said.

"Not my problem." He was stuffing fries into his mouth, his other hand on the burger. When he needed a drink, he leaned over and sipped through the straw. No one was taking his food.

"Depends what you want worse. I could hold you on suspicion of terrorist activity until Homeland Security decides what to do, or just lock you up on assault and reckless endangerment and let the DA's office deal with it. Either way, you're not walking out of here. I'd change my attitude if I was you."

Doans was in the middle of processing a large piece of the burger. "Oh, come on. You've got nothing to hold me on."

"Maybe I'll cut this food fest short and release you then, but I'm keeping the money for evidence. What's to say the story you gave me is true? Could be your friends paid you that pile of cash for telling them where the bomb is. They could be on their way out there to recover it right now, while you're sitting in here stuffing your face.

Maybe they'll come back, wondering where the gringo with their money went, and are looking for you. Who knows?"

Doans finished chewing the burger and jammed a handful of fries in his mouth. "I'd never betray my country like that. You can't keep my money."

"We'll see about that. Get up. You're released."

He hesitated. "What about the rest of my stuff?"

"The deputy will turn over everything but the cash on your way out."

———

She called for a deputy to escort Doans out of the interrogation room and issued orders to release him. He made a desperate grab for the rest of the food, but the deputy smiled as he yanked him away. Heather came in from the observation room.

"You turn the recorder off?" Jules asked.

"Yeah. Why release him, though? We've got plenty to hold him for a while."

"I've dealt with a ton of guys like this. They'll sit here and eat your food." She glanced at the half-consumed meal on the table. "But you never really know if they're telling the truth or not. They all think they're smarter than you and always have some kind of an angle."

"But still, why let him go?"

"There could be a bomb out there, in our home. No one in D.C. has expressed even the slightest curiosity. The only way to figure this thing out is to let him go and follow him. Get out there and see what he does. Don't do anything but observe. Keep me posted."

"But I'm not a deputy."

"Exactly. He'll never suspect you. Don't worry. Just keep an eye on him."

———

Doans was out the door and into the morning heat a little lighter than when he came in — by about a half a pound. He opened the manila envelope the deputy had handed him and took out the handheld GPS. The screen was broken, but otherwise the unit was intact. He took out the other possessions and tossed the envelope to the ground. Conflicted, he was glad to be free, but the money was gone. He kicked a can on the sidewalk. Without the cash, what was he going to do now? Never even thinking that he'd overplayed his hand and the sheriff had outwitted him, he needed a new plan. His car was back at the bar, his cash in the sheriff's office. He started walking south on US1 toward the bar. A few blocks down, he saw a sign for a boat ramp. On a whim, he crossed the street and headed toward it. He was drenched in sweat when he reached the ramp. Depressed, he sat down on the curb to think, wondering where his karma would lead him now.

He watched the stream of traffic at the ramp. Most of the boats were putting in for the day; the only vessels pulling out were commercial boats who started early and had finished their day's work.

Everyone had their own technique — some pros, others not. He was watching one couple in particular. They were yelling back and forth. Sun reflected off the man's head as he stood at the helm of the boat, signaling and yelling for his wife to back up the truck to drop the boat in the water, but she would go no farther than wetting the bottom of the trailer tires in the water. The man was clearly agonizing over her trepidation. An idea crept into his mind as he watched the show.

Ever the Good Samaritan, Doans walked over and offered help.

"She won't drop it back far enough," the man said.

"I can see that. Tell you what. Why don't you hop down from there and back her up? I'll take the boat off for you."

"You'd really do that?"

"For sure. I've been where you are before. Nothing worse than a boat ramp fight."

The man log rolled his bulk over the side, cautiously putting one foot on the fender. He hopped off and opened the car door for his wife, who was happy to comply.

Doans hopped over the gunwale and took control of the helm. He signaled that he was ready and the man backed down the ramp, his wife looking on in horror as the trailer's wheels went into the water. The boat started to slide off, and Doans smiled as the engine started on the first try. Feeling as good as he had in two days, he cut the wheel to the left and pulled back on the throttle. The boat responded and moved backward away from the ramp, bow pointing toward the inlet.

The man pulled the trailer out and was quickly around the bend, looking for a parking spot. His wife was playing on her phone, probably texting her friends what a jerk her husband was.

No one was looking as he pushed the throttle forward. The boat's bow rose, the engine buried deep, and churning the water. After a long pause the boat leveled out and accelerated out towards the gulf.

———

Heather had circled back and was parked on the street under a shade tree just out of sight of the ramp. She hadn't seen it coming — there were always people helping out at boat ramps. It often took a half-dozen guys standing on a tailgate to get enough traction to pull a heavy boat. But this was different. She got on the radio to the sheriff and started toward the ramp at a quick jog.

The man was standing over his wife yelling at her for whatever part of this he could blame on her when Heather reached them.

"You folks OK?"

"No, we are not OK. He won't stop yelling at me. Can't you lock him up until he cools down?"

"That son of a bitch took my boat! He offered to help me because she's so damned worthless, and he took the damn boat. I want to file a report. This is going to ruin my vacation."

"Let me see the registration for the boat. I'll do the paperwork and call it in right now. Unless he knows where he's going and is heading into the back country, we'll find him pretty quick. Maybe get the chopper up."

Heather watched them walk away as she called in a description of the boat. The wife trailed behind, appearing happy with the outcome, imagining an afternoon or two drinking Mai Tais by the hotel pool or shopping in Key West. Anywhere but that damned boat.

37

GILLUM WAS FEELING EUPHORIC. He'd always heard about the mythical rush felt before a mission. Now he was experiencing it first-hand. No cloak and dagger this time. He had direct orders from the Vice President to obtain the bomb and bring it to Homestead. Now that was authority, he thought. He sat in the front passenger seat of a black Suburban, Mac wedged between two crewmen in the back. The rear seat was folded down. Dive tanks rattled, and gear was jammed in every possible space. He'd picked the two crewmen for their reputations. These guys were special forces. They wouldn't question his orders.

There was a yellow VW bug in the drive when they pulled up to Mac's. "I may have company. Why don't you let me go in and see what's going on here? I don't know that car."

"I'll go with him. The rest of you go around the side and load the boat," Gillum said.

Gillum followed Mac into the house. They looked around checking his office first, and saw the medical supplies on his desk. Upstairs was evidence of breakfast scattered everywhere.

"The boat's gone." The crewman burst through the front door.

Gillum was starting to put the pieces of the puzzle together. "Looks like at least Wood and the girl were here. But there's too much food for just those two. Who drives that?" He pointed at the VW visible through the window.

"No idea," Mac said.

Gillum's frustration was written all over his face as he paced the workshop floor. "Never mind them. We need to get out there. You've got to know someone around here that's got a boat we can use. Let me remind you that your ass is on the line," he added.

"I've got the only one I know with the size hoist we need to recover the bomb. All the other salvage boats draw too much water too. Besides, anyone else you'd have to hire, and I don't think you want more folks involved in this."

They were in Mac's office. Gillum sat at the desk, scrolling through the recently opened files. He noticed a GPS program had recently updated and clicked on the icon. A list of waypoints displayed in spreadsheet form. Columns showed latitude, longitude, description and date. He hit the 'date' button on top of the column and scanned the display of the waypoints automatically sorted in chronological order. The top date was only two days ago. That had to be the bomb, he thought. He copied the numbers onto a piece of paper and sat up satisfied.

Pulling out his cell phone, he went to his contacts, and hit a number. "Sheriff, Captain Jim Gillum here, Commander Naval Air Station Key West." He threw in all his titles. The conversation went back and forth for a minute as they exchanged pleasantries. They obviously knew each other and Gillum got to the point. "I need a favor," he paused. "We need a boat. You got a recovery vessel in your fleet?"

"Just a couple of outboards, nothing that big. You've got the whole Navy at your back. Why ask me for a boat?"

"I'm in Marathon. There's a national security issue I'm trying to deal with. I don't have time to call for a boat up here. It's either you or the Coast Guard, and I can't stand the Commandant. Prick wishes he was in the Navy."

"Has this got something to do with a terrorist threat?"

"No, just a recovery of some old bombs." He had no reason to lie.

"I've got bad news for you. You're not the only one after a bomb. I just released a guy who we're following right now. He's trying to sell it to a couple of terrorists. That's a pretty big coincidence here. I've lived here all my life and this is the first bomb I ever heard of."

He thought for a minute, ignoring Mac and the crewman staring at him. If she was right and it was the same bomb, this made things interesting. He took his time thinking through how this development could affect his career. Adding terrorists to the equation made the job a little harder, but the reward much greater. Gillum pictured himself showing up in Homestead a hero. "What about D.C.?"

"I've been in touch with them. Reported it all, just as they tell us to, but no one has called back. They must all be out playing golf, Saturday morning and all."

"The bomb's real. I can confirm that. Don't know about the terrorists, though. First I've heard of it. Tell you what, I'm up here with a team and a local that knows where the bomb is. How about teaming up on this?"

"That'll help me out. The guy I released just stole a boat and is probably heading there now. I don't have time to put together a team. Where are you?"

"We're with this guy named Travis, at his place. We were going to use his boat, but it's gone."

"I know him. I'll bet I know who's got his boat. We better move, there's bound to be trouble. Meet me across at the 33rd Street boat ramp. I can be there in ten minutes."

———

"Pack it up boys, we're moving out. Not you, Travis. You're done. Sheriff's going to help us out from here."

Mac was packing his dive gear. "You can't find the spot without me."

Gillum held up the piece of paper with the waypoints. "Negative. Tie him up." He motioned one of his men toward a chair. "Put him in the chair and bind his hands and feet. Might as well gag him too."

The crewman drew his gun, motioning Mac toward the chair. He handed the gun to Gillum and duct taped Mac's hands to each other behind his back and his feet to the chair. Now restrained, he couldn't resist as the man took a six- inch piece off the roll and placed it over his mouth.

"Now, you be good and sit right here. I promise once the bomb is secure, we'll be back and let you go." He turned to the men. "Let's go. Pull down that door so no one sees him." Gillum had no intention of letting Mac go. Alone in the workshop, he scanned the shelves of the shop area. He noticed a couple of large gas cans, dumped the contents of one into a large oil pan, and set it on the floor below the workbench. A bottle of bleach sat on a shelf nearby. He opened the top, stuck a rag in, and laid the bottle down on the bench so that the rag would drip into the gasoline. The deadly fumes emitted from the mixture would remove Travis from the equation.

38

STEVEN BECKER

SMOKE WAS STARTING to rise off the liquid, and Mac stared at the pan as the bleach slowly dripped into the gas. He didn't have much time before the fumes and smoke reached him or the unstable mix exploded, whichever happened first. He started to rock the chair in the direction of the back door. Getting outside was top priority, then he could figure out his next step. The chair tipped, but he recovered and moved toward the door. It was slow going, but he was making progress. Sweat dripped into his eyes, adding to the burn from the smoke and he focused on the door as the smoke slowly filled the space. The fumes had just started to envelope him when he reached the door. Once outside he sat in the chair gulping air. Several deep breaths later he was ready to get out of the restraints.

He eyed the waist belt PFD he used for paddling, a multi-tool hanging from a carabiner on its belt. It was only a few feet inside. Reluctant to go back in, he looked around but saw no other option. Gas and vapor filled the space now, the wind acting as a fan to keep the fumes in the building. He took several deep breaths, totally emptying his lungs with each effort and held the last breath. Holding his breath, he repeated the process of tipping the chair back and forth, walking it forward with each effort. He moved the back of the chair to the PFD and grabbed for it with his fingers. The carabiner in hand, and his lungs burning, he rushed to get out of the door, but the chair tipped over, dumping him onto the floor. The good air left his lungs upon impact, then he automatically grabbed for air. Fumes filled his lungs. Coughing, he rolled the chair towards the door, trying to get outside and escape the fumes.

He made it outside and once in the fresh air, his head cleared. The tool had a serrated blade, which made short work of the duct tape. Free from his restraints, he took a deep breath and ran into the house. He righted the bleach bottle, stopping the drip. The mixture had stopped smoking now, but he had no idea how stable it was. He ran back outside to refresh his burning lungs and breathed deeply again. A few deep breaths, the last one held, and he was back inside. He grabbed the pan from the floor and moved as fast as he could without spilling the volatile liquid. Once clear of the building, he poured the contents slowly onto the gravel drive. Better a little gas in the earth than an explosion. The immediate danger over, he planned his next move.

He went back in and grabbed his BC and regulator. His mask and fins were on the boat, but he quickly found an extra set. Reviewing the mental checklist in his head, he moved toward his office. He removed a pistol from the gun safe in the back of the closet and placed it in his waistband. At the desk, he keyed the mike on the VHF radio, already on channel 16. He hailed his boat several times with no response. That didn't surprise him; if Trufante or Wood had anything to do with this, you could count on the radio being off.

The computer was still on, the screen opened to where Gillum had left it. He had to re-sort the numbers, listing them in ascending order of longitude, making it easier for him to place them in his head. Novices needed to plot the numbers either manually on a chart with a lat/lon grid, or by using a computer program. Mac had worked with these coordinates for years, and visualized each location. The first two columns showed the coordinates and the third column contained the waypoint number in his GPS.

His cell phone sat on the desk, undisturbed since yesterday. He grabbed it, hoping there was enough battery. He was sure Mel would be attached to her phone and he tried to call, but it went to voice mail. His next attempt was through a text message. He texted her the waypoint number and lat/lon coordinates, laboring over the numbers, triple checking that he'd got them right. The last line of the text asked her to meet him there. His lungs still burning from the fumes only added to his anger and he made the decision to go after Gillum.

————

Gillum was pacing outside the SUV as the sheriff's truck and trailer pulled up to the ramp. The deputy already on site began directing the busy boat traffic to clear a path as Jules backed the triple-axle trailer toward the ramp. There was room for half a dozen boats to put in, and despite the wind, all the spaces were occupied, with several boaters impatiently waiting. He stopped a truck that was just about to back in and directed it to move out of the way. The driver shot a look but obeyed. Once clear he motioned for Jules to back into the space.

The SUV dropped back until the trailer's tires were submerged to just below the bearings. The deputy at the helm held up a fist, signaling for her to stop. He checked that the motor was down and fired it up. The 27-foot Contender slipped off the trailer, the deputy guiding it into a space at the adjacent dock. The Navy crewmen quickly loaded the boat and stowed their gear while the Sheriff got out of the truck.

"Someone better stay on land and coordinate this thing. I'm gonna try and track down the two terrorists here. My deputy will take you." She turned to the deputy. "Keep me posted. Whatever the Captain says goes."

The boat moved away from the dock and the deputy turned

toward open water. After passing the channel markers he acceler-ated. The twin 275 hp engines had the boat on plane in a few seconds and it moved out of sight around the corner. She parked and went to the deputy's car, still under the shade tree. Once inside, air conditioning running, she got on the radio and put out a BOLO for the two suspected terrorists. There were too many people involved in this now to play it low key.

39

STEVEN BECKER

A MAC TRAVIS ADVENTURE

WOOD'S
REEF

THE BOAT WAS MAKING ten knots, pitching forward with each wave. Trufante had the wheel. He leaned against the seat, taking weight off his injured leg. Spray drenched the deck as the bow rose and fell. It was only two foot seas, but driven by the wind, they were whitecaps and stacked up close together. The waves were following now, the waves running with the boat. It would be much worse coming into them on the way back. Wood was below, laid out in a bunk. Sue and Mel sat at his side.

Mel watched his face as his brow furrowed with every bump.

"By the dawn's early light, who taught him how to run a boat?" Wood muttered.

"Easy, Dad, it's pretty messy out there. We'll be at your place in a few minutes."

"Tell him to bring her into the lee of the island. That's the side the bomb is on, and out of the wind. Let me know when we get there." He rolled over, burying his face in the cushion.

Sue motioned for Mel to come out onto the deck. Once outside, she raised her voice to be heard over the engines and wind. "He can't take much more of this. Even if those staples hold, there's no telling whether there's internal damage."

"There's not much we can do until we get there. Once we have the bomb secure, we can just park him out there. Probably where he wants to be anyway."

"If you can talk him into it, I'll call in sick and stay out with him. He shouldn't be alone."

"Thanks." Mel looked down at the text message just coming into her phone. She moved over to the helm and showed it to Trufante.

He squinted at the small screen and smaller letters, her hand bouncing with the rhythm of the boat. "If we were sitting in a bar on land I couldn't make that out. You'll have to read it to me."

"Just says to meet Mac at waypoint 59 in an hour. These must be the coordinates." She texted back.

"Wonder what's going on out there." Trufante turned on the chart plotter and waited for the unit to acquire a signal. An hourglass spun on the screen as the unit calculated its position from the satellites it used to navigate. The display changed to a menu, and he went to the chart view and scrolled to 59. An arrow came up on the chart plotter, showing the location of the waypoint overlaid on a chart. "That's where we found that thing," he said slowly. "Wonder what he's up to?"

"There's Dad's place." Mel pointed to the island in the distance. "He said to go around to the lee side of it."

"Yeah, makes sense. That's where we left the bomb. I'm going to have to go in a big loop to miss the sandbars. It's low tide now, gonna take a few."

"Let me know when. I'm going to look in on him."

Sue was by his side when Mel came over next to her. "How's that leg holding up?"

"Hurts a bit, but I'll live." He grinned at her. "We get back from this, I'll have to get a nurse to help me out."

She smacked his arm. "So what's really going on here? I've been picking up bits and pieces about a bomb. What are you guys really into?"

Trufante put his arm around her. "Well little lady, it kinda goes like this ..."

————

No one had to tell Wood when they pulled around the island. The seas went to glass, the wind buffered by the land. The boat coasted smoothly through the water. He gained his feet and fought his way up the ladder one rung at a time, pausing between each step.

"Actually made it without wrecking. Pull her up onto that sand bar there." He pointed toward the shore. The sand bar was about fifty feet off the beach. "We can ground her. By the time we're done, the tide should float us back off."

Trufante slowly approached the sandbar, nudging the bow, then gunned the engine slightly to ground the hull. The scar left by the boat that crashed was still visible as he stopped. "What's your plan now? We're two cripples and two women. How're we gonna get that thing out a 'there?"

"No worries, it ain't a bomb without the guts. Should have done this before, and never got the Navy involved. I'm gonna try and pull the trigger mechanism and then see if I can get the warhead out of it. Never did it myself, but I used to watch the ordnance men all the time."

"That's a ballsy maneuver. You sure you know what you're doing? I got a lot more beer to drink before I'm ready to meet my maker."

"Just get those girls to pull the paddleboard down. You stay here with the boat. I'll grab some tools and the girls can get me in there. I'll give it my best shot. No telling what the inside of that thing looks like after sitting in salt water for so long - could be nothing left."

"That's good, because Mac texted Mel and wants us to meet him at the spot where we pulled this up."

"Goddam it to hell. Fifty years those bombs have sat down there undiscovered. Now they're both out."

———

Wood lay prone, Mel on one side, Sue on the other, guiding it as the paddleboard slid easily through the water. They reached the shore and helped Wood off the board. Mel and Sue supported him as they made their way towards the bomb. They both glanced at the wrecked boat before moving to the bomb. Camouflage pulled back, the casing shone dimly in the sun. Wood got down on his knees, removed a screwdriver from the box they had brought from the boat and started to remove the access panel. The screws were bound — years of saltwater had corroded them just enough to weld them to the metal.

"Can you find the house from here?" he asked Mel.

She gave him the look only a daughter can give her father. "What do you need?"

"In the top drawer of the tool cabinet is a set of easy outs. They look like little spiral things. Grab them, and there's a battery drill right by it. Better get both batteries."

While Mel headed toward the house to retrieve the tools. Wood tried to get comfortable, his back against the dull metal.

40

DOANS WAS PRETTY MUCH SOAKED by now, the low freeboard of the boat offering little protection from the spray. Next time he'd have to be more picky about what he stole. No wonder that couple fought like that with this piece of crap. The salt water hit his face again as he pulled back on the throttle. He slowed down, surveying the broken water. It was much harder to see the bottom features when it was this choppy. He was halfway to the island, an area he knew was loaded with obstructions. On a typical Keys day, you could watch the turtle grass swaying in the gentle current like wheat in a breeze. The sandbars and shoals stood out in stark contrast to the sandy bottom. Not today, though. The slate grey water was unreadable.

He took his handheld GPS from his pocket and wiped off the broken screen with his shirt tail. While it powered up, he stared at the screen, hoping it still worked after the crash. It was hard to read through the cracked plastic. The screen showed his progress in real time. Ahead was the mark he had put in before running aground and hitting the old man. He navigated toward it, trying to remember where the shoals were.

His mind was drifting when a wave took the boat on the beam.

He looked around and saw another, larger wave—the wake from the lobster boat—coming at him. The next wave caught him before he could correct course, knocking him to the deck. He lay there for a moment waiting for his vision to clear. As he turned to get up he saw a waterproof box secured in the open compartment below the steering wheel. His injuries forgotten he pulled the box out, got to his feet and set it on the seat. The latches opened, he removed the revolver from the foam surrounding it. The cylinder spun in his hand revealing six bullets. *Thank God for rednecks,* he thought as he placed the gun in his waistband.

The island came into view after a half hour beating and he flexed his hands, trying to get the circulation back. The white-knuckle ride had left them numb. The motor pivoted on its mount, the propeller leaving the water as it lifted clear of any obstructions and he slid up to the piling by the beach. It was low tide, but the boat didn't drag the bottom. He found a line in the forward compartment and tied off. Already soaked, he didn't mind hopping over the side of the boat into the water. Once on dry land, he headed up the path.

The clearing was empty when he reached the house. Dead reckoning was never one of his talents and he stared at several trails heading off in different directions. He took the far right one and moved onto the narrow trail. The palm fronds in front of him rattled and moved in a different direction than the wind, as if an animal was about to cross his path, but he ignored the disturbance and continued on.

Finally, tired and mosquito bitten, he could see the clearing through the thinning brush. He saw the old man and a younger woman leaning against the bomb. Travis's boat was grounded on a sand bar fifty feet from the beach. He swept a large palm frond aside and stepped into the clearing, gun drawn. Wood and Sue froze focused on his gun.

"Aren't you the son of a bitch that ran me over?" Wood said, surprised.

"You look okay to me, old man. You got this pretty girl keeping you company?" He leered at Sue. "Looks like you're doing okay from here."

"I can only imagine why you're here and how you're mixed up in all this."

———

Gillum peered through the bouncing binoculars, trying to piece together what he saw on the island, while keeping the contents of his stomach where they belonged. The Sheriff's Contender was downwind of Mac's boat and out of sight, the velocity and direction of the wind masking their engine noise. From their position, it looked like there were three people on the beach, one holding a gun on the others. He handed the binoculars to the deputy.

"Have a look through these, and tell me what you're seeing out there."

The deputy lifted the binoculars and gazed at the island for a moment. "Looks like the guy we're supposed to be watching out for. The boat he stole must be on the other side of the island."

Gillum directed the pilot to move the boat around the point. When they were past it, one of the crewmen threw the anchor as far as he could onto the beach. He started recovering line, pulling the boat toward the shallow beach. Gillum and the two crewmen hopped over the side and headed toward the land, their guns drawn as they approached the clearing.

"Put that pistol down and step over with the others." Gillum entered the clearing first, the two crewmen behind him.

The guy with the gun looked behind him. Seeing he was outnumbered and outgunned, he dropped his gun to the sand, and watched as Gillum picked it up. He moved over by the bomb, awaiting his fate, and trying to keep his distance from Wood.

Gillum chuckled. "Well, Wood, it's been a long time since the two of us were together with this baby."

"Haven't you and Ward caused enough trouble, leaving these

bombs out for whoever to find? You two should have manned up and reported it back when it happened. What do you plan on doing?"

"That wouldn't be any of your business." He moved over and spoke quietly to the two crewmen. One of them took off in the direction of the sheriff's boat. "Let's all get comfortable, now."

———

The crewman reached the sheriff's boat, pulled the anchor out of the sand, and pushed the boat off. He hopped over the gunwale and directed the deputy to head off in the direction of Mac's boat. They quickly crossed the distance between the two boats. A hundred feet away, the deputy turned on his lights and signaled over the bullhorn for any one aboard to show themselves.

A tall man came out of the wheelhouse, hands over his head. When they reached the boat, the Navy man vaulted the three feet and landed easily on the deck. He looked around, reached for a piece of line, quickly turned his prisoner around, and bound his hands behind his back. At the helm, he gave a short blast on the horn, signaling to the men on the beach that the boat was in his control.

"Over the side," he motioned with the gun to his prisoner.

It took several minutes for both men to cross the knee-deep water, already several inches higher with the tide coming in. They reached the beach and waited for instructions.

41

THERE WERE three boards in the rack, just inside the garage door. The fourteen footer was the least stable, but the best for what he had in mind. Fortunately, the wind would be at his back once he got under the Seven Mile Bridge. Until then, it would be bad. The wind got hold of the race board and spun Mac around. Still feeling the effects of the gas fumes he struggled with the board. Finally he regained control and carried it to the dock.

The skinny board was rigged with tie downs for gear on the bow and stern. He used these to secure the buoyancy compensator and tank, then he blew into the BC, partially inflating it to use as a cushion for the small pony scuba tank against the thin fiberglass coating of the board. In a bag secured to the back, he had his regulator. The board would be awkward with the equipment, but he would just have to adjust his stance to compensate. He strapped on a weight belt and headed out into the water.

As he started to paddle, he struggled against the wind, trying to balance the weight as he stroked into the choppy water. He moved backward, trying to get the nose of the board out of the water. The first half mile was going to be the hard part. Paddling into a twenty-knot wind was not for the faint of heart. After he got into the channel, the wind would start moving to his back, pushing him forward.

Several hard minutes later he cleared the end of the canal. Turning right into the main channel, he had the wind at his side now. Counting strokes, trying to take his mind off the struggle, he didn't see the larger wave until it took the board. The next thing he knew, he was in the water, weight belt dragging him under. The leash held the board close, and he pulled it toward him, heaved his body back on and regained his feet. But the board had drifted dangerously close to the seawall. After what felt like a thousand strokes on his right side he regained the channel, the wind finally shifting to his back. He started taking longer and deeper strokes, timing them to catch the waves running behind him, and surf the crests. Where he had struggled to go one mph into the wind, he was cruising at close to nine mph now. He fell into an easy rhythm, several quick strokes to get on the crest of the wave, then a few long slow strokes as the wave played itself out. Rinse and repeat. The Seven Mile Bridge faded behind him as he cruised toward the ledge.

He knew these waters well enough to find the buoy line without the help of a GPS. When he arrived, there was no one in sight, which was a good sign. Following the trap buoys he found the spot and reached for the closest buoy, lay down on the board, and grabbed the line. The board swung around, water pouring over the nose, drenching him. He reached down and removed the leash from his ankle, securing the trap line to it instead and waited while the board swung back with the current. He was effectively anchored now.

Waves bounced the tank against the board and he cringed. Race boards weren't durable enough to take a beating like this; they were made to be light. The tank would break the fiberglass coat and allow water to saturate the foam inside if he wasn't more careful. He decided it would be best to get in the water and start looking, take some weight off the board at least. The sound of his boat propeller's cavitation would be audible underwater and alert him when Mel arrived.

He tried to reconcile himself to the feeling that he might be alone in this as he straddled the board, legs in the water. No idea where Mel, Wood or Trufante were or if they had even gotten his message. He hoped they would be here shortly, but was prepared to find the other bomb by himself. With no plan what to do after, just a gut instinct that this had to be done, he pulled the tank and BC out of the restraints, and screwed on the regulator. Air turned on, he inflated the BC and set it in the water, clipping it to the buoy line with a cara-biner attached to the vest. Fins and mask adjusted, he slid off the board and into the water. The BC strapped to his back, he held the inflator above his head, released the air from the bladder, and quickly sank to the bottom.

———

The rough seas had an effect on the visibility—only ten feet now. He automatically checked his gauges, noting air pressure and depth, his bottom time limited only by his air supply. Although the pony tank was considerably smaller than a standard-size scuba tank, the air would still last an hour, and it wasn't deep enough to worry about decompression. The ledge slid past him as he explored the reef, looking for any sign of metal, straight lines or a man-made shape. Working his way along its length, he passed the spot where he had found the first bomb, an indentation still visible in the sand.

A small hump in the sand caught his attention toward the end of the ledge. If he hadn't recovered the first bomb and seen its size and shape, he would have passed right by. Air flowed from his regulator as he took it from his mouth, and pointed it toward the sand. For once, he wished for an octopus. The extra regulator, used for buddy breathing in emergencies, would allow him to breathe while he was using this regulator to clear the sand. Instead, he alternated the one regulator between his mouth and the sand, blowing the firmament from around the object. His teeth gripped the rubber mouthpiece as he breathed and waited for the sediment to settle before moving on.

He'd been at it for twenty minutes, and was starting to worry about Mel and Wood and whether they were coming at all. He would need them — and his boat — if he found a second bomb. Another breath and he would surface and scope it out up top. He held the next breath, allowing small bubbles to escape from his mouth and removed the regulator, pointing it at the ground again. Sand shifted as the air swooshed out, changing the contour of the bottom. Blinded by the sediment, Mac moved his hand along the disturbed sand and hit something smooth.

42

MEL WATCHED THE SCENE UNFOLD, concealed behind a strand of thick mangroves. She shielded her eyes from the glare and scanned the water. The sheriff's boat was tied off of Mac's. It looked like one man was on deck. She moved her gaze to the men on the beach. Clearly the man in charge didn't know what to do. He probably wanted the bomb, but didn't know what to do with the prisoners. The lawyer side of her brain took over as she tried to figure a way out. She pulled out her phone and checked the time. They were supposed to have met Mac ten minutes ago, although she had no idea why. But first she had to get her dad, Trufante, and Sue out of there.

She'd need firepower and surprise to negotiate this position. Despite her racing heart, she quietly exited her hiding spot and started slowly back down the path toward the house. Once out of earshot of the clearing, she increased her pace and quickly covered the ground to the shed. With no idea where her dad kept anything, she started rummaging through the piles of tools and gear. In a pile of dive equipment, she saw a spear gun. She grabbed the gun—more valuable in her hands than a shotgun—plus an extra spear, and a fresh band. Then she moved stealthily back down the path toward the clearing. In her teen years, her passion for spearfishing had won her several competitions, and although it had been years, the gun felt good in her hands. When she was within a few feet of exposing herself, she stuck the extra shaft in the sand in front of her, checked that the spear was inserted, pulled the band back, and engaged the trigger.

She knew she was outgunned. The element of surprise and her experience with a spear gun were her only assets. Slowly, she moved to a better vantage point and aimed the gun at the closest crewman. Evaluating the threat, she had determined the crewmen to be vastly more dangerous than the officer. She accounted for distance and the weight of the spear, knowing it would drop as it travelled, and pulled the trigger. The shaft buzzed through the air, embedding itself in the crewmen's shoulder, right by his neck.

The Captain spun in a circle, panic showing on his face, and took off toward the water with the second crewman. They were quickly out of range of the band-driven gun, as they dove into the water and made for Mac's boat.

"Nobody move," she yelled, still concealed. She didn't want to let them know she was alone.

She saw Trufante smile when he recognized her. With both hands bound, he rose and walked towards Doans. He rotated to the right, using the momentum to swing his arms and smack the shorter man in the head.

Wood picked up the gun from the sand and pointed it at Doans. "I ought to do you right now, for all the trouble you've caused."

Now Mel came out of the bush, the remaining shaft cocked in the spear gun.

"That's the son of a bitch that ran over your dad," Trufante told her. "Shot me in the leg, too. Good thing he's not as good a shot as you. Why don't you pop him, get me some revenge?"

Mel came out of her Rambo trance. "Let's just tie them up and figure out what to do." She looked remorsefully at the crewman on the ground, who had air bubbles coming out of his neck. Shooting fish was one thing. Knowing that injuring the crewman was her only option at the time and looking at the result of her action were two different things. Her voice cracked, "Sue, could you have a look at him?"

Trufante picked up the rope, walked over to Doans, tied his hands behind his back, and pushed him into the sand. He turned to walk away, but changed his mind, turned, and cold cocked him on the head with the butt of the gun.

"Stop it!" Mel yelled. "No more! Dad, tell him what you need to disarm this thing." She pointed toward Trufante with the spear.

Wood called out a list and she watched Trufante head down the path to the house.

"Wait! I'm going with him. This guy needs a tracheotomy quick. I need supplies." Sue ran after the Cajun.

———

The deputy watched the entire event from the boat. He had a sidearm, but clearly the situation on the beach was out of control. Instead of getting involved, he reached for the radio and gave the sheriff a rundown.

Jules' voice came back clearly. "I want the prisoner back. He's the only link to the terrorists. Get Wood on the radio. I'll see if he knows what to do with the bomb."

"What about the crewmen? One took off with the Navy Captain in the other boat. The other's down."

"Go check it out and get back to me."

———

Mel pointed the spear gun at the deputy coming up the beach.

"It's OK, ma'am. Just want to talk. I think we're on the same side here."

"You can talk while I hold this on you, just in case."

"Suit yourself. Sheriff wants that man back in custody." He pointed at Doans. "She wants to talk to Wood as well." He reached behind his back, and Mel tightened her finger on the trigger of her spear gun. He walked forward toward her, a radio extended in one hand, the other over his head.

"Tru, get the radio and give it to Dad." She moved the spear to point it at Doans.

"He's all yours. Just do me a favor and ask the DA to make sure he gets the book thrown at him: attempted murder, accessory to terrorism and whatever else they can think of."

Meanwhile, Wood grabbed the radio. "Wood here. What can I do for you, Sheriff?"

The radio crackled and Mel heard the Sheriff's voice clearly. "We clear on what's going on here? My deputy is going to take the prisoner into custody and bring him back. Is the Navy man stable enough to move?"

"No way, not for a while. We got a girl here from the hospital says she can probably get him fixed up enough to be moved. It looks bad, but not fatal. If they want to send a chopper to pick him up that would be ok, but with this weather, moving him by boat would be too risky."

"Roger. I'll contact the Navy and see what they want to do. What about the Captain?"

"Bastard took off with Mac's boat and the other crewman. No idea what they're up to. My worst fear is they're after the other bomb." Wood said.

"Great, two now. What about the one at your place?"

"I got that. I'm about to operate. I can disarm it and lose the parts, if you know what I mean."

"You sure you don't want me to call the Navy about it?"

"That's how this started. It's too complicated to get into now. Disarming this is the only option. I'll figure it out. Can't be that hard, this dinosaur's as old as me."

"All right, let me know if you need anything. Out."

"Maybe, put up one of those helicopters you got—see if you can see where they went." Wood handed the radio back to the deputy.

The deputy grabbed Doans by his arms and pushed him out in front of him toward the water. They reached the boat and he shoved him over the gunwale. She heard the engine start and saw one of the men haul in the anchor. The boat quickly turned into a blur visible only by the spray it kicked up.

————

Mel looked around her. Wood was resting against the bomb, the Navy man was still. "I'm going after Mac," she muttered.

"And, how you figure on doing that? Swimming?"

"That idiot that ran you over has a boat on the other side."

"Well, take the Cajun with you. He's about as worthless as tits on a boar to me."

"You sure you'll be okay?"

"Yeah, I got this. Sue'll take care of the Navy guy and I'll get to work on disarming this baby." Mel jumped when he slapped the bomb. "Don't worry. It'll take more than that to set her off."

Her sense of urgency was clear as she headed down the path towards the boat with Trufante hobbling behind her. Regretting that she hadn't searched the man before the deputy took him, she hoped the keys were in the boat.

She picked up her pace, ignoring the yells from Trufante to wait. She had to reach the GPS numbers and Mac before the navy captain.

43

STEVEN BECKER

A MAC TRAVIS ADVENTURE

WOOD'S REEF

GILLUM DIRECTED the crewman to start the motors, and watched the white sand cloud the water as the boat reversed off the sandbar. He cut the wheel, pushed the throttle down, and headed west — the only direction without obstacles. As soon as they were out of gunshot range, he ordered the petty officer to slow the boat. He regretted the other crewman getting shot, but remorse was not on his mind, rather a fear that the injury would cause an investigation—something he would do anything to avoid. With the first bomb now out of his control, his only option to stay in favor with the future President was to find the other bomb.

The GPS was on, showing the location of their boat on a chart, and a waypoint icon displayed three miles to the east. He placed the cursor over the mark and checked the coordinates from the screen against the piece of paper in his pocket. They matched and he hit the GOTO button. The new course displayed on the screen showing bearing and time to their destination. The wind was still blowing whitecaps on the tops of the waves. Gillum gripped the seat and cursed as the boat rocked from side to side as the vessel moved quickly forward in the side swell. The navigation arrow on the GPS pointed dead ahead as the crewman changed course.

"I'll take the wheel. See if you can find some dive gear." Gillum moved toward the wheel, instantly cutting the throttle to something he was comfortable with. The crewman went below, leaving him alone with his thoughts. Things were spiraling out of his control and that worried him.

The crewman came out of the cabin carrying a laundry basket loaded with gear. The next trip yielded a tank. Unaffected by the seas, he slid the BC over the tank, attached the first stage, and the inflator hose. Gillum glanced over as he assembled the gear. Turning the regulator and air gauge away from him, he turned the valve on the tank. Pressure checked, he found a bungee cord and tied down the gear. Next he sorted through the snorkeling gear, finding booties, fins, and a mask.

The boat slowed as they approached the mark. A line of lobster buoys showed the direction of the ledge, where Gillum could see a surfboard swinging in the current, attached to one of the buoys.

———

Mac heard the sound of the propeller. He could guess the range, but not direction. Hoping it was Mel, he worked his way back along the ledge to the trap line he'd descended from, grabbed it and began to surface. As his head broke the surface, he saw his boat, and felt a wave of relief wash over him. Mel was here, then. Air swished into his BC as he triggered the inflation mechanism, and he bobbed on the surface, waiting.

He heard the anchor splash as it entered the water. Within moments the boat's movement stopped. The anchor caught in the sand and the boat swung back toward him, moving closer as line was expertly paid out. The figure on deck let out twice the line necessary had it been calm. The extra line acted as a buffer against the wind-blown waves.

Mac could see the transom clearly now, as the boat settled. Not sure he had been seen, he swam to the paddleboard and lifted his body onto the board. The added height allowed him to see the man at the wheel. One look and he quickly slid back off the board and into the water, releasing the air from his BC in the same movement. Once on the bottom, he added a small amount of air to the BC to regain neutral buoyancy. He hung there, trying to figure out how Gillum had gotten his boat, and what his next move would be.

Seconds later, a splash startled him as a diver entered the water. Mac kicked twice, moving toward a large coral head. It would hide his body, but not his air bubbles. He counted on the lack of visibility, and assumed the ledge would attract the diver, rather than the coral head. Bubbles rose intermittently now as he tried to slow his heart rate and conserve air. The gauge showed only 400 PSI. That meant he only had about twenty minutes of air left.

The diver followed the ledge, as he'd expected. Now, Mac had a decision to make: stay with the diver or surface and take his boat back. The diver was moving away from him, and he figured the man would stay with the ledge until it disappeared into the sand, then reverse and follow it back to the boat. Depending on his speed, it would take from ten to twenty minutes. The diver receded into the murky water. Safe from that threat, he decided on the boat. He had only seen one man on deck, so was fairly confident Gillum was alone, and he was an old man. Mac thought he could take him.

He took off the weight belt and BC, clamping the mouthpiece of the regulator in his teeth. Freed from the weight of the equipment, he took a deep breath and released it, then kicked hard and broke the surface at the transom. The dive platform splashing in the waves concealed him. The platform slammed the water every time a wave hit the boat. It took several attempts to remove his fins and he held them in one hand as he slithered onto the platform, staying low. His head rose, like a turtle's poking out of its shell, above the transom as he tried to formulate a plan to cross the deck before Gillum saw him.

Surprise was his only option. He stepped over the transom and ran at the Navy man.

Gillum saw him coming, but was too slow to draw the revolver and shoot. Mac lowered his shoulder, plowing into Gillum's meaty gut, and knocking the air out of him. The gun fired as he went down. His head hit the deck, bounced, and came to rest.

Mac quickly checked himself and breathed a sigh of relief. Wherever that bullet had gone, it wasn't in his body. He went to Gillum and disarmed him, setting the gun on the driver's seat. He looked over — Gillum was out cold.

The smell of diesel brought his focus back. That's where the bullet was: the port side fuel tank. Fuel was running down the deck, exiting at one of the self-bailing ports, and forming a slick in the water.

44

A MAC TRAVIS ADVENTURE

WOOD'S
REEF

MEL AND TRUFANTE waded through the thigh-deep water to the stolen boat. Mel easily scaled the gunwale, while Trufante, hindered by his wounded leg, log-rolled, landing on his side with a painful grunt. He was still situating himself when she released the line and started the engine. The boat lurched as the propeller bit the water, causing him to fall back against the console.

"You going to help or just sit there?"

"If you'd go a little easier on me, I'd be happy to help."

She ignored him. "Take the wheel, I've got to figure this out. You know where you guys found the bomb?"

"Yeah, I know the area, but it's a mess of channels in there. I need some GPS help."

Her phone showed three bars and an arrow, indicating the GPS was active. She opened the text message, highlighted the first GPS number, and entered it into the hiking program she used when she ran trails back in Virginia. In the text window she repeated the procedure with the second number and hit GOTO. The program went to a new screen, an arrow showing the direction of the coordinates, several data boxes below showing distance and speed. According to the device, they were only three miles away. She held the display up for Trufante to see.

"Nice, but I need it on a chart. Follow that arrow and we'll be digging out from some sandbar. This dude must have been sporting around on some lake with this thing." The unit was a low-end depth finder. No GPS or chart functions.

"Do your best." She climbed on the leaning post used for a seat, grabbed hold of the welded stainless tubing that held the t-top, and pulled herself up for a better view. "I'll yell if I see anything."

A quarter mile before the waypoint she climbed down. "I can see Mac's boat out there. We need to move in slow, kind of serpentine so the Navy guy doesn't know who we are."

Trufante glanced around the boat and noticed a couple of fishing rods. "Grab one of those rods and put it out like we're trolling. I'll set a course so we pass by them. Anyone watching should be able to see that we're dragging a line. That should throw 'em off."

She searched the water in all directions, trying to figure out where Mac was and how he would get out here without his boat. She trusted his resourcefulness, but wished she knew what he was up to. The clicker sounded as she started to let line out, the lure bouncing in the wake of the boat.

"Turn that damned clicker off. I know your dad taught you better than that."

"Like that's what we need to be worrying about now. Get your priorities straight."

"But still. Turn the damned clicker off."

They covered the distance in twenty minutes at a fast trolling speed. Trufante turned slightly, angling to get within fifty feet of Mac's boat. He turned the boat into a large, easy turn, taking them at ninety degrees to their previous course.

"Something's wrong." He pointed to the water aft of the boat. "There's a fuel slick."

"What could have caused that? Look, there's bubbles a hundred feet back of the boat. Looks like they have a diver in the water. No flag, though."

"Isn't that Mac's board off that buoy? Son of a bitch, if he didn't paddle all the way out here."

"He got here on that?" Mel looked at him, shocked.

"Yeah, dude's a stud on that thing."

She had a picture forming in her mind of Mac fighting the seas on the toothpick floating by the buoy. A smile briefly crossed her face, interrupted by the sound of the reel going off. The clicker buzzed louder and faster as line poured off the reel. "Crap, what now? This is all we need."

"That'll give us an excuse to get closer. Set the hook on the son of a bitch. I'll start working closer to Mac's boat as you bring it in."

Mel grabbed the reel, her muscle memory taking over. She'd caught her share back in the day. She turned off the clicker and tightened the drag. The mono line started to pull as the hook set. "Shark. I can see its dorsal fin break the water. Black tip, probably."

"Just bring her in slow. I'm going to start edging over to Mac's boat."

———

Mac saw the other boat. That was all he needed — a wayward tourist. He could see the sun's reflection on the fishing line coming off the stern. What the devil was that guy trolling out here for?

He looked again as the boat moved closer. It was clear now that the fisherman was a woman. The man driving the boat turned toward him, flashing a huge grin, and Mac paused. He knew those teeth. He looked again at the woman, realizing it was Mel, and motioned for them to come closer. Trufante saw him and changed course. Mel had her back to them, still fighting whatever was on the line.

He looked around him, distraught at the thought of losing his boat. The fuel slick continued to grow. It surrounded the boat now as diesel continued to pour from the bullet hole. He paused hoping this would not be the last time his feet touched the familiar deck, then made a quick decision to abandon ship and jumped over the side.

———

The shark jumped, sensing that it was trapped, and Mel didn't react in time. As the shark's body left the water, it twisted and wrapped its tail fin in the leader. The line was no match for the abrasive skin, which quickly sliced through the monofilament. The shark, disoriented and exhausted from the fight, swam slowly on the surface for a moment, letting fresh water circulate through its gills to revive it.

Mac splashed on the surface as he swam toward the boat. Mel gasped, noticing the tail fin as it turned toward him and accelerated. The dorsal fin showed its intention as the shark made a quick pass around him. She felt helpless as it circled again, this time closer to Mac. Suddenly it turned and butted him in the side.

Trufante stood motionless at the wheel.

"Quick—turn towards them! See if you can get us between Mac and the shark," she yelled. She almost fell as the boat tilted with the quick change in course. "Good—now go get him." Her heart pounded as the boat closed the gap. The shark prowled the waters nearby, not sure what to do about the boat. They were close now. "Cut the engine. Don't want to hit him with the prop."

The boat settled in the water as they both leaned over the side waiting for Mac to reach them. They were so engrossed with his plight in the water that they didn't notice the pistol aimed at them from Mac's boat until the voice called out.

45

THE DEPUTY BACKED off the throttle as he hit the no wake zone and rounded the corner entering the yacht club basin. He slowed further, allowing the wind and current to take him to the dock. Once there, he cut the engine and went forward to tie off the boat. Doans was handcuffed to the stainless-steel tubing that supported the T-top, his arms wrapped around the pipe.

Once the bow line was secured, the deputy moved to the stern, grabbed the line, and hopped on the dock. The boat brushed lightly against the rub rail as he secured the second line.

"Stay here. I'm gonna get the trailer and pull us out."

"Like I'm going anywhere," Doans said.

The deputy ignored him and went for the truck. He had just reached the vehicle when the UHaul pulled up. He took no notice, thinking it was going to turn around.

———

"There's the infidel," Ibrahim said. "What's that fool doing handcuffed to the Sheriff's boat? Idiot. Typical American dog."

"What are we going to do? He has obviously failed."

"Yes, he has failed, but Allah be praised, He has given us the tool we need to complete our mission. Look. He has delivered us a boat. Quickly, let's go."

"What about the deputy?"

"If we hurry, we will be gone before he even knows it."

The two men jumped out of the truck and ran toward the dock. They reached the boat and looked at each other. "Untie the rope, Behzad."

Ibrahim stepped into the boat and turned the key. The engine turned over. Behzad untied the lines and followed. Ibrahim pushed the throttle too far forward and the boat jumped. Doans slammed against the stainless-steel tower and fell to his knees. They were about to hit a trailer when Ibrahim looked at Doans, his eyes wide with fear.

"For Christ's sake. Find neutral, then pull back. Slowly." The boat moved backward in response. "Now cut the wheel and push it forward. Easy." Ibrahim followed his directions, satisfied with himself as the boat moved toward the inlet. "It's just like a car. Just take it easy."

"What now?"

"Keep going. Head toward the bridge. There's an island part way down. We can ditch the boat there and walk back on the foot bridge. We need to lose the boat or they'll find us."

Ibrahim was out of the inlet, but still unsure of the throttle. The boat was going too slowly to get up on plane, and the stern sank deep in the prop wash, bow jutting high in the air.

"You've got to give it some more gas to get it to level out."

He punched the throttle, swinging Doans around the pipe and slamming him into the leaning post. The boat resumed its previous posture.

"No, really. Push the throttle. We'll never get there like this."

Ibrahim tried again. This time he got the boat to plane out. It accelerated across the water, his hands white knuckled on the steering wheel as the boat bounced from wave to wave, swerving out of control. The propellers gained an octave every time the boat left the water.

"You can slow now. Just give her enough gas to stay on plane."

Ibrahim slowly got the feel for the boat. Pigeon Key was dead ahead.

He turned perpendicular from the bridge and headed towards the open water of the gulf.

"Where the hell do you think you're going?"

"You will take us to the bomb."

"Negative, Ahab. That thing's bigger than this boat. We go by the island like I said and stay low. The bomb will come to us."

Ibrahim thought for a moment before grudgingly admitting the infidel was probably right. He turned the boat parallel with the bridge.

"Take it wide around the island. I think there's a spot we can pull up and get off this thing."

Wanting nothing more to do with the devil's craft, Ibrahim followed his directions. "We need to renegotiate your fee. You have clearly failed," he said.

"My ass. You would have flipped this boat if I wasn't here. Don't suppose you can swim, either."

"Nevertheless, you have returned without the bomb."

"Just wait. It should be coming over the horizon any time now."

———

The deputy backed down the ramp, set the parking brake, and got out, ready to pull the boat on the trailer. He pulled the winch cable out and looked around, wondering where the boat was. He looked out into the water, confused, and could just make out the blue and red light-bar on top of the T-top as it pulled around the bend.

"What do you mean they've got the boat?" Jules yelled in the radio. "The terrorist guy too? Sit tight. I'll be right there."

She pulled up a few minutes later. The deputy gave a rundown and took the tongue-lashing like a man. She would have gone on, but needed to act and recover the boat. She called in a BOLO for the boat and its occupants over the radio, catching some sarcasm from the Highway Patrol and the Coast Guard. The Coast Guard offered their helicopter, housed nearby at Marathon's small airport.

Jules asked the Coast Guard dispatcher to have the chopper wait for her.

46

STEVEN BECKER

A MAC TRAVIS ADVENTURE
WOOD'S
REEF

"I'M GOING to need your help here." Sue looked toward Wood. The Navy crewman was laid out on a blanket, the wrecked boat shielding him from the wind. She had re-rigged the Bimini top from the boat, providing protection from the afternoon sun.

Wood crawled over and made himself as comfortable as possible, though his side hurt with every movement. The crewman had a towel wrapped around his shoulder and neck, the spear gun shaft protruded from the center. His eyes were closed, his chest rising and falling but his breath was shallow.

"Here we go." She grasped the shaft, leveraging herself to pull it out. "You've got to take the towel and apply pressure as soon as this comes out."

"Slow down, girl, You won't be pulling that out without tearing him apart. That spear's got a barb on the end that will open if you pull backwards. Only way that's coming out is to push it through. Same as a fish hook."

"That's gonna be ugly. Roll him on his side. We'll take a look." They rolled him onto his side. Wood watched as she stared at the man. She looked like she was trying to visualize the interior of the shoulder. Slowly she pushed the spear further into his body, causing him to squirm, though he remained unconscious. Pushing harder now, she wiggled the shaft slightly, working the barb around an unknown obstruction. His body twitched in pain as she worked. Slowly she slid it through him, first an inch, then two. A bulge appeared on the skin where the shaft was ready to come through.

"Got it. Now we have to open this up. How big is the head?"

Wood crawled out of the shade, stood, and walked to where Mel had left the spear gun. He disengaged the band and withdrew the shaft. "Looks like this," he said, wiggling the barb back and forth. "See what I mean?"

"Yeah, that would have torn him up if I just tried to pull it. Let me see that." She took the shaft and folded back the barb, eyeballing how big the exit hole would need to be. Tequila was the only thing available to sanitize the incision, so she poured it liberally on both sides. The sharp bait knife was sterilized with a lighter. Once it started to glow, she quickly punctured the skin with two incisions, creating a small X. Before blood found the wound, she started to move the shaft. As it emerged through the exit hole, she gently pulled it. It came out, blood spurting behind it.

"Got it. Get that towel and put some pressure on both sides. I'll get something to stitch him up."

Without a suture kit, she had to improvise. Fly line backing made of Dacron and a sewing needle were the only supplies available. Another splash of the tequila went to clean the holes again. Wood accepted the bottle, gauged how much was left and drank half. Her shaking hand accepted the remainder.

The needle caused the man to jump every time it passed through his skin. Wood inched over to hold him down as she finished the wound on his back. They rolled him over together and he watched as she started on the front wound. Nothing like watching a competent woman work, he thought as he laid back in pain.

She grabbed a pill bottle from the supplies, tossed two at him, and tried to get the sailor to swallow a couple. "Found these in your medicine cabinet. They're old, but should still work."

The sailor was resting comfortably on his back now. Still unconscious, but out of danger. "Good job, girl. Now you gotta help me operate on this baby before these kick in." He popped the pills in his mouth and slapped the bomb.

————

Wood had his tools laid out like a surgeon. He moved to the access panel covering the trigger mechanism. "This is the tricky part. One spark hits the wrong spot in there and this could blow." The tequila had accelerated and amplified the effect of the pain killers Sue had given him. He needed to finish before their full effect hit his system. For now, his pain was at bay and his nerves calm.

The cordless drill spun as slowly as the trigger would allow, boring a pilot hole through the fifty-year-old screw head. He repeated the procedure with the remaining eleven screws.

"Why so slow?"

"It's metal. The slower the better. You wouldn't think so, but rip off at high speed and you'll burn the tip of the drill bit. Sparks fly off, hit something sensitive, and that's the end of it. Any more questions?"

She looked down. He removed the drill bit and inserted an easy out, a cone-shaped piece with a spiral wrap. As he drilled these into the pilot holes, the screws started to emerge. Once they were out, he removed the panel and the bomb's guts saw daylight for the first time in fifty years. The Python 35 trigger mechanism was undamaged, but the barometric pressure sensor — the device which was set at the depth the bomb was to explode — had corroded.

"Damn. Lucky this thing hasn't blown yet." He took the wire strippers and eased a section of insulation about midway off each of the two wires connecting the switch to the trigger. Stripping the ends of a loose section of wire, he wrapped each bare end around his incision in the trigger wires, making what looked like a bridge between them. The connection sparked, causing him to jump back and slam Sue in the head. "Damn, girl, I could use some space here." He eased his hands back inside the case, more careful this time. Using the wire strippers he wrapped the bare ends of wire around each other. Next he cut the wires close to the sensor and pulled it out.

"Okay," He withdrew from the casing and took a deep breath. "That thing's cut out of the loop now."

The Python was held in by four large screws, undamaged by the salt water which, he extracted, lifting the trigger out of the bomb. Then he removed the firing pin to disable it. "Done. She's safe enough for a baby to play with."

Sue relaxed now. "That's it? No more boom?"

"That's right, girl. Still have to take out the core, but it needs this here to set her off. Fission bombs need a small detonation to trigger the nuclear material, which starts bombarding atoms, setting off the actual explosion." He sat back against the bomb and felt the adrenaline wash out of his system. The creases on his face resisted the rare smile, not from the drugs, but from the success at disarming the bomb. The fifty-year nightmare had only one act left, and that was up to Mac, Mel and Trufante. His body fell to the side as the pain killers took full effect.

Sue grabbed him and propped him up. "I'm going to look in on my patient if you're OK over here."

"I'm good. Maybe take a walk back to the house and find me some more of that tequila. Kind of help out those pills."

"I'm going to veto that prescription. You stay right here. Maybe I ought to have a look at your wound as well."

47

STEVEN BECKER

A MAC TRAVIS ADVENTURE

WOOD'S REEF

Behzad and Ibrahim looked around as they climbed onto the dock and wobbled toward land. There was no sign of activity anywhere.

"So, you have a plan?" Doans asked as he followed them.

Ibrahim turned. "We no longer need you. As you say, the bomb is coming to us. We only need to wait and intercept it. The sheriff can pick you up and deal with you. Maybe we'll be generous and call, so you are not out too long and sunburn your white skin."

"You don't need me, fine. But the sheriff is going to put a helicopter up. They'll spot this boat in minutes. I'll be happy to tell them where you are and what you're up to."

Ibrahim spoke quietly to Behzad, who ran off toward what appeared to be a maintenance shed. "I knew better than to get mixed up with you. My friend has proved to have questionable acquaintances. We will free you, but you will stay with us. Do not think you can make a deal with the authorities—not that they would believe you. I will be watching you and have no remorse in the death of a lying infidel. Understand?"

Behzad returned with a set of bolt cutters, and Ibrahim instructed him to cut the chain connecting the bracelets. Doans extended his hands as far as he could, and Behzad slid the tooth of the cutters onto the chain and started to close the levered handles.

"You need to get the link all the way in," Doans corrected him.

Behzad repositioned the cutters and pushed the handles together, this time meeting resistance. He used the seat for leverage against one handle and pushed the other against it. The chain snapped.

"You need to find a gym, my friend." Doans moved his arms around, relishing his freedom.

Ibrahim looked overhead, motioning them to silence and looked up. "Helicopter. We must get out of here."

"Hold on, I've got an idea." Doans went forward and grabbed a dock line from the hatch. He returned to the helm and spun the wheel until the engine straightened behind the boat, then tied the line to the steering wheel. He looked over his shoulder to make sure the motor was still straight and tied the other end of the line tightly to the leaning post. He signaled Behzad, who climbed onto the dock as he started the engine. Checking the rig one last time, he pushed the throttle forward, hopped onto the dock and pushed the boat off.

Standing on the dock, he watched the boat slide through the bridge pilings and head to the open waters offshore of Bahia Honda.

"That'll buy us some time."

"How far back to Marathon?" Ibrahim could just make out the entrance to the Knight's Key channel.

"A couple of miles or so." He glanced at the deserted section of bridge. The old road had been decommissioned when the new span was put in. Open to foot and bike traffic now it dead ended at Pigeon Key. "We wait until dark. There's nobody on the bridge now. We'd be too visible. The sheriff puts up a chopper, they'd spot us for sure. Around sunset, there'll be more of a crowd. Then we can walk without notice."

He was scanning the area, looking for a hiding place, when he heard the sound of an outboard motor working slowly toward them. "Must be a tour coming back. We've got to get under cover."

A loose piece of trellis covering the foundation piers of a nearby building caught his eye. "Come on."

Before ducking under the building, he watched the helicopter set a course for the abandoned boat.

––––––

Hands shaking and still trying to catch his breath, Gillum held the flare gun. His head pounded from striking the deck, but it was the angle of his fall that had put him in the right position to see the bright orange case containing the gun. Remembering his munitions training, he knew a bullet would be worthless to blow the smaller boat, but the pyrotechnics of the flare might trigger an explosion. He pulled back the trigger, releasing the flare. It propelled toward the other boat and landed on the deck. The explosion he hoped for never happened, but a small fire started. He watched as the two occupants jumped into the water on the far side of the boat. Just as they cleared the deck, the fire took. The ensuing explosion caught them in midair, accelerating their trajectory toward the water.

Wreckage scattered across the surface covering an area as big as a football field. As he watched the debris fall, a burning piece landed on the fuel slick behind Mac's boat and ignited it. The flame spread quickly following the leaking fuel toward the boat. Gillum watched it with feverish eyes. He scanned the water, looking for signs of life, as the fire crept onto the boat itself and moved toward the fuel leak.

In the water, his diver broke the surface, took stock of the situation, and yelled for Gillum to grab a fire extinguisher. He dumped his tank, hopped the transom, and headed for the cabin where he grabbed an extinguisher. The sound of the discharge woke Gillum from his trance and he watched as the diver suppressed the fire. With the slick still burning in the water, the diver emptied the canister on the surrounding flames, watching as they burned themselves out.

Gillum was back in command of his faculties now, looking for the gun. He spotted it and went back to scanning the water. He wanted no survivors. The bomb recovery had now spun so far out of control and involved so many people it would be impossible to cover his tracks. At least an accident at sea might get rid of some of the players without an investigation.

Gillum noticed movement on the water and aimed. He fired two quick shots, but both missed, thrown wild by the waves.

"Let me give that a shot." The sailor held out his hand for the gun.

Gillum resisted and fired two more wild shots. Defeated, he handed the gun to the sailor, barrel pointed toward him.

"Whoa, sir, redirect that please."

Gillum looked up, not catching on for a few seconds. Then he changed his grip, allowing the sailor to grab the gun.

The sailor braced himself against the side of the boat and synchronized his breath with the rhythm of the boat rising and falling with the seas. Gillum was just about to take the gun back when the boat lifted on a wave and he heard the gun fire. His gaze went to the figure out in the water and noticed it jerk suddenly.

48

BILL GORDON STEPPED off the plane in Key West. He'd flown in from Jacksonville on orders to "deal with the situation." Rank did not often matter when representing the Inspector General's office. The office held enough power over military personnel that enlisted men, as well as officers, bent over backwards to curry favor. This held true especially for commanding officers, whose future was often directly affected by the Inspector General's periodic reports. He expected the complete cooperation of Jim Gillum.

His cab arrived at the base gate, where he flashed his credentials with practiced ease and was admitted. Upon entering the administration building, he was immediately notified that Gillum was "out on a field exercise." He sensed something wrong — the first red flag. From everything he'd read in the file chronicling Gillum's fifty years of service, work — especially field work — was not a common thread. Gaining promotion through attrition and seniority appeared to be his MO.

The XO came out to greet him, and they spoke quietly for several minutes.

"Get Garrett for me," the XO finally told the duty officer. "Find out where Captain Gillum is and who is with him. We'll be in my office."

Garrett arrived several minutes later. The three men were assembled in the XO's office, Garrett again reciting his story, both men intent on every detail. The phone interrupted him. The XO answered, made some quick notes. "Gillum signed out an SUV and flat-bed trailer this morning. He's got two divers from the Underwater Training School and the local guy he detained. This is not good." He turned to Garrett. "Get a truck and bring a couple of guys with you. You're going to Marathon."

The XO returned a minute later with a radio that looked more like a satellite phone. He handed it to Gordon. "Captain Gillum is not answering his cell phone. I'll try and raise him or the divers on the satellite-linked two-way radio. They should have one with them." He turned on the unit, set the frequency and began to hail. "Captain Gillum or crew, please respond." He repeated this over several times before he got an unexpected response.

———

Sue picked up the radio, looked at Wood, and shrugged. He nodded back, indicating she should answer.

"Hello?"

"Press the button on the side, girl. It's not a phone."

She pressed the button. "Hello?"

"This is Commander Gordon NCIC, with whom am I speaking?"

"Sue Phillips, RN." She added the RN with a quick wink to Wood.

"Miss Philips, please explain how you have that radio in your possession."

Wood signaled for the radio. "This is James Woodson, Petty Officer, retired. What can I do for you?"

"We are looking for Captain Gillum and two divers with him. You have the radio. How did it come into your possession?"

"You investigating that son of a bitch?"

"Let's just say I have an interest in finding him."

Wood gave a thumbnail sketch of what had occurred.

"Can we set a chopper down there?"

"Negative. There's not enough open area here." He glanced at the small clearing cluttered with the boat wreck and bomb. "The way the wind is blowing, anything's gonna be tough."

"We can do a low drop from a chopper. We'll be feet wet in twenty. Should take thirty minutes to reach you. Is the seaman stable or do we need a doctor?"

Wood looked at Sue. She glanced at the sailor, resting comfortably now. "Just a trauma kit and IV with some antibiotics and pain killers. Better make that for two," she said, eyeing Wood.

"Roger that."

———

The rotor wash hit the water as the helicopter hovered over Wood's Island. The pilot did a quick reconnaissance, looking for a spot to offload. He steered in a circular pattern, quickly deciding that his information was correct. The clearing was as Wood described it—covered almost entirely with mangroves and too small to land even without the bomb and wreck. He would need to drop his cargo in the water. The helicopter moved fifty feet away, to an area where the water looked clear of obstacles, and the pilot gave the thumbs up as Gordon moved toward the rear. A green light came on by the cargo door, and the inflatable was cast out first. On impact it immediately started to inflate. Three large waterproof cargo boxes were next. One contained the outboard engine, the others medical equipment and weapons. The crew bailed next, feet down and together, dropping the ten feet into the water. They were in shorty wet suits, each with a yellow inflatable PFD around his neck.

Once in the water, the outboard was skillfully mounted to the inflatable and the men eased over the side. The two other boxes were loaded and the motor started. Seconds later, they coasted to a stop on the beach.

———

The first man ashore was a medic, carrying a dry bag. Sue directed him to the injured sailor and watched him get to work setting up an IV drip and checking the dressing. Satisfied, he moved over to Wood and followed the same procedure as Sue explained his history.

Gordon, after having introduced himself, was huddled with the other two men around the bomb. He was clearly disturbed that the access plate was off. He approached Wood. "Where's Captain Gillum?"

"That horse's ass took my buddy's boat and took off. I should say he *stole* the boat. Son of a bitch."

Sue went over to him. "He's hurt and should be in the hospital, but he's out here playing Army with you guys."

"You can have your damn IV," He pulled the needle from his arm. "Could use something for the pain though."

"Before we give you any pain killers, we need some answers."

"Just hook it up and start the antibiotics. I'm worried he's got an infection. He's starting a fever," Sue said.

Gordon signaled for the corpsman to start the drip, but then turned back to Sue and Wood.

"A little respect wouldn't hurt. I'm the best friend you have here. Why don't you two give me a rundown about what happened here, and start with why that bomb is opened up."

"Son, respect is something earned."

Gordon ignored the jab. He looked into the bomb's carcass. "Harmless, huh?"

"As long as that reactor core is out it is. The detonator might give a little blast, but it's pretty safe. What about that fool Gillum out there trying to find the other bomb? You know there's two of them, don't you?"

Gordon put his best poker face on. He had hoped this was over and he could make a quick case against Gillum, but apparently not. "They're not answering the radio. I had it pinged to get their location."

"You don't need to be wasting time with that GPS nonsense. You just head out on a course towards the NE about 65 degrees. Watch the sandbars and you'll be on it in a couple miles. Mac's trawler oughta be there, and that other fool's outboard. They'll be sitting right on it. My daughter and Trufante'll be on the small boat."

Gordon ordered the medic to stay behind and monitor the two patients. The other two men followed him back to the boat. One stayed behind and pushed it off the beach, jumping in when it was deep enough to start the motor. Then they were off in a spray of foam.

49

MAC SURFACED and scanned the debris, looking for Mel and Trufante. A seat floated by, smoke steaming from the burning cushion. Desperate for a better vantage point, he pulled himself from the water and climbed on. He just started to focus on his boat, relieved that it was still intact, when the first bullet entered the water. His shoulder jerked back, but he didn't feel anything for several long seconds until he saw the blood in the water. Then he felt the pain.

He was treading water, blood streaming from the shot to his arm. He tore back his shirt and realized that there were two holes, entry and exit. At least the bullet had passed through, but he needed to stop the bleeding. Blood was pouring from the wound, leaving a slick in the water. Desperate, he kicked to tread water as he removed his shirt and wrapped it around his arm, tightening it with his teeth to fashion a primitive tourniquet. The flow was stemmed temporarily, but he knew it wouldn't hold. A piece of fishing line floated by, moving through the water slithering like a snake. He grabbed at it and started wrapping it around the shirt. With nothing to cut it, he continued to wrap, figuring the end would appear. The line in the water started to tighten, and then went slack, as a dorsal fin cut through the waves on the surface.

The fin moved closer, attracted by the blood in the water. It started circling around the edges of the blood slick.

———

Gillum yelled at the sailor to keep shooting.

"I don't see him. He took a shot for sure." The sailor opened the revolver and spun the cylinder. "There's only one bullet left, you got any ammo?"

"Doubt it. Did you see the bomb when you were down there?"

"Yeah, I'd just started digging around it when my air ran low. Looks old for sure. Not in good condition either. The case is rusted out. I came up to see what you wanted to do with it." He headed into the cabin, searching drawers and cabinets for bullets.

Gillum was thankful to be alone, if just for a moment, to process this information. Finally, things looked like they were going his way. They had a boat and he'd found the other bomb. One was better than nothing. The bomb at Wood's was far from his mind now as he concentrated on the situation at hand. He just needed to recover it and get out of here. It was almost five now — still an hour or so of daylight to get the bomb up. His best scenario to avoid an investigation and garner the attention of Ward was to secure this bomb. He might have to drive through the night, but he could make the rally tomorrow with this bomb and secure his retirement.

The sailor emerged a moment later, empty handed. "Nothing."

"Never mind. We won't need any. We need to recover that bomb and get it to shore."

The sailor scrounged through the deck storage, pulling out pieces of rope and cable he could rig a sling with. "We're gonna need some torque to pull it out. You sure it'll hold?"

"Yeah, just tie it on and we'll pull it free."

The sailor swapped tanks, climbed over the transom, and did a giant step entry off the dive platform, arms full of rigging.

———

Mac heard the splash from the boat as the diver entered the water. The shark sensed something as well. Its instincts told it to go deep, and that's what it did, pulling Mac behind. Fortunately, there was enough slack for him to take a deep breath before the shark pulled the line under. He managed to hold his breath as he bounced off the bottom, unable to control the shark's movements. He was squinting, trying to avoid any obstacles, when the dive tank came into focus. With all he could muster, he kicked toward the tank, temporarily halting the shark's progress.

Fear subsiding, the shark refocused on its prey, its senses easily picking out the blood stream coming off Mac's shirt. It turned and made a run for him. He saw the line go slack, but the shark was out of his field of vision, so he used the opportunity to go for the tank. As he was about to grab the air hose, he glanced over his shoulder and saw the shark bearing down on him.

The years of training paid off now; he released the air in his lungs, grabbed for the regulator, and took the breath he sorely needed. In one movement, he grabbed the second stage hose connected to the air gauge and pulled the tank free. Using the knife attached to the BC he cut the high-pressure hose attached to the gauges. The air hose recoiled in his hand but he gained control in time to shove it in the shark's face as it attacked. The shark took the shot of air square to the head. Stunned for a moment, the anger in its eyes was clear as it regained its wits and came back toward Mac.

Mac had the hose bent back on itself, temporarily stemming the air flow. He watched the shark as it came at him. Slower this time, wary of its prey. Mac released the bend and stuck the hose in the shark's mouth as it approached. With everything he had, he held the hose until finally, the shark twitched and rolled. He took several breaths watching for any movement. With the shark belly up now and no longer a threat, he transferred the multi-tool, knife extended, to his right hand. His left hand gripped the air hose, again bent back on itself as the knife quickly cut through the fishing line. The tool's pliers gripped the bend in the air hose as he tied a piece of line around the handle. The airflow was cut off now, and only small bubbles exited the hose. He finished tying the loose ends of the line around the wound. The blood appeared to have stopped, only a slight misty trail coming from the t-shirt now. He couldn't feel anything, which worried him in the long term, but he knew the benefit in the short term. As long as he didn't pass out from shock, he would be able to make a go at saving his boat.

Mel crossed his mind for the first time since he'd been shot. The experience, the emptiness inside at her loss, was a new feeling for him. He knew this was not the time to analyze his feelings though, so he took stock of the situation and began to formulate a plan to take out the Navy man and get his boat back.

50

Trufante labored through the chop. The wound from the spear was open and burned from the saltwater, but otherwise he was OK. Mel was out cold, a head wound visible. The bow of Mac's boat was still fifty yards away, bouncing in the chop. The boat they had been on was completely obliterated. He pushed the seat cushion, with Mel draped over it, ahead into the waves. With his arms holding Mel and only one leg for propulsion, he was tiring quickly, and felt like he was going backwards one stroke for every two he took. The tide was pulling him in the wrong direction. But he knew better than to stop for breath. The current would pull him even further away if he lost momentum.

Exhausted, he finally reached the bow of the boat and grabbed the anchor line. For the first few seconds, he felt like he might pass out and he was breathing so loud, he was sure anyone on the boat would hear him gasping for air. After a few minutes his breath settled, but his arms felt like they were going to fall off. The anchor line was far from stationary, as the boat bounced with each wave. He'd need to make a move fast if they were going to make it at all. He looked over at Mel, still unconscious, and hoped for a piece of line or flotsam to float by so he could secure the seat cushion to the anchor line. But the current had moved the debris pile in the wrong direction.

Releasing the anchor line, he let the current, now in his favor, push Mel and the cushion towards the transom. When he reached the dive platform, he tried to lift himself up to assess the situation on the boat, but with one hand holding Mel and the other grabbing the platform, he had no leverage to gain a vantage point. He kept as low as possible while he crawled onto the platform itself. His six foot wingspan allowed him to hold the cushion with one hand while the other pulled at the transom, and he peered into the boat. Gillum was at the helm, facing what was left of the speedboat, seemingly entranced by the drifting flotsam and flames. Glancing quickly around the deck, he saw a dock line still attached to a cleat. In order to reach it he would have to release the cushion, leaving Mel adrift, climb over the transom, and get back with the end of the line. All without being seen and without her drifting away. A pretty good trick for a two-legged man, never mind a man with one leg out of commission.

Fortunately, his good leg was long enough to clear the transom. His hand released the cushion and he lunged for the line. Catlike, he grabbed the end and pulled himself back onto the platform. Line in hand, he slid back into the water and stroked towards Mel who had drifted several feet. He hadn't realized he'd been holding his breath until he regained the cushion and swam back to the boat. With the cushion tied to the line, he slid both her arms through the handles. It supported her and she was temporarily safe. He climbed back on the platform, staying low, and trying to regain some strength.

With his back resting against the transom, he waited as his breath slowly came under control. He inhaled and set his good leg back over the gunwale. He tried to lift his injured leg, but it was like a log. Fearing he was about to crash to the deck he reached out, grabbed a trap buoy and tossed it over the side in an attempt to distract Gillum. The Captain turned to look, his attention on the decoy, as Trufante eased his frame onto the deck. Not as quickly as he would have liked, but at least he hadn't alarmed Gillum. He reached for the bait knife they used to cut chum for the traps and made his move. In what seemed like an eternity, he got his stiff leg over the transom and moved toward the Navy man.

Gillum heard him and turned. When he saw him, he grabbed for the weapon and fired. The shot went wide and into the water. He fired again, but the hammer just clicked, so he threw the gun at Trufante, who approached with the knife.

In the end, Trufante was too slow. Gillum had plenty of time to reach for the gaff, stored in clips under the starboard side. He swung and connected, the blunt end of the gaff striking Trufante on the side of the head. The Cajun staggered and went down. Exhausted from the swim and hampered by his injury, he was no match for the Navy man. Gillum stood over him, adrenaline pumping, ready to land the final blow. Then something struck his head.

———

Mac looked at the air gauge. He had only minutes remaining. Left with two choices — facing Gillum on the boat, or the diver in the water — he chose Gillum. The diver posed a bigger threat, trained in underwater combat. He also considered his limited air supply. Cutting the high pressure hose to repel the shark had left the tank on fumes. Gillum, although in possession of a gun, seemed the easier target. And it didn't hurt that he had a score to settle with the captain. He ascended, careful to surface directly under the boat. His hands kept the bouncing hull from smashing him as he worked his way, upside down, toward the bow. Once at the anchor line, he removed the equipment, inverted his body, crossed his legs over the line, and started to climb, cursing his wounded arm. Although more difficult, the element of surprise and ability to find a weapon other than the small multi-tool he had in his pocket made the bow the best entry point. The transom was too close and visible to the helm, where he figured Gillum to be.

His feet reached the deck first and he pulled himself up the line until he had enough leverage to swing his hips and push his body forward onto the deck.

Once aboard, he slithered towards the wheelhouse, where he took cover behind a bulkhead. He peered around, waiting just long enough to see if he'd been discovered. Forward was an air hatch to vent the cabin. The cover was closed. He opened the multi-tool and chose the file — the thickest and hopefully strongest blade. He inserted the tip in a gap and started to pry. The hatch opened easily, with a little pressure, and he eased slowly through the opening. Inside, he went forward to the bunk, lifted the cushion, and removed an access panel. Inside lay a shotgun.

There was activity on the deck as he moved forward, using the furnishings for cover. Waiting in the shadows for his eyes to acclimate to the bright sunlight, he watched the two men scuffle. The sun was four fingers off the water, about an hour until it set. Blinding at this angle, he could see the pear shape of the captain, but not who he was fighting. He moved quickly towards the men and in three steps he was on them, the butt of the shotgun slamming into Gillum's head, knocking him to the deck.

Trufante regained his senses and squinted up at Mac. "Damn good to see ya."

"Yeah. What about Mel? What happened to her?"

"Check off the transom. I left her on a seat cushion, tied off."

Mac covered the distance to the transom in two strides and hopped onto the dive platform. Mel was there, just as Trufante had left her. Hand over hand he reeled in the line, pulling her onto the platform, using his body as a cushion. Even unconscious, her body felt good against him. He put that thought on hold, lifted her over the transom, and carried her to the bunk.

51

WOOD'S
REEF

THE RADIO CRACKLED and Gordon's voice came over the static. "Woodson, this is Gordon, over."

"I hear you," Wood answered.

"I'm sending the chopper back to you. You should see it in a few minutes."

Wood scanned the horizon, using his hand as a visor to block the glare from the sinking sun. He didn't see anything, but as he put down his hand he heard the low rumble of the chopper's engine.

"Can't see that, can you?" Sue asked.

"No matter."

"I've been watching you. Pretty sure you need glasses."

"Hell with that. I can see just fine."

Gordon was back on the radio. "I've got the pilot on your frequency. I want to get you guys and the bomb out of there. Can you sling it for him and get the wounded sailor in the basket? There's only the pilot and one crewman in the helicopter."

"Yeah, I'll do that for you." He felt no urgency in Gordon's voice. He thought of Mac and Mel out there looking for the other bomb, and here they were just taking their time, screwing around with a harmless one. "Let's get this moving. You know this thing's defused now, don't you. We ought to be chasing down Gillum."

"Roger that. There's another chopper headed out to look for them. Out."

Now the pilot picked up the conversation. "I'll be overhead in a few. I can drop a sling to you to get the cargo sent up. I want to get the casualties on first. After the slings we'll drop a basket. Can you signal where you want it?"

"Got it."

The chopper was back overhead now. Sue waved her arms over her head and yelled at the pilot to drop the basket by her.

"Can't hear you," Wood said sharply.

She stared him down and focused on the basket dropping from the chopper, swinging in the wind, a tag line dangling from it.

"Grab the small line. You can use that to guide the basket in." The line was almost there when a gust blew it to the side. She jumped for it and missed. On the ground she grabbed her ankle.

"Can you help me here?" she said from the ground, clearly in pain.

"Yeah—I got it."

Wood waited for the line to come close enough to grab. He signaled the pilot when he had it.

The pilot dropped the cable lower until Wood held up a fist, letting him know it was on the ground. Then the chopper hovered as Wood removed the rigging supplies and dragged the wounded crewman into the basket. With Sue sidelined, he strained with the weight of the man and felt something moist drip down his side. He labored to roll the pilot into the basket, the drip turning to a flow as warm liquid oozed from the wound. "Ready to lift." Wood spoke into the radio.

The basket lifted, swinging in the breeze as it was raised to the waiting copter. A hand reached out of the open door and grabbed the basket as it came closer and it disappeared inside the cargo hold. A few minutes later the basket reappeared empty. Once on the ground,

Sue was able to get in by herself, saving Wood the exertion. He signaled again and waved to her as she was lifted.

Alone now, Wood went over to the bomb and set to work with the rope. The bomb had rigging points welded to it that seemed to be strong enough, even after all the time in the water. He clipped the lines to each point and moved the yoke to the center, anticipating the balance of the bomb. A raised thumb, letting the pilot know he was ready, and the cable dropped from the chopper, with just the hook now. Wood retrieved it and clipped it to the yoke, then signaled for the pilot to lift and crawled out of the way. The cable strained as it broke the bomb free of the sand. It started to swing, almost clipping Wood, but the pilot reacted quickly and moved out over the water, raising the cable as he went.

"I'll drop the hook and harness for you." The pilot's voice came over the radio, but Wood shook his head.

"Negative on that. I'm not getting on that thing. I got a boat here," he answered.

"I have orders to get you as well. There are some folks anxious to talk to you."

"This thing's not over and I'm not going on a joy ride with you guys." He wound up like a pitcher and threw the radio into the water.

He stared at the sky watching as the door to the chopper closed and the pilot set a course for Marathon.

Wood was alone for the first time in days — an awful long time to be around people for his taste. He sat back, temporarily enjoying the quiet and his freedom, but the liquid seeping from his side and the fate of Mel and Mac snapped him out of his reverie. He leaned onto his good side and raised the shirt from the wound. The dressing was still in place, but it was covered in blood, yellow pus seeping from the edges of the bandage.

He got to his feet, using the spear gun for a cane. Pain flashed through his side with each step.

He stopped and dug a hole in the sand by the mangroves, well above the high tide line, where he buried the core. The Python trigger went into the backpack Sue had used to bring supplies down from the house.

As he moved down the path, the fire in his side burned more with each movement, forcing him to stop several times. He finally reached his boat and removed the camouflage. Spent from the effort, he leaned back against a tree to catch his breath, and waited until he had gained enough strength to move the boat.

Once in the water, he would be home free. The wind had quieted and the tide was moving toward the mainland. The ride would be a lot smoother than it had been this morning. His strength was leaving him as he went for the trailer axle. It was now or never. He lifted the bow of the boat off the ground, using the axle for leverage. With a grunt, he pulled the boat forward into the well-worn grooves in the sand. It moved downhill, picking up speed as it rolled toward the water. He couldn't control it, and had to jump out of the way as it went past. The axles hit the end of the rut and stopped with a bump, launching the boat backward into the water. Wood grabbed the backpack with the detonator and slowly waded out to the boat. Once there, he slid over the side on his belly and with a cringe, pulled the starter cord. Thankfully the engine started right away and the boat was up and running on a plane, moving away from the setting sun.

52

A MAC TRAVIS ADVENTURE

WOOD'S
REEF

"GOT A PLAN?" Trufante asked as he grabbed a beer from the refrigerator. He was coming up from the cabin after checking on Mel. She was still unconscious, but seemed comfortable. There were no visible wounds besides the bruise near her temple.

"Grab me a bottle of water. Maybe ought to get one for him, too." Mac motioned at Gillum, who was trussed up like a hog.

"You can't treat a captain of the US Navy like this," Gillum spat.

"The only reason you're not in twenty feet of water tied to a lobster trap is that uniform. It's the man inside that counts, and you're a piece of crap. I'll make sure they run you out of the Navy. Maybe a little jail time would do you good," Trufante spat back.

"Give him a little water, Tru." Mac watched the show, more worried than he let on, but there was nothing he could do until the diver returned.

"Gladly." Trufante took the water bottle, opened it, and squeezed the flimsy plastic. The contents gushed onto Gillum's face, a fraction of the liquid reaching his open mouth. Trufante dumped the remainder of the water on his own head and tossed the empty bottle at him.

"Diver should be up any time now. He's been down a while. We need to be prepared for him. I don't know how he's going to react," Mac said.

Just as he finished speaking, the diver broke the surface of the water. He finned for the dive platform and climbed on, not noticing anything different about the boat until he had dropped his tank and climbed into the cockpit. There, he was faced with Mac and Trufante. Mac cocked the shotgun.

The diver leaned over the side and casually cleared his nose. "Always gets me when I'm down that long." He surveyed the scene in front of him. "What do y'all have in mind?"

"Names Travis, this here's Tru and this is my boat." Mac looked towards Gillum, disgust clear on his face, "I'm taking him back to stand trial. Let his superiors deal with him. But first I want that other bomb. I found it down the ledge about fifty feet. Not sure if you saw it or not." Mac grunted.

The diver paused for a moment, thinking, then nodded. "I'm good with taking the Captain to trial. I've seen enough of his cowboy act, and he's sure not acting the way a Navy man should. I've been taking orders up to this point, but this hasn't seemed right to me. My help would depend on what you have in mind for the bomb."

"I'm afraid that if it stays down there the wrong person will find it. Not many come into this part of the backcountry, but enough do. It needs to be brought in and handed over to the authorities, someone who will disarm and dispose of it. I hate to even think about what might happen if the salt water degraded the core and released radioactive material into the water." He looked around the boat. "This will all be gone then. Enough reason for you?"

"I'm good with that. I know some guys outside of his chain of command that can help." The diver looked at Gillum, his lip curling in disgust.

"You good to dive again?"

"Yeah. I doubt I'm at risk for the bends, didn't crack thirty feet.

I'm good." He double checked his depth gauge; the red needle had gone to thirty feet indicating this as his maximum depth.

"Got some food here." Trufante yelled up from the galley. He'd disappeared a few minutes before. He was making some sandwiches, a fresh beer by his side. "Don't know about you guys, but it's been a long time since breakfast."

They each took one of the offered sandwiches and wolfed them down, not realizing how hungry they were.

Mac wiped his mouth on his t-shirt, wondering how Trufante could be so nonchalant. He headed towards the forward berth. After a quick check of her pulse and breathing he was satisfied Mel was not in imminent danger. He watched her rest. She reminded him of a baby—angelic while asleep and demonic when awake. Without thinking about it, he leaned over and kissed her forehead. She stirred and turned away from him as if spurning his advance, so he left her, went back up, and changed his tank out for a fresh one.

"We're gonna do this the same as the other one. You might as well rest a bit." He turned and spoke to the Navy man. "I'll find the bomb and let this buoy out on the site. You guys move the boat right on top of it. I'll set the anchor where I want it and surface. Then we can both go in and get the bomb out."

Mac caught the crewman's glance as his eyes followed the blood dripping from his wound to the deck.

"Maybe ought to have a look at that first. Probably better if I go down," the diver said, starting to gear up without waiting for a reply.

He grudgingly gave in. Another shark drawn by the blood from the wound would only hinder the recovery. Trufante put down his beer long enough to help Mac clean and properly bandage his wound. Arm patched, Mac paced the deck waiting for the diver to surface.

Mac and Trufante sat on the transom, feet resting on the dive platform. Mac was uneasy, alternating between glancing at the cabin door, hoping Mel would appear, and scanning the water for the buoy. Trufante looked more like he was enjoying a day at the beach, as if he had no idea of the danger they were in. Mac rose quickly as the buoy broke the surface and headed to the helm. "Tru, go up and let off on the anchor line. I think you can leave it hooked. The current'll drift us back on the buoy."

The boat floated towards the marker and Mac yelled for Trufante to tie off the line when it hit the dive platform. They repeated the procedure they had used on the first bomb. Although two were wounded, the recovery went smoothly, and they were soon heading back to Marathon, bomb braced on the deck.

The sky was starting to darken and Mac turned on the running lights and settled back in his chair. The wind had dropped, taking the seas with it. The waves were mere ripples on the water now, the bow of the boat cutting through them like butter. Still anxious about Mel, he relaxed for the first time in days, one bomb secure on his deck, the other safe at Wood's.

53

THE SUN WAS SETTING NOW, but the three men remained in their hiding spot under the house. Except for the spiders, it wasn't bad. Cooler than outside, at least. The tour boat had come back about an hour ago and there had been a steady stream of traffic passing by ever since.

"We need to move soon. When will these people go away?"

"How should I know?" Doans answered. Ibrahim was getting antsy. Behzad was passed out.

"As soon as it is dark, we need to go. If there are casualties, it is Allah's will. We have been too long here already. The bomb could have been brought in and we would never know."

"You are not going to serve your god in jail either. You know they're looking for us for stealing that boat. We go when it gets dark," Doans agreed.

———

The Inspector General's office at CNIC in Jacksonville was busy. Several men and women were in a conference room, monitoring the activity in the Keys. They were locked into Gordon's radio channel, hearing everything broadcast. This was mostly background noise, as the contact was intermittent. The only action was the blur of fingers over the laptops operated by a handful of technicians — one researching the Vice President's connection to Gillum and Key West, several others researching types of bombs that could be out there ... and how to defuse them. The terrorist connection reported by the sheriff in Marathon had added a layer of tension to the room. There was an open link to Homeland Security, who were suddenly interested.

"Okay, people." Everyone looked to the front of the room. "Here's where we are. We know Gillum, Woodson and Ward served together. It looks like it was Gillum as aviation ordnance man and Woodson as engineer. Ward was the pilot. We're still digging, but all the nukes look like they're accounted for, although plenty of ordnance was ditched or dumped." He turned to the radio man. "Get Gordon to take a picture of that thing with his phone and send it. Then we can identify it."

He turned back to the room. "If it *is* a nuke then these three, and that includes the VP, are up to their eyeballs in some kind of coverup. I think we need to have a look at Ward's phone records."

"No way," one of the women answered. She was an attorney involved to make sure this investigation stayed legit. "You're not going to get the Vice President's records without a court fight. We don't have time. There is another way, though. Gillum's cell phone is Navy issue. We don't need permission to check that. We can back trace the numbers. See if we can connect any dots."

"Excellent. Let's get that moving."

Someone else started typing. It took a minute while the room waited in silence. "Pulling up now ... Here we go. There have been a half dozen calls from a DC number in the last forty-eight hours. Same number, checking ... Here you go. It is registered to Ward's traveling secretary."

"There's enough to confirm his involvement. Now let's find out what we're dealing with and neutralize the bomb." He got up to leave. "I'm going to call the White House."

There was still activity on the island as the sun descended below the horizon, but it looked like it was all moving in the direction of the dining hall. "We go now." Ibrahim said. He shook Behzad to wake him, amazed he'd been able to sleep.

They pushed out the loose section of lattice and moved toward the road in single file. Doans led, the two terrorists trailing behind.

"This way. Just be cool. No one is going to question anything in the dark. As soon as we hit the old bridge, it's only a couple miles to Marathon."

Behzad looked green at the thought. "I'm hungry."

The other men, more worried about saving their skin or completing God's work, ignored him. The group moved swiftly toward the old section of the Seven Mile Bridge and started to walk in the direction of the lights on shore. It was deserted for the first mile or so, then they started hitting tourists watching the sunset or walking in the cooler evening air. As they got closer to land, the bridge became more crowded, but no one gave them a second look as they crossed the threshold to land.

"The boat ramp. How far?"

"About a mile. Why there?"

"We have a truck there. It is also the most likely place for them to bring the bomb ashore. We will wait there."

"Not me, I got you this far. I'm out."

"Infidel." Ibrahim withdrew Cesar's gun from his waistband. "You squandered $25,000 of God's money. You think you can walk away from that? You will do as I say. Walk." Ibrahim was disgusted with the American. He vowed to send him to hell as soon as he was no longer needed.

Doans didn't respond. He just walked forward.

The lights were closer now, but still a mile away. They walked in silence, Ibrahim not really noticing Doans. He watched Behzad's body language—slumped forward and head down. He realized he was on his own now. With Allah's blessing he could do this. He stayed alone in his thoughts, praying to Allah to help find the bomb.

They walked in silence towards the boat ramp. It was quiet now, lights from several boats visible coming in from the gulf. They went to the U-Haul truck. "Now we wait."

"What about some food?" Behzad asked. The chemicals had finally worked their way out of his system and he was famished.

"Here." Ibrahim tossed him the keys to the truck. "Get enough for several meals and get back here quick. Water as well." He'd had enough of his old friend.

———

Behzad turned the key and breathed a sigh of relief as the engine turned over. He pulled out of the parking lot. This was the first time in two days he had been out from under the constant scrutiny of Ibrahim. He briefly thought about heading back to Key West, and trying to put his old life back together, but realized he'd burned too many bridges. Cesar wasn't going to take the loss of the money or the embarrassment lying down. He pulled into the Publix supermarket parking lot instead, and headed for the entrance.

The cart swerved as he navigated the aisles, an open bag of chips in the child seat. He ate handfuls at a time, leaving a trail through the store. His cart loaded, he paid and exited the store. As he was pulling out of the lot, he noticed a bar and package store around the corner. With some cash still left, he was sure he had earned a drink.

———

Ibrahim and Doans made an unlikely couple hanging out at the boat ramp. They sat on the curb, waiting for Behzad. It'd been a while, almost too long, and Ibrahim was starting to worry, when the sheriff's boat pulled up to the dock. The two men receded into the cover of the mangroves and watched. Minutes later, a sheriff's cruiser pulled up and dropped a man off by their pickup and trailer. The deputy backed the truck up onto the ramp and waited as the deputy on the boat drove it onto the trailer. He gave a thumbs' up and the truck pulled it from the water. The truck pulled up next to the cruiser, windows rolled down, the deputies chatting.

———

"I'm going to see what they are up to. I need to know if they have any idea where we are." Doans said as he skirted the brush, moving toward the vehicles. Just as he was about to close the distance and get into hearing range, he was caught in the headlights of a truck moving toward the boat ramp.

Jules saw her prey, hunched over like an animal, eyes glaring in the headlights. She hit him square on with the search light and increased speed toward him, yelling out the window for the deputies to pursue. Trapped on the peninsula of the boat ramp, Doans was back in cuffs in minutes. Actually double-cuffed, the bracelets from his last detainment still around his wrists.

"You've caused enough trouble for one day," Jules said as she pulled Doans' head down onto her rising knee. Doans fell forward, blood streaming from his nose. She grabbed his collar, lifted him to his feet, and launched an undercut to his gut. Back on the ground, searching for air, Doans pointed toward the brush and motioned for the sheriff to come within hearing range.

"I'll give you the terrorists. Just stop."

"Over there? One or two? They armed?" Jules rattled off the questions while using hand motions to direct the two deputies to the mangroves.

"Just one. The others got the truck, went after some food. He's got a gun."

Jules removed her gun and smacked Doans on the back of the head. "Stay here while we take care of this."

Doans fell to the ground.

————

Ibrahim saw that Doans had given him up, and started to run. He got off two wild shots. The deputies zeroed in on their source and gave chase. Searching for a way out, he ran toward the entrance of the Marathon Yacht Club, a squat, single-story building next to the boat ramp, busy on a Saturday night. He went for the door, kicked the host out of the way, and started for the dining room.

The sheriff's men entered behind him, guns drawn and gaining ground. Ibrahim went for a woman at one of the waterside tables, grabbing her by the neck and lifting her to her feet. The deputies slowed, lowering their weapons to protect the hostage.

Then a deafening shot came from behind them and Ibrahim dropped to the ground. The lady, realizing she was unharmed, ran crying for her husband. Jules holstered her gun.

"I've had enough of this crap. Get him out of here."

The deputies ran over to where Ibrahim's body had hit the ground, and looked back at the sheriff in surprise. The body was gone.

"Over there! He crawled down there and went into the water. Bleeding pretty bad," one of the diners yelled.

The deputies ran over to the rail and searched the water. There was some blood in the water, but with the ebb tide, it quickly dispersed. The terrorist was nowhere in sight.

54

WOOD'S REEF

THE WATER WAS glassy as they entered Knight's Channel. Mac kept the flashing red buoy on the right, lining the boat up to clear the green marker on the left as they entered the harbor. Then he passed the wheel to Trufante and went below to check on Mel. Worry crossed his face as he looked down at her, resting like a sleeping baby. His gaze focused on her. Her high school days were long gone, and she wasn't the radical he thought she'd become; he let his new-found feelings loose in his mind. She was still unconscious, but didn't appear to be in pain. As he adjusted her slightly, trying to make her more comfortable, he noticed her cell phone sticking out of her hip pocket.

He removed the phone and set it on the counter next to the bunk. A text message flashed and disappeared, and he hit the power button. The screen lit, fuzzy through the salt coated case. There was no contact attached to the message, just a phone number with a message: *Ms. Woodson please contact me. Bill Gordon, USN urgent.* Mac hit the respond button and chose the call back option. The phone went straight to voicemail. He hung up without leaving a message.

He took the phone with him onto the deck. "What do you make of this?" Mac handed the Navy man the phone.

"Don't know. Your buddy," he motioned to Trufante, "was talking about some Navy guys that came to that island in a helicopter. Could be that was him."

"I called the number, but it went to voicemail. If he's on a chopper, he probably can't hear it. Any other way to get through?"

"Yeah, I can make a call. I know a guy at the base in Key West can probably patch us through to the helicopter. Hope he's on duty."

Mac handed him the phone.

———

Gordon's blurred image came on the screen in the White House situation room. The camera vibrated from the helicopter and the audio was garbled from the rotor noise. The handful of people assembled, including the President, now fully briefed, listened intently.

"Gordon, give us a status report please," the Chairman of the Joint Chiefs asked.

Gordon ran down the chain of events as he knew them. He informed them that the bomb hanging from the helicopter was harmless, the core and primer removed. He explained how they had checked the site where he thought the other bomb was, and that they'd only found wreckage. They were currently on a course back to Naval Air Station Key West.

The connection went silent for a few minutes, while the men in DC consulted each other. Then the Chairman broke the radio silence. "We have a report from the sheriff in Marathon, via Homeland Security, that there might be two terrorists loose in Marathon. They are searching for one that was shot by local law enforcement. The other is believed to be driving a UHaul truck. They have apprehended one, but he doesn't appear to be the leader. Looks like he's an American selling out his country for a payday.

"Change course to Marathon and land at the 33rd Street boat

ramp. They won't know the bomb has been disarmed. We want to use it as bait to draw them out."

"Yes, sir, changing course. Who do we coordinate with on the ground?"

"We're setting up a secure line with the sheriff's office. Let her handle the ground, she seems pretty competent. The connection should be live in a few minutes."

"Roger, what about the other one?"

"There's a Coast Guard cutter headed out to the coordinates you gave us. We should have a report from them shortly."

————

Mac heard the rotor before he saw it. Then the chopper became visible, its navigational lights blinking like strobes in a night club. He grabbed the binoculars from the helm and focused on the bird. There wasn't enough light to see any markings, but it looked military. And it appeared to have something beneath it. Every time the white tail light blinked, it threw enough light to reflect off the surface of the casing. His eyes adjusted to the light and background, and he saw the clear shape of the bomb.

He tapped Trufante on the shoulder and pointed skyward, to the helicopter that was now circling and descending. "Follow that."

The channel was too narrow to make a turn, so Trufante slowed the port engine and disengaged the starboard. He compensated for the counterclockwise spin of the boat caused by the one engine and pulled back on the starboard throttle. The sound of metal on metal made him wince as the transmission fought to reverse. Once engaged, he pushed the port side control while pulling back on the starboard. The boat spun on its axis, churning water and turning one hundred eighty degrees. Still within the channel, he pushed the throttle on both engines forward and headed back out.

The helicopter dropped from sight as the boat crossed under the Seven Mile Bridge. It was gone when they reached the other side.

"Got to be the ramp," Mac said. "That's the only spot with enough room to land. They're too close to be heading for the airport. The ramp is the only other spot I can think of."

————

Ibrahim was in the water up to his neck, hidden in a mangrove patch, just offshore of the rocks. Flashlights combed the brush, focusing more on land than the water, but they were getting closer. He'd covered his face as well as his wound with mud. It may have disguised him, but blood was still seeping from his side. He heard a helicopter getting closer and craned his neck to get a view of the sky, looking for the inevitable searchlight that would show his hiding spot.

That's when he saw the bomb and felt the breeze as the helicopter descended fifty feet from him. Mangroves swayed like a hurricane, revealing him, but no one was looking. The sheriff's men were now working to direct the pilot to the Navy trailer. They were all focused on bringing the bomb down safely, setting blocks to match its contours. Once it was settled, they started to tie it down to the trailer's bed.

He was so focused on watching the bomb that he didn't notice the nudge at his side. It wasn't until something engulfed his waist that he awoke to his situation. The shark pulled him out of the mangroves and rolled him underwater, breaking his back. The last thought Ibrahim had before he lost consciousness was of Behzad.

55

THE BOAT RODE EASILY, cutting through the glassy water. Wood was about to cross under the bridge when he saw the other vessel. The red light on the right side told him it was coming at him. He changed course to avoid it, moving over to the next span of the bridge. The boats entered the bridge simultaneously, and the following wake of the larger boat threw his smaller craft into the piling, tossing him to the deck.

"Goddamn idiots!" he screamed.

He turned to look at the offending boat while trying to regain his footing. The wake from the larger boat slammed against his again. He felt warm fluid trickle down his side and knew the wound had resumed bleeding. Biting his lip from the pain, he crawled to the helm and spun the boat around, going under the adjacent span. The pain eased slightly as he got the boat running on plane again.

———

Trufante looked back at Wood's boat, almost in their prop wash. He almost ran up on them as he slowed to obey the no-wake buoy marking the entrance to the boat ramp. Trufante, still at the helm, looked back as he set the port engine in neutral and reversed the starboard side, cutting the wheel to the left.

"Wood's back there," he yelled.

Mac was at the bow, line ready in his hand, waiting to jump onto the dock to tie the boat off. He ran to the back of the boat, waited for the smaller boat to coast to a stop, and threw the line in his hand to Wood, who caught it and tied it off to the bow cleat. Mac pulled the line tight, allowing the two boats to brush hulls. Fiberglass hit metal as he offered Wood a hand and helped him over the gunwale onto the deck. Backpack in hand, Wood winced in pain, almost falling over from the effort.

Mac noticed. "You need to lie down and let me have a look at that."

"No time now, and my nurse is on that helicopter." He pointed to the chopper on the ground, and looked at the bomb sitting on Mac's deck. "Cover that thing up. It looks like a three ring circus around here. The less of 'em that know there's two bombs, the better."

Trufante got to work covering the bomb and Wood turned to Gillum, tied up like a roped calf. He looked at him and turned back to Mac. "We'll take care of him next. Where's Mel?"

"Got hurt, she's resting in the cabin."

"Damn, hope she's alright, but there's nothing I can do now. I'll get Sue to look in on her. I like that gal, surprised she's interested in you." He looked toward Trufante.

"Glad to see you're feeling better. Ornery as a gator in a hurricane."

Wood grabbed the backpack, crossed the deck, and struggled onto the dock. He crossed paths with Sue, who gave him a look of concern before continuing toward Mac's boat. Gordon was sitting in the helicopter, quiet now with the engines powered down. He was on his cell phone when Wood approached.

"We've got that fool captain trussed up on Mac's boat and enough evidence to stop that freakin' Vice President. You got a plan?"

Gordon eyed him as he wrapped up his call. "That was DC, the President, actually. He gave us enough rope to hang the VP. He thinks Gillum's bringing this bomb up to Homestead so he can look like a hero. We're gonna turn the tables on him and try and flush out the terrorists."

"Good, I'm in."

"You're most definitely out. You have the thanks of a grateful nation, but look at you. You're in no condition to go anywhere but back to a hospital bed."

Wood stalked back to Mac's boat, heavily favoring his bad side. "Dump that piece of crap on the dock." He pointed at Gillum. "Let's get out of here before they figure out what's what. The man said they were taking the bomb to a rally in Homestead. I got a mind to take this primer up there and stick it in Ward's face. Then see what he says."

"What's all this?" Mel asked, emerging from the cabin, Sue behind her. Wood and Mac both went to her, but she waved them off. "I'm fine. Just a bit of a headache." Sue confirmed her diagnosis adding a probable concussion.

"Look, we've got to do something about this. If that son of a bitch gets elected you won't even recognize this country in four years. Don't fight me on this," Wood started.

"Fight you? Dad, for once we're on the same side. Let's get out of here."

"You guys do what you need to. I'll keep your secret," the Navy man said. "Let's get him up on deck and I'll frog march him to Gordon. He's got a hard-on for him."

Mac and the crewman lifted Gillum onto the dock and called up to Gordon.

"Here. He's your problem now! We're out of this," Mac shouted.

He quickly released the lines, yelled to Trufante to power up and pushed off the dock before anyone could question him.

The cockpit was crowded as Mac's boat pulled out. Trufante still had the helm. Sue was forcing Wood down to the cabin, and Mel was typing furiously on her cell phone. Mac secured the tarp over the bomb and signaled Trufante to go. The diesels churned the water brown as the boat kicked up on plane and headed back toward Mac's.

Mac went over to Mel. "Glad you're okay."

She nodded in acknowledgment. "I got an email out to my boss about Gillum and the Vice President. I asked him to get the press involved. We need to get to Homestead and finish this."

"What do you have in mind?"

"I'm working on it. Can you go down and see what's up with Dad?" She dismissed him and went back to her phone.

Mac went down to Wood. He wondered how this was going to play out and what to do with the bomb lashed to the deck. The Navy had let them go in the confusion at the dock, no one realizing the bundle lashed to his boat was the live nuke. Sue had Wood under control now, changing his dressing, so he went back to the wheel and stood by Trufante.

"Girl likes you," Trufante said.

"Hell she does. She's more interested in her phone and her damn crusades."

"Nah, I've seen her looking at you. Girl likes you."

"Sure likes to be in charge is what she likes." Mac knew his part in this was pretty much over. It would take Mel's legal brain and action to sort it all out. The question was, where did that leave him?

56

BEHZAD WAS FEELING GOOD. A couple of shots and some school teachers from Naples out for a good time was all he needed to forget his troubles. The club was filling up as the night wore on. He sat at the bar, the pile of cash laying on the blemished copper top decreasing as his popularity increased. He was the life of the party, and living large.

Suddenly the door opened and a tall man walked in. Behzad's gay-dar went on red alert, ignoring the party going on around him. The man sat down across the bar. Behzad quickly got the bartender's attention, which was easy to do with the tips he'd been throwing around. The man accepted the drink he sent over, and motioned Behzad over to join him.

Thirty minutes later, they were on the way out the door together. Behzad was floating. This was just what he needed to wash the past few days from his soul. As they went toward the stranger's car, he stopped in his tracks, staring out at the road. He saw a Navy truck at the stoplight, bomb tied down on the trailer behind it. His euphoria faded as he realized his predicament. He'd burnt too many bridges in Key West to return there, now he had no place left to go but to follow the bomb and finish the plan. The stranger might provide a few hours of relief, but he knew it was fleeting. So he said a quick goodbye and ran for the truck. The back tires screeched as he pulled out of the parking lot, heading north on US1 toward his destiny.

———

Mel was still engrossed in her phone as they pulled up to Mac's dock. She looked up and took a breath while Mac and Trufante tied up the boat. The mood on the boat was subdued, the adrenaline having run its course. All except Wood, who came barging out of the cabin, Sue standing in the doorway, raising her hands in frustration behind him.

"Let's go. Mac, get the truck. Mel, get off that damn phone. We gotta go."

"What are you talking about? We're done. I've relayed all the information to my boss. He's going to get the press to tell the story."

"Girl, the election is in two days. The press is in that bastard's back pocket. He was crooked as a bent axle when I knew him fifty years ago, and I don't expect he's changed. I let this happen then. I need to fix it now."

Mel looked at Sue for help, but she gave her the *nothing I can do about him* look. So she tried to reason with him. "You're in no shape to be doing anything besides taking a ride to the hospital."

"I need to see this through. If it's the last thing I do, so be it."

Knowing resistance was futile, she helped him onto the dock. "All right. What do you have in mind?"

"Me, you, and Mac are going to Homestead. That's where the son of a bitch is going to show that bomb off like he's some kind of war hero."

"I don't trust that guy Gordon either. He's got his own agenda. With Gillum arrested, I can't figure what he's up to." Mac said.

Trufante gave him a questioning look.

"You and the girlfriend stay back here and watch this other one."

He looked at the camo covering the lump on the deck, making it clear what he was talking about.

Trufante's smile lit up and a long arm extended toward Sue. "Roger that, boss."

Mac threw the pack over his shoulder and went for his truck. Mel and Wood walked behind him, determination in their strides.

———

Trufante looked toward the road as Mac pulled out of the driveway, the three crowded in the front seat. He pulled two chairs up to the dock, his smile lighting up the walk as Sue came toward him with two beers in each hand, drops of water dripping from the ice-cold bottles. She sat down, opened a beer, handed it to him, and set the others on the ground. Trufante was grinning larger than a Corona commercial as he clicked bottles with her and took a long draw on the beer.

———

Gillum's cell phone went to voicemail again. Ward had been speed dialing his number for two hours now, and he was starting to get nervous. The rally was hours away, and he'd had no contact from Gillum. This was going to be the grand finale of his campaign. There was no room for a mistake. Not now.

He'd made an unexpected stop at the Home Depot in Kendal, making it look like a spur-of-the moment decision to show him as an average Joe. His Secret Service detail had been close to stopping him, but he'd overruled them. They'd watched over their charge as he'd waltzed into the store, shook a few hands and perused the tool aisle.

The tools now lay in front of him. A screw gun, bits, screwdrivers, and wire cutters. He emptied the papers from his briefcase and set the tools out carefully on a towel liberated from his quarters at Homestead Air Force Base. With everything secure he closed the briefcase, buckled the latches and sat down with a fresh tumbler of Scotch. He closed his eyes and visualized the future President of the United States disarming a nuclear bomb. He saw the response of the crowd in his mind, the hawks cheering his ease with handling a weapon of that magnitude. The doves awed by their candidate's ability to actually disarm a nuclear warhead. He drained his glass and tried Gillum again. After all these years, he still didn't trust him. The only thing that could derail his finale was the ineptness of a career Navy Captain. How ironic. He resolved to end the man's career if this didn't go off as planned.

57

BEHZAD'S RESOLVE started to fade as he approached Islamorada. He'd made it all of an hour before Paradise stopped seeming like such a good idea. The lights from the tiki bar drew him in like a mosquito to a bug zapper, and he pulled the truck off to the side of the road and hightailed it to the bar, hoping to make last call. Luck or Allah was on his side, as the lights were still dim, the music loud, and the crowd rocking. He sauntered up to the bar and threw a wad of cash on the tile top. The bartender, knowing big tips came late at night, was right over, happy to serve. A round for the bar was quickly poured out, and the pile of cash lightened. Behzad had two drinks and a half dozen shots lined up in front of him. Last call was imminent and he downed two of the shots quickly, the harsh tequila burning his throat. Two more and he was back on the train to Paradise.

Then the lights blinked, signaling last call. The bartender came by and he ordered another round for the bar. Revelers came up and thanked him on their way out. The lights were on high now, and the music was off. The mood ruined, but his resolve heightened, he downed the remaining two shots still in front of him and headed back to the truck. It was three in the morning and he was in no condition to drive. He spotted a Waffle House across the street and walked over, swaying as he went.

———

"Careful with these fools," Wood said as Mac cruised through Islamorada. This was a dangerous time of night in the Keys. It was just after last call and a surge of drunks would all be hitting the road at the same time, and with US1 only a lane in each direction, it was easy picking for the Highway Patrol.

"We've got some time. Maybe we ought to get some food and let the drunks find their way." Mac pulled into a Waffle House lot.

Mel had been quiet on the way up, focusing on whatever she was doing on her phone. "Good deal. The rally is at 10am. We can get something to eat, then drive up to Florida City and get a room."

They walked into the Waffle House. The only empty table was by the bathrooms. They reluctantly sat and Mac looked around. The place was full of partiers, loud and obnoxious. They waited for several long minutes without service, several unruly patrons bumping into their table on the way to the restroom.

"Let's go. This place is bullshit." Wood turned and headed toward the door. He pulled the handle and winced in pain. Mel quickly stepped up to help him when a Middle-Eastern-looking guy crashed into them.

"'Scuse me," the man slurred.

They walked right by him. Just another drunk looking for some late-night food.

"You care to give us a clue what's going on with that phone of yours?" Wood asked. Mac pulled back into the northbound lane. He accelerated and reached the speed limit, carefully dodging traffic as the road split going through Key Largo.

"Just taking down a presidential candidate. If it wasn't so scary, this would almost be fun," she replied.

"That's my girl. Cut that bastard at the knees and let the rats feed on him."

"Nice. How about we just put him out to pasture?" Mel responded.

"Whatever, so long as we stop him," Mac injected, worried more about the second bomb presently on the deck of his boat.

"I'd like to see it put right as well, but is it worth your whole life? Looks like a little living wouldn't hurt you. "You spend all this time jousting at windmills. You're a smart, good looking girl. Look around, there's more out there than courtrooms and offices."

"And you like what is going on here?"

"Hey," Mac stopped them. "Let's focus on what we have in front of us. Leave the life issues for later."

It looked like she was pouting and he regretted saying it.

She looked down at the blank screen on her phone, deep in thought. A few days ago, she would have lit into him — torn off his head — but now things seemed to have changed. "Maybe you're right."

They travelled in silence as the traffic lightened. They were feeling the warmth of each other, side by side in the truck, isolated from the rest of the world. They knew they were tied to each other now and this made them family.

Mac looked over and noticed her staring out the window, Wood asleep with his head on her shoulder. "Maybe when this is over you might want to spend some time down here. I saw your face on that boat. You like it, whether you want to admit it or not."

"Are you asking me out, Mac Travis? With my grumpy old man sitting right here? That's balls."

"Never mind. That's not what I meant. And look at him, he's out cold." They were silent for a minute, listening to the rhythm of Wood snoring. They both chuckled.

Mac tentatively reached for her hand, grateful when she didn't pull back. "Yeah, maybe I am asking you out. Let's just call it an open offer."

"Under consideration," she said, but did not release his hand.

The traffic was nonexistent moving north. Southbound traffic was intermittent, with trucks pulling boat trailers and tractor trailers, both preferring to navigate the road at night. The lights of Florida City were visible in front of them now.

"I'm gonna pull into that motel over there and see if we can get a room. I don't think I can sleep, but we can get cleaned up, check on Wood, and make a plan."

———

Mel went into the convenience store connected to the gas station. She grabbed food, and drinks, and pretty much wiped them out of first aid supplies. The clerk gave her a questioning glance as he took her credit card. She answered back with one of her own. He withdrew back to the security of the counter, swiped the card, and handed it back.

It took both of them to get Wood to the room. He was laid out on the bed, naked from the waist up. Mel stripped the dressing from his side. It was saturated with blood and a greenish ooze. Not good. Wishing she had some antibiotics, she force-fed him three aspirin to work on the fever. The staples still held, and there didn't appear to be any additional bruising around the wound as she bandaged him back up.

She and Mac both took long showers, then sat at the small table, the convenience store buffet of jerky, nuts, and some energy bars spread out in front of them. She looked at the crack in the curtains, light starting to seep in.

"The rally's at Bayfront Park at ten. It's a little after six now. We should get out of here and check it out. I've got a friend from the *Miami Herald* who will meet us there."

"What about him?"

"I think we should leave him. He'll be madder than mad, but he's in no condition to do anything. I don't want him to do something stupid and hurt himself. If I know him, he'll try to get past the Secret Service and punch out the Vice President."

In the end, they left a note and headed out the door, hoping he would sleep until they returned.

———

Behzad was fading in and out of consciousness as he tried to stay on his side of the yellow line. He'd pulled over twice to rest, but his head was pounding so hard that he couldn't sleep. He approached Florida City as the sun was rising, and stopped at the first gas station he saw to ask directions. As he was about to get out of the truck, an old man crossed in front of him.

"Hey, man. You know how to get to Bayfront Park?" Behzad asked.

"Yeah. I could use a lift there myself. Give me a ride and I'll get you there."

"Man, that's cool. You got some aspirin in that backpack, you got a deal."

"Matter of fact I do." He went to the other side of the truck, threw the pack onto the seat, and pulled himself into the cab.

"What's the matter with you?" Behzad asked as the guy grimaced in pain.

"Some son of a bitch ran me over with a boat." He leaned over and opened the pack, removing the aspirin. He popped three himself and handed the bottle to Behzad. "Save me a couple, would you?"

STEVEN BECKER

A MAC TRAVIS ADVENTURE
WOOD'S
REEF

BAYFRONT PARK WAS STARTING to fill when Mac pulled in. They parked and walked over to the picnic area, close enough to the stage to see but away from the crowds. They could talk here without being overheard. They sat side by side waiting for the reporter friend of Mel's that had agreed to meet them.

"What do we do now?"

"I'm going to leave that up to Jose. He can break the story in tomorrow's papers. By breakfast, everyone in the country will know about Ward. Let the masses vote him down. As bad as this looks, I've been researching and can't find any law that he's broken."

"Shame he'll get off and just retire."

"Yeah it is, but that's the law."

Jose Reyes walked up and gave them a badly disguised once over. The wear and tear of the last several days showed clearly and Mac noticed him pause and stare at the bandage on his arm. He moved towards Mel and gave her a quick hug. She introduced him to Mac and they sat down at the picnic table. Mel recounted the story with Mac filling in details. The reporter took copious notes. The excitement on his face grew as they explained Ward's involvement.

"This can all be confirmed?"

"Guy named Gordon from the Inspector General's office knows just about everything we've told you. I doubt he'll speak on the record, but he can confirm the facts."

"It's political dynamite. Why me? You have the connections to get this out in your own name. Take all the credit."

She looked at Mac. "I've been reconsidering some things lately. I think it's better to remain anonymous here."

"I can't thank you enough. This could be a Pulitzer."

"Don't get too excited." Mac looked towards the crowd gathering at the stage. "Stop that bastard before you start accepting any awards."

————

The UHaul pulled into the crowded park. Behzad ran over two curbs trying to park the truck, but his resolve had not faltered. Sleep deprivation, the chemicals and the alcohol that had passed through his system in the past few days had affected his thought patterns. In his paranoid state all he could think of was Paradise. There couldn't be hangovers or drug dealers ready to kill him in Paradise, he thought. He saw the bomb parked by a stage. Signs and banners were scattered through the park showing the smiling countenance of Joe Ward, a face he remembered as the Vice President. It didn't add up in his confused state, but it didn't have to. A Vice President, a crowd and a bomb. All he had to do was get close enough.

The two men climbed out of the cab, each looking like they had survived a war, pain evident on both their faces, though for different reasons. The old man grabbed the backpack and headed toward the podium. The Navy trailer was parked next to it. Behzad could see the shape of a bomb visible underneath the flag carefully draped over it. He grabbed the gun from underneath the seat, placing it in his waistband.

———

Joe Ward moved toward the stage as the band played patriotic tunes. He took his time shaking hands and finding the prettiest women to hug a little too tight. He'd never been one to kiss babies, so he avoided that entirely. Finally he made the platform and waved to the crowd and band to wind down.

He approached the podium to start his speech. The crowd remained in a frenzy. He smiled and waved, in no rush for this to be over. It felt like the first of many victory celebrations to come. He glanced at his campaign manager standing just offstage who was moving his hand across his throat, signaling him to stop. He held his hands up, palms forward for several minutes before the crowd quieted.

The speech he had recited many times before in the last few days rolled easily off his tongue and he smiled as he thought of the drama to come. As his prepared speech closed, he grabbed the microphone and headed off the stage toward the bomb with his Secret Service agents frantically trying to cover his impromptu actions. He reached down and grabbed the briefcase from the side of the stairs where he'd stashed it earlier and headed toward the parked trailer.

The crowd parted as he made his way toward the bomb. He climbed the bumper and stood next to the flag-draped shape. "I want to make sure we take the time today to commemorate all the veterans of this country, and especially celebrate the end of the Cuban Missile Crisis. Fifty years ago, I flew combat missions with bombs like this strapped to the belly of my plane, looking for Soviet subs to drop them on." The crowd quieted as he pulled the flag off, revealing the dull sheen of old metal.

He set the briefcase down on the stage and opened it. Agents tried to form a perimeter around him and the trailer, but the crowd edged closer, trying to get a look at what he was doing.

Ward held up the drill. "Now, fifty years later, I am going to decommission this bomb. We have moved past the need for nuclear weapons and I vow to do this to every one of them."

The crowd was getting edgy, realizing that a nuclear bomb was in front of them. Ward removed the access panel, and looked blankly at it. There was nothing in the compartment. He tried to recover and think of a way to save the moment.

Suddenly, Wood appeared on the stage, holding a back pack over his head. He reached in and pulled out the primer. "Looking for this?" Secret Service agents scrambled to reach him, but he held the primer over his head. Not sure of his intentions or the danger posed by the primer they kept their distance. "Don't trust this man. He covered up the fact that this bomb was dropped into the ocean fifty years ago. Fact is, he dropped it himself," he paused for effect, "and left it there, to be discovered by anyone who came along. He didn't take it seriously then, and he wouldn't take it seriously now. He'll do it again, I guarantee it."

————

Behzad saw his chance, now that the agents were all focused on the strange old man he'd picked up. He had followed him to the stage, not having a plan. Now he was standing beside him. Without thinking about it, he removed the gun and fired.

At the concussion of the gunshot, the primer ignited, its force destroying everything within ten feet. The bomb disintegrated, it's empty shell turning to shrapnel. People scrambled backwards, trampling on their neighbors trying to get out of the blast area. Ward, Wood and Behzad were all down. The agents left standing scrambled to cordon off the area and help any survivors.

————

Mac jumped onto the table when he saw the disturbance. They were on the perimeter of the crowd, no reason to be in the mix until they saw Wood hold the primer up. He hopped down and they raced toward the stage, fighting against the surge of people fleeing. They reached the Secret Service agents and were stopped there, though they could see the carnage. Mel buried her head in Mac's shoulder. He put an arm around her, unable to look away.

EPILOGUE

STEVEN BECKER

WAVES LAPPED against the hull of the boat as the divers came up. Mac threw the bag with its three lobsters onto the platform and helped Mel onto the ladder. Tanks off and a cold beer in hand, they looked at the sun as it set over land, five miles away.

"You know, he went on his own terms," Mac said.

"I know. It doesn't make it any easier, though."

Mac didn't answer. He went to the bow and pulled the anchor. Back at the helm, he swung the boat toward the north. "Let's drag a couple of baits and cruise around for a while. It's time we talked this through."

Mel swung the lure over the side and started to let out line. Satisfied the artificial bait was riding right, she engaged the drag and set the clicker. She repeated the process with another rod, setting the bait further back this time. Rods in their holders, she grabbed two more beers and sat next to Mac at the helm.

"I'm going back to D.C. tomorrow," she said.

He looked devastated. "I thought we had something here."

"We do." She took his arm. "But the only way this is ever going to be over for me is to go back and tie up the loose ends. I don't want Joe

Ward to be remembered as a martyr or hero. I need to get the truth out about him and Gillum. I feel like we've just started to unravel this."

Mac nodded. "I understand. You know where I'm at when you're ready."

"That might be sooner than you think."

As they embraced, the port side rod went off. A fish jumped in the distance. Mel ran to the rod and started the fight. A plane seemed to come at them, slowing and losing altitude. It appeared to stall then, and something dropped. It was soon out of sight, too far off to see what it was, and the fish was close enough to gaff. The plane forgotten now, Mac's gloved hand reached for the leader, his other hand gently setting the gaff below the fish. He quickly pulled up on the gaff and, in one movement, had the fish over the side and into the box.

ABOUT THE AUTHOR

Always looking for a new location or adventure to write about, Steven Becker can usually be found on or near the water. He splits his time between Tampa and the Florida Keys - paddling, sailing, diving, fishing or exploring.

Find out more by visiting www.stevenbeckerauthor.com or contact me directly at booksbybecker@gmail.com.

facebook.com/stevenbecker.books

instagram.com/stevenbeckerauthor

**Get my starter library First Bite for Free!
when you sign up for my newsletter**

http://eepurl.com/-obDj

First Bite contains the first book in several of Steven Becker's series:

Get them now (http://eepurl.com/-obDj)

Mac Travis Adventures: The Wood's Series

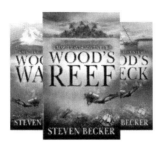

It's easy to become invisible in the Florida Keys. Mac Travis is laying low: Fishing, Diving and doing enough salvage work to pay his bills. Staying under the radar is another matter altogether. An action-packed thriller series featuring plenty of boating, SCUBA diving, fishing and flavored with a generous dose of Conch Republic counterculture.

Check Out The Series Here

★★★★★ *Becker is one of those, unfortunately too rare, writers who very obviously knows and can make you feel, even smell, the places he writes about. If you love the Keys, or if you just want to escape there for a few enjoyable hours, get any of the Mac Travis books - and a strong drink*

★★★★★*This is a terrific series with outstanding details of Florida, especially the Keys. I can imagine myself riding alone with Mac through every turn. Whether it's out on a boat or on an island....I'm there*

Kurt Hunter Mysteries: The Backwater Series

Biscayne Bay is a pristine wildness on top of the Florida Keys. It is also a stones throw from Miami and an area notorious for smuggling. If there's nefarious activity in the park, special agent Kurt Hunter is sure to stumble across it as he patrols the backwaters of Miami.

Check it out the series here

★★★★★ *This series is one of my favorites. Steven Becker is a genius when it comes to weaving a plot and local color with great characters. It's like dessert, I eat it first*

★★★★★ *Great latest and greatest in the series or as a stand alone. I don't want to give up the plot. The characters are more "fleshed out" and have become "real." A truly believable story in and about Florida and Floridians.*

Tides of Fortune

What do you do when you're labeled a pirate in the nineteenth century Caribbean

Follow the adventures of young Captain Van Doren as he and his crew try to avoid the hangman's noose. With their unique mix of skills, Nick and company roam the waters of the Caribbean looking for a safe haven to spend their wealth. But, the call "Sail on the horizon" often changes the best laid plans.

Check out the series here

★★★★★ *This is a great book for those who like me enjoy "factional" books. This is a book that has characters that actually existed and took place in a real place(s). So even though it isn't a true story, it certainly could be. Steven Becker is a terrific writer and it certainly shows in this book of action of piracy, treasure hunting, ship racing etc*

The Storm Series

Meet contract agents John and Mako Storm. The father and son duo are as incompatible as water and oil, but necessity often forces them to work together. This thriller series has plenty of international locations, action, and adventure.

Check out the series here

★★★★★ *Steven Becker's best book written to date. Great plot and very believable characters. The action is non-stop and the book is hard to put down. Enough plot twists exist for an exciting read. I highly recommend this great action thriller.*

★★★★★ *A thriller of mega proportions! Plenty of action on the high seas and in the Caribbean islands. The characters ran from high tech to divers to agents in the field. If you are looking for an adrenaline rush by all means get Steven Beckers new E Book*

The Will Service Series

If you can build it, sail it, dive it, and fish it—what's left. Will Service: carpenter, sailor, and fishing guide can do all that. But trouble seems to find him and it takes all his skill and more to extricate himself from it.

Check out the series here

★★★★★ *I am a sucker for anything that reminds me of the great John D. MacDonald and Travis McGee. I really enjoyed this book. I hope the new Will Service adventure is out soon, and I hope Will is living on a boat. It sounds as if he will be. I am now an official Will Service fan. Now, Steven Becker needs to ignore everything else and get to work on the next Will Service novel*

★★★★★ *If you like Cussler you will like Becker! A great read and an action packed thrill ride through the Florida Keys!*

Made in the USA
Columbia, SC
06 September 2023

22536971R00167